J. A. BOULET

1956
LOVE
&
REVOLUTION

"A beautiful series of a family's struggles. One in which you almost become a part of them. You share their loves, their triumphs, and their losses. There are good times here, but I had tears in my eyes at times too." - Our Town Books, USA (The Olason Chronicles Series Review)

"I also applaud the "Final Note to Reader" chapter included at the end of each of her novels. She takes the time to go into further detail about the research performed for the military battles she describes her character's going through. Not only does this contribute to the realism of her novels, but it also pays homage to all the brave souls who served and perished to give their life for the Royal Canadian Navy during WWII. If you enjoy historical fiction, I would highly recommend this book as a must-read!" – Steven A., USA (The Wars Between Us Review)

"Reading this historical fiction account of the swiftly crushed Hungarian Revolution brought tears to my eyes." - Lynda Engler, USA, Author of Ice Crash: Antarctica

Also by J. A. Boulet

The Strong Amongst Us

The Strong Within Us

The Wars Between Us

The Origins

J. A. BOULET

1956
LOVE
&
REVOLUTION

Published by J. A. Boulet

Book cover design: White Rabbit Arts at The Historical Fiction Company

ISBN: 978-1-7781999-5-0

This book is dedicated to my late Hungarian parents, Mike and Maria. Their strength and perseverance continues to thrive in my heart. So many Hungarians lived through the brave events of 1956, including them.

Note to Reader

This book is a work of historical fiction. I have attempted to be accurate with many of the historical events, although some details have been intentionally skewed to fit within the story. This is a fictional saga of bravery, love and patriotism. Even though many of the historical details are accurate, this book should be read as fiction.

J. A. Boulet May 10, 2023

Part I

The Winds of Change

CHAPTER 1

It was August 1955, and Elona was tired. She grabbed her bucket and wrung out the mop one last time. She had been cleaning at the theatre all night, and it was now early dawn. Something about the purple-lightening skies always enchanted her. Budapest was a quiet city at 4:30 am, almost peaceful. But Hungary was nothing close to peaceful lately. So many things were happening in her country that it made her stomach churn. Politics hadn't been something she cared much for, but lately, it seemed every Hungarian held hope that their country would reinstate a more economically-sound government.

They lived through so many years of repression, paying exorbitant taxes for Hungary's industrialization and war reparations to Russia, among so many other fees, that every single Hungarian paid almost two-thirds of their income out to the government. This left so little for food, cigarettes or anything else. It was a tough life of constantly working with little chance of enjoyment.

Elona was only twenty-one years old, but she felt like she was eighty.

She stepped outside onto the dark street and turned back to lock the theatre doors. Her pail and mop were already beside the door when she noticed she had left the dirty water in the bucket. She sighed and cursed softly. Elona was not going to open up the heavy double doors again and return all the way to the other side of the washrooms to dump her bucket.

She pushed the keys deep inside her pants pocket and picked up the pail gently, sneaking to the alleyway. Elona tiredly tipped her bucket in the alleyway, dumping it upside down to empty it completely so she could return home with a much less heavy pail. She didn't drive, and her bicycle was broken, so she didn't even have that luxury anymore. A headache started at her temples, and she massaged her face gently. Maybe, one day things will get better.

She looked up as male voices echoed down the street. She wondered who would be in the streets at this hour. There wasn't much crime because of the state police, so she usually had nothing to fear.

Then a chill ran down her spine.

It must be the AVH, the State Protection Authority. She had her documents with her but was always fearful of the AVH. They could do anything to Hungarians, it seemed, without cause. They even confiscated anti-communist families' homes and sent the people to camps. The AVH was no better than the Gestapo.

Elona stayed in the shadow of the alleyway as the officers appeared, walking casually down the deserted street. There were four men in full uniform with differing colours. They were smoking cigarettes and chatting amicably. Her heart skipped a beat as one man looked directly in her direction.

She tried to keep as still as possible while the men continued their conversation.

"Imre Nagy needed to go," one man said. "He's nothing but trouble to this country."

"We have enough trouble just doing our jobs to keep the peace here," another man countered. "After Stalin's death, our entire society is beginning to unravel."

The third officer nodded but didn't add to the conversation. He was quiet and reserved, with an almost intelligent look to his face.

Elona was fascinated by his face. She stared at him from the dark corner of the alleyway and found herself entranced by his mannerisms. He had a gentle but strong gait. Something about him told her that he was in charge. He must be a Colonel or something.

Elona grimaced and chastised herself. She was a married woman! She shouldn't be gawking at an officer!

"You are quiet tonight, Colonel Laszlo," the fourth policeman said. "Nothing to add? You are always so reserved about politics."

Laszlo nodded down the street. "I think there is someone in that alleyway, Jozsef."

All four men glanced in the same direction.

Elona knew she had to do something. She couldn't just stay in the alleyway, and she couldn't run. So she grabbed her bucket, stepped out onto the street and began to confidently walk home. Her back felt like it was on fire from all the eyes on her. She continued walking, once slowing down to adjust her mop so they could clearly see that she was just a cleaning lady.

The first tall officer shouted. "Halt! Get your papers out."

The four men approached her as she stopped and fumbled in her bag nervously. She had nothing to be nervous about, Elona told herself. She had been stopped before at 4 am.

The group closed in. She had her documents ready, and her arm stretched out with the papers in her hand.

Laszlo was in the lead and stopped directly in front of her.

He was an olive-skinned handsome man with ice-blue eyes that pierced right through her soul. She could see that those very same eyes would most likely be an icy threat to any enemy.

Laszlo took the documents from her hand and shuffled through them. "Elona Molnar. Twenty-one years old," he held the papers open, inspecting them for authenticity. "Why are you out on the streets at this hour?" His eyes lifted, staring right through her.

"I just finished work," she said meekly, half-afraid and half-intrigued. "I am a cleaner at the cinema."

"The Corvin Cinema?" Laszlo pointed to the building behind them.

"Yes," she answered more assertively.

"You clean there until 4:30 am?"

"It is the only time of day to clean without interruptions. I start at midnight and clean until I am done. My husband didn't help tonight, so I will need to return tomorrow."

"You are married?" Laszlo asked, somewhat surprised.

"Yes, my husband was tired from working all day," she replied. "He just got a job as a bakery chef. We both have to work to pay for things." Elona stumbled over her words, struggling to articulate what she was trying to say. "To pay for everything. There is never enough money and so many bills."

The first officer leaned over Laszlo's shoulder to look at the documents. As he did, Elona noticed the uniforms were very different. Two of the men wore blue policemen uniforms, but the Colonel had a very unusual brown uniform with two stars on his collar, one she had not seen before. The man beside Laszlo also wore the same brown uniform but without the star emblems. "You are not AVH," she said, the relief in her voice evident.

Laszlo spoke first. "No, we are Magyar," he said in Hungarian. "My two friends are from the local police, and Tibor is a fellow Hungarian Army soldier."

The shorter policeman, Jozsef, spoke hastily. "He's not a full colonel. We just call him that because he's from way back when the Germans left in 1945."

Laszlo grimaced. "I'm a Lieutenant," he stated firmly. He didn't like this information given to a stranger on the street, even if she was just a woman. Silence descended on the group as Laszlo handed the documents back to her.

She stuffed the documents back into her bag. "You've been in the army since the Germans left," she said softly, almost to herself.

The night closed in around them. "Yes," Laszlo responded, his mind drifting back to a terrible time. He didn't need to tell this woman anything more.

"He was one of the first to enlist," Jozsef added. "He hated the Germans."

"That's enough!" Laszlo barked. All three men straightened and went silent. They were not willing to risk suffering from Laszlo's wrath.

Elona looked down. "I'm sorry," she said. "It is not my place to ask such questions. I just thought you were all AVH. I'm relieved that you are not."

Laszlo squinted his eyes at the small woman. She had dark blonde hair, small beautiful green eyes and a short stature. He estimated that she was only five feet tall. Compared to his height of six feet, she was tiny.

"May I go now?" Elona asked. "I do need to get home."

The taller policeman snickered, and she wondered what was so funny. Elona shuffled nervously.

Jozsef glowered at his mate. "Stay safe, Mrs. Molnar. Walking around the streets at this hour is not advisable," Jozsef said, nodding to the petite woman.

"You all have made Budapest a safe city from crime," she said. "The only people to fear here are the AVH."

Laszlo grimaced and shifted his feet. "AVH have their jobs to do, just like all of us."

"They're Russians," she whispered under her breath.

Tibor stepped forward, but Laszlo stopped him. "She's right," Laszlo said. "They are Russian, and the Russians are the ones who saved us from the Germans."

Elona looked up into his blue eyes. "I am sorry to have offended you. I meant no such thing."

Laszlo nodded briefly. "Be on your way, Elona, before one of my friends gets a stupid idea." He shooed her away with his hand. "Go home to your husband."

"Thank you." Elona grabbed her pail, slinging the mop over her shoulder and walked briskly down the street. She could feel the stares of the men at her back but somehow knew that she was safe. Laszlo was an interesting man, she thought. She would have liked to learn more about him.

Elona gazed up as the sun struggled to rise, casting a display of purplish rays across the skies. She felt the pail rhythmically tap her leg as she walked and looked up again, thanking God for the peaceful police interaction. And no AVH tonight.

Elona arrived home an hour later. It was a long walk, and she was exhausted. She opened the door slowly, trying not to awaken the sleeping family. She had no children, although her mother lived with Elona and her husband.

Her mother was a chronically light sleeper. Elona wondered if all citizens who survived the German reign couldn't sleep. She was only a child during that time, but even Elona had trouble sleeping sometimes. Ironically, Elona's mother was strangely sympathetic toward the Germans and absolutely despised the Soviets. Elona never quite understood how her momma could think that way after all the horrible things the Germans had done.

In 1944, 500,000 Hungarian Jews were deported and murdered. Elona shook her head at the horror. She was only ten years old but remembered it well when many of her classmates disappeared from her school.

Elona removed her worn boots. As she sat down, Elona noticed the bottom of her right boot sole was partially detached. She rubbed her face in exhaustion. She would try to sew it back together again. Her family was very poor right now. When she was younger, there was a time when she didn't even have shoes. Elona had to tie cloth onto her feet, and that served as her only footwear. She was lucky to have these boots, but they were reaching the end of their life, and she had no money to purchase another pair. Footwear was a priceless possession to have in Hungary.

As she placed her boots on the shoe rack, she remembered the story of the Hungarian Jews who had to remove their shoes on the banks of the Danube before they were shot. There were 20,000 of them. They were executed by the Arrow Cross Party just for being Jewish in 1944. Elona grimaced at the memory. She was lucky to have shoes and blessed to have green eyes.

"The world is such a terrible place," she whispered to herself. Elona looked up to the ceiling, searching for answers. "When will it ever get better?" she asked the ceiling softly.

The floor creaked, and she could hear soft footsteps padding through the old house. Elona must have awoken her mother. She straightened and stepped into the kitchen as her mother appeared in her long cotton gown.

Her mother was a short, stout woman in her forties. Life had been hard for her, and she looked sixty. Her hair was almost all dark grey now.

"Anyu," Elona said, using the endearing Hungarian word for mother. "Go back to sleep."

"I was worried about you," Anyu replied. "You were gone all night."

"I was cleaning, you know that," Elona responded tiredly.

"I know," Anyu said, nodding. "Ferenc should have gone with you. He's a selfish man who only cares about himself." Anyu sat down heavily at the pitted wooden table. Her hair was messy and thin. She ran her fingers through it in frustration.

"He takes care of us, Anyu," Elona retorted. "He found this home and provides for both of us. Don't be so harsh."

"You provide for us more than he does!" Anyu said loudly.

"Keep your voice down," Elona whispered. "You'll wake him. He needs to go to his new job today."

"Ferenc snores like a freight train," Anyu responded. "Nothing wakes him up."

Elona chuckled. Her mother was spirited, and Elona loved her dearly. She hugged her mom around the shoulders and kissed her on the cheek. "I'm going to bed," Elona stated. "I'm exhausted. Maybe things will improve in this country one day, and we can all live a better life."

"Things were good when your Pappa was here," Anyu said softly. "I miss him," she added.

"I know you miss him," Elona said sincerely. "I miss Apu too. Hopefully, they'll release him soon, and he can come back home."

Elona's words stoked the fire within Anyu's heart. "Bloody Russians!" Anyu shouted. "Those evil AVH Soviets took my husband away. And for nothing! He didn't do anything! He was just doing his job." Anyu scowled as her lip quivered.

Elona hugged her again. "I know, Anyu. It wasn't fair what they did. It ruined all our lives."

"The article he wrote didn't have any anti-communist tone in it at all!" Anyu cried. "They just wanted to replace him with a Soviet journalist to fill our heads with Russian propaganda."

"Possibly," Elona replied. "The AVH are no better than the Gestapo."

"This is the truth," Anyu agreed. "At least the Germans knew how to govern. Imre didn't even give Apu amnesty because his sentence was longer than two years. Many others had been released, but not my husband."

Elona sighed and patted her mother's shoulder. "Go back to bed, Anyu," she said. "Maybe one day soon, the Hungarian government will change, and we will get our lives and Apu back."

CHAPTER 2

Imre Nagy had so much optimism for Hungary. He had done what his Moscow commanders had asked of him and began instituting reform after Stalin's death. Imre had reduced investment in heavy industry, then brought in a new system of produce delivery, also making it possible to opt-out of agricultural co-ops and a significant price reduction followed. Imre reduced state control of the media and encouraged economic reforms within his own party. These were all steps in the right direction, he mused.

In August 1953, Nagy had released political prisoners with sentences of less than two years and ended internment camps. He had even brought up the idea of Hungary joining the United Nations.

Imre adjusted his round glasses on his nose, wondering where he went wrong.

Just a few months ago, in April, Moscow had dismissed him as Prime Minister and reinstated that wretched Rákosi to undo everything he had accomplished for Hungary. Rákosi was a communist thug that had pounded Hungary into a terrible state of economic decline. He had brought in forced industrialization and created socialist towns, damaging the economy into stagnation. Rákosi even went as far as to tear down the Regnum

Marianum church just south-east of Heroes' Square and erect a giant statue of Stalin on its holy grounds.

Nagy shook his head at the absurd mistakes Moscow was making in Hungary. After fighting alongside his Russian comrades in the Red Army and even living in Moscow himself for fifteen years, this is how he was repaid.

Imre refused to accept that he was no longer Prime Minister. He would rally his supporters. Nagy struck his fist in frustration on the wooden table. The cups toppled, and he stood in fright, catching a ceramic cup before it smashed. He stared at the cup in his hand as an analogy formed in his mind. Imre smiled satisfyingly.

He would do the same for his beautiful country. Imre Nagy would catch Hungary before it smashed to the floor.

$$\gimel$$

Laszlo deeply inhaled the smoke from his cigarette as he peered down the street. Tibor was beside him, as usual. They had just finished a day of ammunition cleaning and sorting. It was a long day, but things were light around Budapest lately.

He found himself musing about the latest government changes. Imre Nagy was a right-leaning communist, but Laszlo had to admit that the man did manage to reform his country. The economy had begun to improve. Imre's biggest failure was encouraging political reform. Nagy should have just stuck to economic reform.

Tibor lit a cigarette and exhaled tiredly. "I wonder where Rákosi will lead us from here?" Tibor asked.

Laszlo looked over at his younger brother and grinned. Not many people knew they were brothers, and he wanted it kept that way. Laszlo was a private man. He kept his family life separate from his work life and preferred it this way. "Rákosi has already plunged us back to 1952, repealing all the reforms that Nagy did. One step forward, three steps back."

"It doesn't help Hungarians at all," Tibor noted. "Magyars are angry now. Everyone I talk to had high hopes of getting Hungary to start running as an independent country."

"Yes, this is true," Laszlo responded quietly. "I started wondering if reform was possible myself."

Tibor laughed. "You?" he cried good-naturedly. "The career soldier who secretly stood beside the Red Army. I don't believe it."

Laszlo scowled at his brother. "Shut your mouth," he snapped. "You have no idea what it felt like being a twenty-year-old fighting to get the Germans out." Laszlo stood and pointed a stern finger down onto the table. "You were only ten years old! I was ensuring a future for you!"

Tibor pulled back in his chair at his older brother's explosive temper. He held up his hands in defeat. "I'm sorry," Tibor said quietly. "I was only a kid; you're right."

"Don't you forget it!" Laszlo said, his voice thundering against the tanks stationed at the barracks entrance.

Tibor sat silently, knowing that one more word could unleash the trauma his brother had experienced. He heard from other soldiers that Laszlo had killed many men during the war against the Germans. Tibor wondered what it would feel like to kill another human being. He supposed it would give him nightmares for years, maybe even his entire life.

The wind blew at their faces suddenly as if to silence them both. After several minutes, Laszlo threw his cigarette butt on the ground, crushing it with his foot. "Let's have something to eat," Laszlo said stoically. "We're done for the day."

⟩

Ferenc was late coming home, and Elona was frustrated. She had slept badly and awoken to wrap cabbage rolls and make perogies with whatever she could find in the kitchen. There was hardly any meat left, so she added more rice to the cabbage roll mixture to disguise it. No cheese was left either, so she chose to add potatoes and onions in the perogies instead. She was trying her best to feed her family with their meagre supplies, and her husband couldn't even show up for dinner on time.

After two hours, he finally came home.

She looked away when he stepped into the kitchen. Elona could feel the resentment building in her heart. Nobody in her family liked Ferenc. She began to wonder if she had made a mistake in marrying him. He had pursued her so relentlessly in the first year. When she finally gave into his advances, he lavished her with attention, but once they were married, he quickly became disinterested. Elona concluded that it was just part of being married.

"What's for dinner?" Ferenc asked.

"Cabbage rolls and perogies," she responded bluntly.

"Smells good," he responded.

"Everything is cold," she retorted. "Anyu and I have already eaten. We waited over an hour for you."

"I was busy cleaning up," he said. "It was only my second day at the bakery." He rummaged in his bag. "I brought some day-old bread and gombòc." He pulled out the bread and plum dumplings, placing them on the counter.

Elona turned her head, peering curiously over her shoulder. She loved gombòc! The sugary round dumplings with plums inside were her favourite dessert since she was a small girl. She stood and walked to the counter, reaching for the dessert.

"Heat my food first," Ferenc said arrogantly. "I'm hungry. Then you can have your dessert."

Elona scowled angrily at him, and her mouth opened to protest. She pursed her lips closed and grabbed his dinner from the refrigerator, plopping it onto a cooking pan and shoving it in the oven. It was not uncommon for women to be treated like this; she knew it was just the way of her culture. The women were expected to dote on their men. Wives brought their husbands food and drinks, then happily cleaned all the dishes afterwards. Sometimes it made her feel like she was only a servant. Elona would lie in bed at night staring at the ceiling, thanking God that Ferenc didn't demand sex too often. He had forced himself upon her last week, and she had to close her eyes during the marital act. Being intimate with him sent shivers of revulsion down her spine now. He didn't want sex with her too frequently, but when it did happen, Elona imagined she was a queen in a luxurious bed with a loving king at her side. It was the only way she could complete the intimate act without sacrificing her sanity.

He was not an ugly man. On the contrary, Ferenc was quite handsome with his longish hair slicked back and his dazzling charm. This is how he had initially won her over. His looks could melt any woman's resolve.

But lately, his lack of respect had begun chipping away at her self-esteem. The picture of him in her mind's eye had changed dramatically. She no longer saw him as attractive like so many other women did. Elona thought he was now a revolting, cruel man.

She sat down and curled her palms under her chin, looking straight at the wall, attempting to hide her emotions.

Ferenc leaned over and kissed her head. "You're a good woman," he said.

She smiled, but what she wanted to do was spit in his face. "I'm going for a walk tonight before the sun goes down," she said slowly. "I will get your dinner when it's warmed, and then I'll be back before dark." She grabbed a gombòc and took a large satisfying bite.

⟩

Elona walked through the bushes, inhaling the fresh air of the riverside. Her spirits lifted as soon as she heard the ripples of the Danube River flowing. She had taken Ferenc's bicycle and parked it in the bushes. It took almost a half hour to reach the secluded spot, but it was well worth it. This was one of her favourite places in the world.

She parted the bushes and reached the edge of the riverbank. Elona smiled as a strong breeze flowed into her face. She sometimes wondered if her life was as good as it would ever get. These moments by herself meant more to her than anything else. She felt free from the constraints of her family, her job and her life. Nothing mattered here except herself.

Elona sat down on the grass by the riverside and inhaled the fresh air. The secluded spot was on a barely visited trail in southern Budapest, known as Pest County. Elona learnt from her mother that Budapest was once three different cities, Buda, Pest and Old Buda. In 1849, the famous Chain Bridge was completed over the Danube, linking the two cities of Buda and Pest. Twenty years later, Old Buda joined the large city.

Elona laid back on the grass, gazing up at the skies. Her home city had a violent past, with many wars fought on its soil. She ran her hands along the grass, digging her fingers into the soil. Elona knew that she had the strength of ancient warriors buried somewhere deep within her blood, although lately, she felt just repressed.

The river rushed past her. The waves gurgled and sploshed with undying continuance as if her troubles were just rushing along down the river to be forever forgotten.

Hungarians were proud people, she thought. They loved their country and wanted to defend it at all costs, but world events always seemed to swirl in murderous chaos around central Europe, with Hungary caught in the middle. Hungary was originally larger than its current size, being part of the Austro-Hungarian empire. WWI had changed that, and it had split into a fraction of its original size. She didn't agree with the political beliefs that always seemed to tear her country apart. Elona, like many Hungarians, just wanted their country back from the hands of communist and fascist leaders. Budapest was a beautiful city! The rolling countryside was breathtaking with its mineral spas, forests and mountains. Hungary was truly a wonderful place if only the politics could be sorted out.

Most of her friends agreed with her. Elona loved her friends from the University. She had met many of them back in her first year of university. Things had been better then. Her father had started working at the Budapest newspaper when she was twelve years old. Suddenly her entire childhood was just a poor dismal past. Apu had dramatically improved their lives by working for the newspaper. Elona had footwear, ate well and went back to school. They were respected, and Elona joined the many other youngsters in starting her first year at Budapest Technical University.

In early 1953, her father was arrested. It started a landslide of hardships for the family. Her sisters and brothers had all married, leaving home, and Elona was left as the youngest child still at home. She was a surprisingly intelligent woman and excelled at university. Elona was determined to be like her father and raise their standard of living.

After the arrest of her father, though, her family plunged back into poverty. Her mother could no longer find any work because she was married to a criminal in the minds of the state. No one would hire her as a seamstress, labourer or anything.

Elona completed her first year of university and then found a job as a cleaner at the cinema. She never went back to school. Food and shelter were more important than education. It was wrong and unjust for the government to treat the family this way, but it was their life now. There was nothing Elona could have done differently.

She would go back to the university once her father was released from jail, Elona concluded.

But it was never that easy.

Elona had been working at the cinema for two years now. She still maintained her friendships with her fellow university students. They were like family to her. Gizella was as close as a sister to her. They had taken many of the same courses together. Elona was supposed to meet Gizella tomorrow for coffee with another close friend, a cleaning co-worker named Béláné Havrilla. Elona was looking forward to escaping with her female friends, even if only for a few hours.

The murky Danube splashed at her feet, snapping her out of her thoughts. Elona immediately pulled her feet away from the wide river. She knew how to swim but didn't trust the currents in the river. Some of her friends defied the laws of nature and swam in the river anyways. She chuckled at the memories.

Her husband never even met most of her friends.

The sudden, sombre thought shot through her heart as a train whistled in the distance. She exhaled heavily, wondering how she would repair her life. It seemed every step she took just led deeper and deeper into the wrong cave.

She stood and wiped the grass off her pants. It was time to go back home. She squared her shoulders and pulled the bicycle from the bushes, leaving her secret sanctuary behind to face her problems again.

Chapter 3

"Elona!" Béláné shouted from the street.

"I'm coming!" Elona shouted back as she hurried outside down the front steps. She ran towards the sidewalk. "My husband took his bicycle to work today! I don't have anything to travel with."

"Where's your bicycle?" Béláné asked.

"It's broken."

Béláné hopped off her bicycle. "Let's have a look at it," she said, walking her bike onto the grass. "I'm sure we can figure it out."

"Are you sure?" Elona responded. "I'm not so good with tools."

"I'm sure we can both figure it out," Béláné responded. "You're a smart lady, and I'm good with putting things together."

"Okay," Elona said, leading Béláné around the property to the back yard.

As they rounded the corner of the house, Elona felt instantly ashamed. The weeds and overgrown grass covered everything, making the backyard look horrendous and uninviting.

Béláné didn't say anything. They arrived at the bicycle lying on its side in the tall grass. "This is not good for your bicycle,"

Béláné said. "You should keep it in the shed or the house. It will rust, and the oils in the chain will dry up."

"Ferenc doesn't let me keep it in the shed," Elona replied. "There's no room."

Béláné hefted the bicycle up and inspected it, lifting her eyebrows questionably. "So your husband would rather have your bike outside, broken and in disrepair?" Béláné said, shaking her head. She was only two years older than Elona, although Béláné seemed much more mature. Having grown up partially in an orphanage had forced her to learn self-reliance at an early age. She wandered her eyes across the unkept yard.

Elona exhaled heavily. "I have been questioning whether I have a good husband anymore."

"By the looks of this yard, he doesn't take care of cutting the lawn either," Béláné said, waving her hand across the yard.

Elona lowered her head, ashamed.

"I'm sorry," Béláné said, grimacing. "We all have our problems with daily life right now. Let's try to fix this bike. What do we need men for anyways?" Béláné pulled the bike upside down, resting it on the steering wheel and seat. She inspected the bike closer. The bike chain clattered loosely onto her knee. "It looks like your bike chain just fell off. I'll try to get it back on and tighten it. Where does your husband keep his tools?"

"I will go get his tool box! It's in the house." Elona ran to the house, returning a few minutes later, lugging a rusty metal toolbox.

Béláné rummaged in it until she found some mechanic gloves and pulled the chain back onto the front sprocket. "Hold this here while I get the chain on the back gear," Béláné instructed.

Elona held the front part of the chain as Béláné loosened a nut and pulled the chain onto each sprocket on the back. "I think we need to start turning the wheel," Elona said.

"Yes, you're right," Béláné said, nodding as the two women worked to fix the bicycle. Béláné retightened and loosened the nut several times. After several frustrating minutes, they had the chain on. She looked down and grimaced. Almost all of the grease was on her gloves and not on the chain. "Do you have any gear oil?"

"I don't think so," Elona said. "I don't know where he keeps that stuff."

Béláné removed her gloves and thought hard. "What else could we use?"

"Maybe we could use lard? I have lots of that!" Elona laughed.

"Let's do it!" Béláné shouted happily as Elona rushed back into the kitchen.

Elona returned with a tub of lard, smiling broadly. "I hope this works!"

"I suppose it will," Béláné said. "Gear oil is probably made of lard anyways!" They broke out into raucous laughter.

Elona bent over laughing, clutching her abdomen with tears in her eyes. "Women probably invented it during cooking!" she shouted. Another round of jeering laughter erupted from them both until they almost lay on the grass, heaving from uncontrollable laughter. Elona dipped her finger in the lard and smoothed it onto the gears, chuckling from the laughing fit.

Béláné watched as she spread it on with buttery consistency. She shook the tears of laughter from her eyes and smiled. "Okay, let's spread it throughout the chain by moving the pedal slowly." Béláné circled the pedal until the entire chain was coated. It seemed to have fixed the problem.

Elona beamed. "You fixed my bike!" she shouted happily.

"No," Béláné responded. "We both did."

Elona smiled happily. "Let's go for our coffee now! Thank you so much, Béláné!" She hugged her friend graciously.

They both pulled Elona's bike upright and prepared for the ride into the centre of the city on the Buda side.

Laszlo led his battalion through the training exercise inside the tanks. Each tank was numbered, and some were not tanks but looked similar. They were armoured personnel carriers, with the top wide open. These were used to transport equipment and personnel to combat zones. Laszlo had worked in the infantry when the Red Army fought against Germany, serving for many years before being promoted to Lieutenant. At the beginning of 1955, he was transferred to the 8th Tank Regiment.

"Remember to focus on your specific duties," Laszlo barked. "If you are driving the tank, pay attention to driving it. If you are the artillery corporal, pay attention to your targets. The last thing you want to happen is the tank crashing into a structure because someone wasn't paying attention."

The corporals nodded and listened. They were mostly new recruits or transferred from other divisions. Laszlo wasn't sure what the government was planning, but the unrest from the last two years was concerning.

"I want a small team in each of these tanks and one team in the APCs," Laszlo stated. "Check the board for the team you'll be on, and I'll meet you at the tanks this evening. We're going to complete a night training exercise. Be back here at 11 pm sharp."

Laszlo left the recruits and lit a cigarette, walking towards the gates of the regiment. He had been feeling angry lately and needed to get away from the army, even if it was just for an afternoon. He leaned against the steel post and smoked the remainder of his cigarette. His brother was at the barracks. Laszlo would ask him if he wanted to take a break. Laszlo blew small plumes of smoke at the sky, wondering where his life would lead him from here. He no longer had the same passions as he did when he was younger, even though Laszlo strictly maintained that the Russians were the saviours of Hungary. He was a lieutenant, after all; Laszlo was required to say these things. He had felt it in his heart when he was young. But now, Laszlo didn't know if Hungary's saviours had turned into the same faces as the enemy.

Maybe every government was the enemy, he mused. Maybe the only people who were genuine were those who didn't exist in any government positions at all.

Laszlo threw the cigarette butt harshly down onto the ground. He crushed the glowing red ember with his boot. He supposed that God didn't lead him to the position he was in for no reason. Lieutenant Laszlo Vadas was meant for greater things.

"Gizella! You look so fine!" Elona screeched as they arrived at the university's dormitory.

Gizella stepped out, wearing a white collared blouse under a dark grey v-neck sweater. She wore a light grey skirt with shiny black boots. Her hair was bright blonde and styled in the current rolled-curls style of the 1950s. She was an attractive, smart woman, and Elona found herself slightly envious.

"Elona!" Gizella shrieked, running towards her friend. "You look so radiant today! I haven't seen you in almost three months!" Gizella crashed into Elona, hugging her fiercely. "We need to see each other more often! Don't keep me waiting! University can be such a bore. We only learn what we are told to learn from this Russian state."

Béláné smiled as she watched the two women reunite. She grinned nervously. "You should be careful of saying such things out loud. The AVH are everywhere." Béláné ran her fingers through her hair uncomfortably.

"No fear! We are at the university, Béláné," Gizella said, pointing out the obvious. "The Student Council has more power against the government than other institutions. We will invoke change in our beautiful Hungary! You mark my words." Gizella walked over to Béláné grasping her arm gaily. "Come! Relax! We are together in the beautiful summer sun today to enjoy each other's company! Let's find a nice place to eat!"

They walked to their bikes, mounted them and cycled towards the Pest side. "I know some quaint coffee shops near the old Central Market Hall," Elona remarked loudly. "You'll love it."

"At least the government is fixing the war damages to the Market Hall," Béláné yelled into the wind. She pumped her legs on the bicycle, riding in the middle of the three-bike line as they crossed the bridge. "I remember it so well going there as a very young girl with the orphanage group. It was one of the highlights of my dismal childhood." Béláné laughed, making light of her past.

Gizella shouted from the rear, "I wonder if they are fixing it too fast. There was a lot of damage! We pay them ridiculous taxes, and they could at least fix it right! I think they are more concerned with controlling us and taking all our hard-earned taxes back to the Kremlin."

"Shhh!" Elona shouted back, grimacing. "We won't be that far away from the Parliament building soon! Watch your tongue!"

Gizella pursed her lips and wiggled her nose. "Okay," she replied, laughing. "I will be good!"

The girls rode across the bridge and soon felt their tires rumble over the paved cobblestones of the old Market Hall area. The building itself suffered a bomb hit during WWII and was damaged badly. It was originally built in the late 1890s by Sam Pecz, a professor from the Technical University. At the time, mayor Charles Kamermayer had taken part in the Public Food Committee to find a solution to the numerous unsanitary food markets. People needed food, and Budapest was a bustling city with a bright future. So they devised a plan to build the 10,000-square-foot indoor market to contain all the food vendors in one place. There were already many fish and vegetable markets on the Danube, and it was the perfect site. Sam Pecz was commissioned to design it and built the Central Market Hall during the 1890s. It was officially opened in 1897. It was one of the world's most advanced market halls, complete with inspectors, refrigeration and lighting systems. After the bomb damage, the market hall was closed, and repairs began in 1950. Some questioned that the repairs were being hastily conducted, and others didn't care. They just wanted the market back.

The group neared the repaired neogothic gate of the grand brick and iron entrance. Elona breathed in a sigh of hope for her country. She loved Budapest. Elona looked behind her, and her two friends were also staring up at the enormous damaged building under repair. Many famous leaders would visit the Central Market Hall, and it was once a great source of pride.

Elona parked her bike at the entrance and dismounted while the other two women slowed.

"It suffered so much damage, and look at it now!" Béláné screeched, frowning. "I don't come to the city centre enough. I can't believe the progress they've made on it!" She parked her bike alongside the other girl's bikes.

Elona grabbed her hand and skipped gaily towards the market vendor tents outside as Gizella ran to catch up. Elona reached her hand back, and Gizella grasped her left hand as they laughed like children. Their faces soon changed as the crowds overcame them. The throngs of people in the makeshift market were numerous, and they kept their hands clasped so they would not lose each other. They squeezed past locals and tourists, grasping each other's hands in a single line until they finally reached an area filled with the delicious strong smell of coffee. The nutty caramelized aroma drifted in the air deliberately to entice the market customers.

Elona stopped in front of the vendor stall. It sold several bags of coffee beans from around the world, some ground coffee and some whole beans. They sold coffee by the cup, and several desserts adorned the displays.

Gizella's stomach growled hungrily as she stepped forward. "I will pay," she announced to her friends.

"No, no," Elona argued. "I can pay."

"You can both pay for lunch," Gizella responded decisively, ending the discussion. She opened her small purse as the women ordered their coffees. Gizella paid and joined the other two girls awaiting their expressos.

The coffees arrived with foamed cream on top. The women grabbed their drinks and stood together, sipping the delicious strong drink.

The market bustled around them as the women debated where to eat lunch. "I would like some polish sausage for lunch!" Béláné said excitedly. "I saw a vendor stall back there, selling sausages from around the world!"

"Perfect choice!" Gizella remarked.

$$\supset$$

Laszlo ate his lunch with his brother as the thong of people pushed past their table. Many people showed respect instantly upon noticing the Hungarian Army uniforms. Several citizens displayed fear in their eyes and lowered their heads.

It disturbed Laszlo that his own countrymen feared him. He was their protector, after all. Laszlo had never worked with the AVH, nor would he ever subject himself to such evils. The AVH had instilled such fear in Hungarian citizens that it seemed all police enforcement and army officials were lumped into the same category. This was so far from the truth. The Hungarian Army was populated by average Hungarian men. Some were born into the military, like Laszlo and his brother. Their grandfather had served in WWI and had died. But not before Laszlo's father was born. The military was the only thing they knew. His father had served in the Hungarian Army also, raising his sons in a strict military family. It was almost like Laszlo and his brother were destined to serve the Hungarian people.

But the Hungarian people now feared them. It wasn't right.

"Good food here," Tibor mumbled between mouthfuls of cabbage rolls.

Laszlo nodded. "Yes, it is good food, and it's nice to get away from the barracks. We should have changed into civilian clothes, though." Laszlo looked up as a group of ladies approached their table.

"I don't mind," Tibor said, filling his mouth with more food.

"You are too hungry to notice a thing!" Laszlo said, laughing as the outdoor market teamed with activity around them.

Béláné shrieked at the display of sausages from around the world. She couldn't even decide on which to try first!

"You need to choose already!" Elona said in exasperation. "Gizella and I have already gotten our food. We are going to find a table. A family is leaving over there! We will try to grab it! Hurry, Béláné!"

Elona and Gizella walked towards the far side of the eating area to the freed table. A family of five moved in front of them slowly as Elona seethed. Two of the smallest kids in front of them were only toddlers and walked very slowly. Elona wished the parents would just pick up the children! Gizella impatiently tried to get around the family to no avail. Elona and Gizella shuffled slowly behind the family, anxiously waiting to get to the table.

As the family moved away, they saw a group of foreigners sit down at the table. Elona's face fell in disappointment. They would have to eat standing up! Elona frowned disappointedly and searched the tents for another free spot.

"You can sit here, Elona Molnar," a deep man's voice said nearby.

Elona looked in surprise at the man seated right next to where she stood. It was the handsome Hungarian soldier that had questioned her a few days ago! He was seated at a table for six with only one other soldier seated.

"You aren't expecting more?" Elona said in confusion, looking at the empty chairs at his table.

Laszlo frowned. Nobody wanted to sit beside the military. "No, it's just me and Tibor," he responded.

"I would greatly appreciate it," Elona said, holding her food tray. "We tried to get a table, but it was taken before we could get there. I have my friends, Gizella and Béláné, with me, though. Are you sure?"

"There are four empty chairs just for you and your friends," Laszlo motioned with his hand to the empty spots as Tibor looked up with his mouth full of food.

Elona moved towards a chair and motioned Gizella to sit. Gizella's face changed curiously to a mixture of outrage and confusion. "This is Lieutenant Laszlo and his fellow comrade from the Hungarian Army. They were very kind the other night when I was walking home alone from the cinema." Elona pinched Gizella's arm gently and whispered, "Be nice. They're good people like anyone else."

Laszlo overheard the whisper and appraised Elona. She seemed to be a woman of simplicity. Her blondish hair was wisped behind her ears, and she was plainly dressed in a grey skirt and white shirt. But it didn't matter because her green eyes shone brightly like a pair of sparkling emeralds. She had a bewitching face that could entrance any man.

Tibor swallowed and eyed the two girls. He stood and pulled a chair out for the smartly dressed, pretty blonde. "Have a seat," he said politely. "We are just having lunch, just like you. No bother to us at all."

Laszlo stood as well, pulling the chair out for Elona. "Sit," Laszlo said. "We'd enjoy the company over lunch, and it doesn't look like there are any other tables anyways."

Elona and Gizella smiled at each other briefly and placed their food down on the table. "Thank you so much," Elona said genuinely, taking the seat on the proffered chair.

Laszlo nodded and was suddenly gripped by momentary confusion about what to say next. He had such little experience in real civilian life. Laszlo looked to his brother for help. Tibor ate hungrily, drowning his lack of social skills in his food. Laszlo picked at his food and sipped his coffee.

"You have the same coffee as us!" Elona remarked gaily, nodding at his cup.

"Yes," Laszlo said, thankful for the woman's conversational skills. "It is the best coffee in the city."

"I should properly introduce you," Elona said happily. "This is Gizella. I remember your name, Lieutenant Laszlo, but I have forgotten your comrade's name."

"Tibor!" Tibor suddenly leaned over and clasped Gizella's shoulder eagerly.

"You can address me as just Laszlo," Laszlo gestured across the table and met Gizella's eye.

Elona watched the two interact, and she felt a strange lump of jealousy in her throat. She stuck her fork in her sausage and cut it with her knife. Elona chewed the morsel and wondered what trickery was playing in her head. Gizella was very pretty and obviously more desirable, she knew. Elona felt like she was often standing in the other woman's shadow. That was normal for Elona. But she couldn't understand where her attraction to Laszlo was coming from, and the immediate jealousy was confounding. It was unwarranted and completely unreasonable. She was a married woman, after all.

Laszlo relaxed back in his seat and then placed his hand on Elona's shoulder. "It is a pleasure seeing you again, Elona," he said politely.

Elona smiled as a radiant stream of warmth spread through her body. She looked across the table to distract herself from blushing.

Gizella sipped her coffee and opened her napkin. Almost immediately, she began talking to the younger Tibor. He smiled at her, and Gizella smiled back.

Elona could sense some instant chemistry going on between them. This was odd because Gizella was always vehemently against the military and the current government hierarchy.

Elona grinned at the irony of Gizella finding a young military man attractive. She watched as Gizella and Tibor talked animatedly. Tibor smiled at her again, and Elona noted something about the younger man's face. He looked strangely like Laszlo. The same ice blue eyes and the nose or the chin were the same. Elona couldn't really determine which feature it was, but it made her think the two men were related.

"I found you!" Béláné said, standing beside Gizella and staring at Elona in surprise. Her eyes shifted to the two men warily. She held her tray uncertainly out in front of her.

"Sit down!" Elona replied happily. "This is Laszlo," Elona said, gesturing with her hands. "And this is Tibor. They are both Hungarian soldiers who were quite kind to me when I was walking home from the cinema one morning."

Béláné laid her tray on the table and pulled the chair out, seating herself. She looked at the two soldiers and found herself fearful but angry at the same time. She looked down and tried to keep her gaze from fixating on the handsome men at the table.

"This is my other friend, Béláné," Elona said, introducing the men. "She used to work at the cinema as well."

Laszlo waved a hand. "Nice to meet you," he said. Laszlo looked across to Tibor and noticed that he was still talking to Gizella. Laszlo kicked his brother under the table.

Tibor looked up at Béláné in shock. "Oh! Hello!" he said, responding to the introduction as quickly as possible.

"How long have you been serving?" Gizella asked him with a smile on her face.

Tibor grinned handsomely. "Seven years already," he replied. "I started as a teenager. My entire family is military. Even my mother served as a nurse during WWII." He flipped his soldier's hat down over the floppy mass of hair on the top of his head. It peeked out from under the hat as if his hair was troublesome to contain.

Gizella smiled and sipped her coffee again. She just noticed that she had barely eaten any of her food! She placed a morsel of sausage in her mouth.

"Where do you all know each other?" Laszlo asked.

"Gizella and I met at the Technical University," Elona answered.

"You also attend university?" Laszlo said hastily. He immediately regretted it.

"Yes, I used to," Elona replied. "It's a long story involving a good share of politics. I had to work to support my family, so I withdrew after the first year."

"Oh, I'm sorry," Laszlo said. "It's unfortunate, but it does happen to many families in Hungary."

"Under this government, of course," Béláné quietly mumbled.

Laszlo overheard and ate quietly, finishing the food on his plate. He was only a soldier. People didn't realize that he didn't make the rules; he only followed them. The government, of course, has always controlled the military forces. Sometimes it is just actions, and sometimes it is not. Military personnel were trained not to think for themselves, but most people don't seem to understand that military men have hearts too.

Elona watched from the corner of her eye as Laszlo grew silent and retreated into himself. She wondered what he must be thinking. Being a soldier must be tough, she thought.

"You've been in the military for a long time," Elona said, addressing Laszlo. "I remembered you said something like that. Or maybe it was one of the fellows with you that day."

"Yes, I started in late 1944," Laszlo stated. "It's a long story."

"You should tell me one day," Elona said, laughing. "We can both share our long stories!"

Béláné stared at Elona and Laszlo curiously. There seemed to be something going on between the two. She couldn't understand it but knew that a miserable marriage could make a woman seek attention elsewhere. Béláné hoped this was not the case. She had a healthy dose of admiration for Elona. She was one strong family woman.

Gizella was laughing at something Tibor had said. She placed her hand on Tibor's forearm as they both chuckled about something.

"What are you laughing about?" Elona asked, smiling. She was truly amazed at the change in Gizella.

"Oh, nothing!" Gizella replied, chuckling. "One day, I'll tell you!"

Tibor smiled secretly like a small boy that had just won some candy.

Elona chuckled. "Alright," she said. "Whatever you say."

Laszlo pushed his plate away and lit a cigarette. "Do you want a cigarette?" he asked Elona.

"Oh, no, thank you," Elona responded. "I am one of the strange ones who don't smoke." She laughed.

Laszlo lifted his eyebrow. That was strange. Mostly everyone smoked nowadays. It relieved stress, and this country had its share of stress. "You are a unique woman, Elona," he said bluntly and immediately felt his cheeks grow warm.

Elona beamed brightly. "Well, thank you," she replied. "You are unique too. I think, like everyone else in this country, we instantly fear the military and all law enforcement. But you two have changed my opinion of that. You are men like anyone else. Well, much stronger and physically fit than others, but otherwise, you have," Elona stumbled over her words. "I guess I'm just trying to say that you have emotions and a heart. You're human like anyone else." Elona glanced to the side, trying to gauge his reaction. She was really scrambling over her words. Both men were very physically fit. It was evident by the way they held their bodies upright, and their abdomens were flat. She found herself staring at Laszlo's thighs seated on the chair and wondered if his lower body was as muscular as his arms seemed to be.

Laszlo caught her gaze and let her eyes roam over his body. He felt an instant sensation in his pants and tried to hide his physical response. It was difficult to maintain composure when a woman was intently staring at his body.

Béláné coughed uncomfortably. "Ladies, I would like to pick up some vegetables and food from the market before we leave." She stuffed food in her mouth, hoping the two smitten women would come to their senses.

Elona's eyes snapped up, and she felt instantly ashamed. She had been staring at another man's body, and she didn't even realize what she was doing. How rude and brash of her! Elona hid her face and ate the rest of her food hungrily, completely ignoring the attractive soldier beside her.

Laszlo glanced at her bewilderedly. He could not understand women. She was, only seconds ago, staring at his legs and complimenting him. Now, she treated him like he was invisible. She ate her food quietly, almost intent on leaving quickly. What did he say to change her mood?

Elona looked up. "Gizella, hurry up and eat!" she said. "We are leaving soon. We all need to pick up some things from the market."

Gizella turned her head and stared at Elona as if she had just realized there were other people at the table. "Oh!" Gizella said in surprise. "Okay, I will eat! I can take whatever I don't finish back with me."

Laszlo wondered what had just happened. He lifted his hat and smoothed his hand over his shortly-cropped hair. It was time to leave, he felt. He noticed Tibor's plate was empty as well. Laszlo stood. "Well, ladies," he said. "No need to rush your outing. You can have the table. Tibor and I need to get back to the barracks."

Tibor looked up and stood instantly. He bent down suddenly, grasping Gizella's hand and kissed it softly, to everyone's surprise. "It was very nice meeting you," he murmured softly. Tibor looked up and noticed everyone staring curiously. "It was nice meeting you all!" He tipped his hat and joined Laszlo. They both disappeared, engulfed quickly into the crowd.

Elona looked down at her hands and felt an instant, confusing emptiness.

CHAPTER 4

This Elona woman confused him. It had been three weeks now, and he couldn't get her out of his head. Laszlo thought back to every detail of the impromptu lunch they had all shared, and the feeling that it arose inside him was something he couldn't wrap his head around.

Laszlo stared up at the ceiling in his barracks room. He lacked the social experience to understand women or himself, for that matter. But he did know that there was a definite attraction between them both, and she was a married woman.

That was never good.

Maybe he should talk to his friend Jozsef. He knew much more about these things than his younger brother did.

Laszlo sat up on his bed and decided to contact his friend. He rummaged in his locker for his civilian jacket and brushed his hand along his favourite instrument, a shining accordion. He would have to take it out one day soon and play some songs. It always soothed his soul to play music. Playing accordion was his hidden passion.

Not too many military men understood his enthusiasm for music. It was his stress relief, a way for him to relieve the pressure of all the awful things he's seen and done. Killing another man, whether it was the enemy or not, cuts into a deep place in a person's heart. Not too many people understood this because nobody ever talked about it.

Laszlo felt a heaviness in his heart every single day since WWII, and music was the only thing that helped to lift his melancholy. He grabbed his accordion and lowered it into the case. He would take it with him today. After his visit with Jozsef, he will retreat to his secret spot along the river. He needed some time to himself.

⫟

"You shouldn't be so worried that she is married," Jozsef said. "If her husband is not with her, then he is the one losing out. Who knows, they probably have more problems than you think in their marriage. It is often the case." Jozsef inhaled on his cigarette and blew out a cloud of smoke. "Just remain friends with her. Who knows, she may be divorcing soon. Then you'll be the first in line." Jozsef chuckled.

Laszlo laughed lightly. "Maybe you are right," he said. "I suppose I have been thinking more of my own situation than anything. She would have her own problems."

"Exactly," Jozsef agreed. "Her reactions are her own doing. You said she looked at you with obvious attraction, then suddenly grew quiet. She likely felt confused and faithful to her husband, so she corrected her behaviour."

Laszlo nodded in agreement. "You are probably right."

"It has nothing to do with you," Jozsef added. "Just remember, you can be attracted to her and still be a good man. Do nothing about it. Just accept it. She's a pretty woman."

"Yes, she is," Laszlo agreed.

"I remember," Jozsef said. "Her green eyes were mesmerizing. Even with her work clothes and mop, she was oddly bewitching."

Laszlo leaned back into the passenger seat of the truck. "Yes," he replied. They were parked along a dirt road outside of the city. They grew silent and simply enjoyed sitting in the truck, smoking cigarettes and gazing at the countryside. Jozsef had picked him up earlier in his vehicle, and they had gone for a drive.

Jozsef was on his day off and out of uniform. He had been a policeman for three years now. He enjoyed it more than the military.

"Why did you leave the military anyways?" Laszlo asked. "I always wondered that."

Jozsef straightened his neck back into the truck seat. "Too much politics in the military," he responded. "I like working for the police better. It's more about the city and the people."

"I suppose you're right," Laszlo replied, staring out as the morning fog lifted over the countryside. It was a picturesque scene, and they both loved it. They hadn't expected it, so they leaned back in appreciation, staring as nature displayed art before them.

"Hungary is such a beautiful country," Jozsef stated.

"It is," Laszlo agreed, finishing his cigarette.

"It's unfortunate that so many wars and bloodshed have scarred this land," Jozsef said. "I wish one day we can take back our country and run it as Hungarians."

Laszlo grimaced. So many people were beginning to think this way. He agreed, of course, but couldn't directly say anything for fear of having his views repeated to a Russian informant. "This is how most people think now," Laszlo said vaguely.

Jozsef nodded at his friend's usual vagueness. He understood somewhat. Laszlo had risen too high in the military to engage in such conversation. Treason was a real threat nowadays, and Laszlo maintained a quiet mouth.

A long silence grew between them. Laszlo couldn't add much more to these types of political conversations. The two friends continued smoking cigarettes in the truck for several minutes, appreciating the Hungarian countryside. The fog lifted more and more until it was gone, absorbing into the sky. The green fields glimmered back at them in the morning sun. Laszlo smiled. He felt oddly happy. He was going to play his accordion today.

"We should get going," Laszlo said. "You can drop me off at my vehicle. I have some things to do."

Jozsef nodded and started the engine. "Yes, I have to take the truck back," he said.

$$\gamma$$

Laszlo placed his accordion on the back seat of his Mercedes and slammed the door. It was an old Mercedes, but it was like driving gold in Hungary. All cars were publicly owned, and private ownership was banned. Nobody owned land or property, except for a few struggling farms within the cooperative. Driving a car was extremely rare.

The vehicle was owned by the Hungarian Army. When he had become lieutenant, it was the car he had been given to use. Jozsef's truck was also a police-owned vehicle. Only government officials, military personnel and law enforcement drove vehicles. Laszlo had developed a knack for mechanics and would sometimes spend his days off tinkering with his car.

It had several mechanical problems, but Laszlo always found a way to fix it.

He sat behind the wheel and started the car. The engine roared to life satisfyingly. Laszlo pulled out onto the road and travelled south along the Danube.

⤇

Elona swung her legs off the bed. She had slept well past noon, needing the extra hours from her night shift cleaning at the cinema. Elona gazed back at the empty bed. Ferenc had already gone to work. She rarely saw him anymore. He never came home until late; by then, she was already on her way to work.

She missed the physical intimacy of a man. Elona loved skin-to-skin contact, hugs in the middle of the night and occasional sex. Curiously, she didn't miss Ferenc, though. She had no desire remaining for him. Elona thought back to the days of her youth when she was with her first love. The boy had fled Hungary to Western Europe. Elona had cried for many months, then finally accepted her fate of staying behind in Hungary.

She was older now, Elona thought. Maybe one day, she will find a way to escape to another country for a better life.

Elona pulled on her thin socks and slipped on a long peasant dress. She had no one to impress today. Elona felt the calling of solitude today. She would go to her private spot along the Danube and dream of escaping from the confines of Hungary one day.

⤇

Laszlo slowed the Mercedes to a stop at the bushes' edge, parking the car so it was hidden from view. He didn't want anyone to find him. This was his private sanctuary where he could play music for hours and soothe his damaged soul.

He shifted into neutral, pulled the emergency brake, and shut off the car. Once he opened the car door, he immediately took a deep breath of country air. It smelled so different out here, Laszlo mused.

He took the accordion out of the backseat and walked towards the river's edge with the instrument in his arms. Laszlo found a cleared spot and sat down on the grassy elevated riverside. It had a slight incline and dipped down until the land reached the water. Laszlo opened the case and lifted the accordion out, setting it on his lap. He thought briefly of the songs he would play, then nodded to himself, knowing which ones he would start with.

Laszlo didn't play songs from books anymore; he created his own music. He had originally started out performing music from popular songs when he was young. In the past few years, he had started developing his own songs, writing down some notes to remind himself until he memorized the entire song. He had a talent for music that few people knew.

He laced his fingers over the edges of the accordion and lifted it closer to his abdomen. He began to play a melancholy song about love. Laszlo played the entire song and grimaced at every mistake. He repeated the entire song over and over again until he had played it two times without errors.

Laszlo licked his lips and started again. This time, his deep voice filtered out into the countryside, singing along with the accordion. He hit higher notes eloquently and lower notes easily, making the birds chirp in response. Laszlo smiled and felt his heart expand with the forested area. He sang the song meekly at first, then repeated the song over and over again until he perfected it. Finally, he sang with gusto, crooning out the crescendo with all he could muster.

He finished the song and took a deep inhale, exhaling with force. Laszlo was glad he had come today. He deliberated over the next song, tinkering with a few melodies until he settled his mind on another melancholy song.

He positioned himself again and then stopped, his heart hammering in his chest.

The bushes rustled near the river.

Laszlo froze and listened intently. He heard another rustle very close. Could it be an animal? Laszlo's hand immediately slipped to his pistol. He listened to another rustling and deducted immediately that it didn't sound like an animal. It was human.

Before he pulled his pistol, a slight woman appeared in the clearing. She had messy hair and a shocked look on her face.

"Oh, my! It's you," Elona said. She stood transfixed on the spot, looking at Laszlo, his accordion and then gazed up towards the dirt road at the Mercedes in the bushes. "I didn't know you played the accordion." She gazed up at him, confused. "You play the songs beautifully. I just followed the music through the bushes." Elona looked around in bewilderment. "I come here often. It's a surprise to see you here."

Laszlo stood frozen. He was flabbergasted and couldn't seem to formulate any words. He mumbled something incomprehensible.

"I'm sorry to have interrupted you," Elona said, smoothing her peasant dress. She must look like a wild child, Elona thought. She had not even brushed her hair after waking up today. Elona turned to leave.

"Don't go," Laszlo said in a deep voice.

"Are you sure?"

"Yes, I'm sure," Laszlo replied. "I only come here to play occasionally."

"Don't let me stop you," Elona said. "You are talented. Please play another song."

"You'd like to hear another song?"

"Yes, definitely," Elona replied. "I heard most of that last song several times before I found you. You perfected it. Please continue."

Laszlo nodded and bent down over the instrument. He pulled his arms apart, forcing the instrument to expand and releasing a rich tone of deep notes for his one-person audience. He licked his lips and played the entire song without singing, making several mistakes.

"It takes me three or four tries before I can play it without mistakes," Laszlo stated.

"Please continue," Elona said softly, stretching her body out on the grass, gazing towards the river. "Pretend I'm not here. I love your music."

Laszlo repeated the process, playing the song many more times until he had completed it with few errors. He gazed at Elona on the grass as she lay peacefully with her toes almost in the river. It was nice playing music without having to deal with the awkward meeting. It was highly unusual that he would meet anyone here, but like the luncheon, events were happening without his intervention. Laszlo accepted that this was the path his life was genuinely being led towards.

He felt something warm in his heart today. Laszlo enjoyed sharing his love for music with this engaging woman.

He started singing and followed with the accordion. His deep voice floated over the deserted countryside, crooning about a lost love and a life unfulfilled.

Elona turned herself over, lying on her stomach and placed her elbows into the grass, propping up her chin. She smiled warmly and felt herself become immersed in the music. Her skin tingled when he sang about an unfulfilled life. Elona knew that feeling all too well. Her entire life, with the exception of a few hopeful years, was stuffed with unfulfilled dreams and lost goals. She felt transfixed to the music, to his strong deep voice and to the man himself as he sang with his eyes partially closed, completely engulfed in his musical passion.

The song grew to a crescendo, and the skin on her arms raised in tiny goosebumps as she felt the misery of the past ten years somehow crumbling from Laszlo's shoulders. He was truly sharing something special with her; Elona knew this in the pit of her stomach. She felt honoured to be the recipient of such soulful music and could almost glimpse into his soul.

The song ended, and Laszlo lowered his head down to the accordion, his lungs breathing in heavily to recapture air. Years of smoking had definitely changed his voice and his ability to hold a note for very long. Ten years ago, he would have been able to sing much better.

She began to clap softly.

Laszlo looked at her now as if he had forgotten she was there. He smiled. "You liked it?" he asked breathlessly.

"I loved it," she replied. "Your voice is so rich and soulful. You are so good at the accordion. What was that song called?"

"It is just one of my creations," Laszlo said. "I call it Lost Love."

"You created that song?" Elona asked, astonished.

"Yes," he responded. "Is that unusual?"

Elona paused. It was unusual, but she wasn't going to say so. "I am astonished at your talent," she said.

"Thank you," he said quietly.

"Where did you learn how to play like that?"

"When I was a boy, my parents sent me to music classes because I would sing in my room." Laszlo unhooked the accordion and placed it down on his lap. "So I learned accordion because it was the only instrument in the house."

"Well, you play so wonderfully," Elona said. "The emotion in that last song touched my soul. Did you write it about someone?"

Laszlo keyed a few notes and then stopped. "Yes, it was about my ex-fiancé."

"You were engaged?"

"Yes, sort of," Laszlo said. "I hadn't bought the ring yet, but we had talked about it many times."

"What happened?"

Laszlo froze and grimaced. "Look," he said, suddenly uncomfortable. "It's not something to talk about lightly." He pursed his lips, unsure how to tell this woman the grisly details. "Something terrible happened."

Elona sat up and walked closer to Laszlo. She lowered herself to the grass less than two feet away and held her hands to her lips in a steeple. "You can choose to tell me or not," she said. "This is your decision. Either way, I will be content and joyful that I heard your pain through your music."

"She was a Hungarian Jew," he said abruptly.

Elona gasped.

"She was taken away on one of the Jewish trains," Laszlo said. "I never saw her again."

"I am so sorry," Elona said sympathetically.

"It was a long time ago," he said quietly. "The pain is still there, but somehow it is more bearable. I guess after time, you realize that life goes on. The living continues on, and the dead are no longer part of your life in physical form. Only the memories remain."

Elona reached over and spread her arms around Laszlo, hugging him warmly. She felt so utterly sad for him, and her heart pumped wildly, thinking back to all the Jewish shoes along the riverfront.

Laszlo accepted the hug. It was awkward because he still had the accordion on his lap, but nevertheless, it was a warm hug that he rarely ever got. He smiled into her hair and could smell a faint scent of flowers and citrus.

She let go of him and sat back down, smoothing her dress nervously. "The Germans were so cruel," she said, noticing his body relax and then stiffen.

"Yes, they were," he said blankly.

Elona mused briefly over the details like she had discovered a missing piece. She dug back in her memory of something they had talked about. She wrinkled her nose, trying to remember, then it came back to her. Laszlo's friends had said something about him being with the army since 1944 and his hatred of Germans. The realization hit her with the speed of a locomotive, and she simply blurted out her thoughts. "That's why you joined the army," she said, a chill running up her spine. "You were fighting for her ghost."

Laszlo placed the accordion down and stretched backwards on the grass. For several moments he was quiet. Then finally, he spoke. "Yes, I suppose you are right."

"I'm so sorry for your loss," Elona repeated. She sat cross-legged on the grass, staring at this gentle but harsh man. She now saw him in a completely different light. "You are an admirable man."

Laszlo stared up at the sky. The clouds looked like fluffy white cotton strips floating in formation. He had never thought of himself as admirable. "Thank you," he said plainly. "I am just a man. Some say I am too quick to anger."

Elona drummed her fingers on her knee. He did seem a bit short-tempered with people. She had assumed that was because he was a lieutenant. "Isn't that a personality trait required to rise to the position of lieutenant?"

Laszlo had never thought of it that way. "I suppose," he said simply.

Elona sensed that he wasn't a man who spoke about himself too much. She tilted her head and touched his arm. A shot of electricity coursed through her arm into her heart. Elona felt an instant attraction to this damaged man. But more than that, she felt a strange kindred spirit with him. Elona couldn't really name it or find a rational explanation, but she felt connected to him. "Well," she said softly, her hand still on his arm. "I think you are a strong man, in mind as well as physical form."

Laszlo looked at her hand on his arm and felt the instant chemistry tingle throughout his system. He wanted to kiss her. His body instantly wanted her. Laszlo tried to calm his strong physical response. It had been an extremely long time for him. Some days it felt like he was an animal in a cage. He urged his mind to say something thoughtful instead of testosterone gibberish. "You are a strong woman as well," he said in a deep smooth voice.

The tone of his voice shook her to the core. Elona had no idea why she was being drawn to him so strongly. "I had my share of troubles," she said softly, her eyes downcast, catching a few glimpses of his muscular body.

Laszlo pulled his arm from her touch and shoved his elbows behind his back, propping his upper body up. He was glad to have the focus taken off of himself. "Tell me your story,"

Laszlo said, finally feeling somewhat more comfortable talking with her.

Elona blinked and wondered how much to tell him. He was from the Hungarian Army. She felt like a political tightrope hung between them. She was still afraid of speaking her true voice for fear of prosecution. Maybe he was a spy? The absurd thought flitted in her mind as she formed her words. "I think I told you before of my university hopes," Elona said. "I was one of the brightest students."

"Yes, I remember," Laszlo said. "You were forced to end your university term to work, but you didn't say much more."

"I had to work because my father was arrested," she blurted out. "He worked for the local newspaper for many years. The AVH came to our house two years ago and arrested him for writing an article that was considered treasonous." She paused. "You have to understand. Apu did not write anything bad; he simply wrote about the reforms necessary in Hungary, the same things that Imre Nagy had implemented several months later." Elona stopped uncomfortably, attempting to word it properly. "General Rákosi took offence and sent his officers to remove Apu from the newspaper."

"Matyas Rákosi hasn't made the best decisions," Laszlo immediately responded. In fact, he hated the man, but he would say no more. Laszlo bit his tongue and allowed her to continue.

"Yes, Rákosi is not very good at reform," Elona said, trying to stay on the political tightrope with Laszlo. She gently bit her lower lip as she continued. "After the arrest, my mother struggled to support the family on her meagre income as a seamstress. But then, soon after, she lost those jobs as well. No one would hire her anymore because she was married to a criminal." Elona swallowed and quickly stammered out the rest of the story. "My siblings all left to get married, and only I remained at home.

I quit university and started working to support my mother. Soon after, I married as well. It was an instant decision. I could not go back to my childhood poverty." She paused, then quickly finished her story. "My mother lives with us, and my dream of having a journalism degree is now on hold."

Laszlo lifted his body to sitting and grasped both her hands. "I was right," he said, looking into her eyes. "You are a strong woman. You have done what you had to do to take care of your mother. You are the admirable one."

Elona blinked. "Thank you," she said. "I try to remind myself that there are many people with much more troubles in Hungary than myself. I am not Jewish. I am still alive, and I am healthy."

"That is the truth," he said slowly. "There has been so much misery in Hungary. Soldiers are not immune from it either."

Elona squeezed his hands softly. "I suppose you have seen a lot of ugliness, especially in 1945."

"Yes, I have," Laszlo said, his eyes clouding over to a different time. "I was young and furious at the Germans for stealing my happiness." He stopped suddenly, and the words choked in his throat. The images of war immediately assaulted his mind, as if the date 1945 had cracked open a floodgate. He closed his eyes, trying to will the horrors from invading his thoughts so suddenly. Laszlo opened his eyes and looked right through Elona as if she was a ghost.

Elona gripped his hands tighter, sensing something was wrong.

Laszlo closed his eyes again.

"Are you okay?" she said with deep concern.

Laszlo blinked. "I cannot speak of war," he said. "My mind does not allow it." An image of a young teenage German boy lying face up with his lower body torn in half invaded Laszlo's brain. The sound of distance shots peppered his ears. He told himself it was the past, not the present, but his heart hammered in his chest as if he had been transported in time. Laszlo started to sweat. Then his cruel mind reminded him that he was the one who had killed that young boy.

"Laszlo!" Elona said firmly, concern washing over her. She gripped his hands tighter. "You are a hero. Don't ever forget that."

Laszlo gazed at Elona as his eyes slowly came back into focus. "I am only a man," he said, exhaling a weary sigh as the teenage boy faded into the dark recesses of his mind.

"You have had to face too many horrors," Elona said, relieved to see his eyes focusing on her again. She was momentarily alarmed at the abrupt shift from reality she had just witnessed. "Anytime you want to talk, I am here."

Laszlo looked down at their hands gripping each other. "You are a sweet girl," he said, his voice lower than usual. "The horrors of war are not spoken. They are forever buried in a place where I don't dare go willingly." Laszlo exhaled another deep breath, thankful that the bad memory had passed. "It is a dark place," he stated calmly.

Elona felt her heart burst open with patriotism and love for this damaged man. He had done his part in saving Hungary from the Germans, and she suddenly felt extremely grateful. "Well, if nobody has ever told you," Elona said sincerely. "Thank you for your service to Hungary. It is a selfless act, and you are a good man."

Laszlo sat frozen to the spot. Nobody had ever said any such thing to him before. He shifted ever so slightly closer. He wanted to hug her and tell her how grateful he was to have met her. Instead, Laszlo gazed into her deep emerald eyes.

Elona felt an odd magnetism pulling them together. She felt so grateful to this man for rescuing her country and was overcome by emotion. Elona leaned over quickly and kissed his cheek. "You are a true hero," she said.

Before she could say another word, Laszlo turned his cheek and kissed her soft lips. He pulled away briefly, unsure if he had stepped over her boundaries. Before he could think more about it, she kissed him back. Her lips pressed against his, and her body fell into his arms effortlessly. Laszlo wrapped his arms around her waist and pulled her into his embrace. It was an awkward position with both of them sitting. He shifted his body, pulling her to his side and laid down on the grass with her. They broke the kiss briefly, and Laszlo took the opportunity to run his fingers along her mat of wild hair. He traced his thumb down her hairline and along her square cheekbones. She was a pretty woman; some would say she had masculine features, but Laszlo could see more than just her face. He had a glimpse of the strong woman inside, and that was the most beautiful thing ever.

They kissed again. It was only small gentle kisses, but it meant so much somehow as if they were consoling each other's wounds. It was the most tender thing Laszlo had ever experienced in his life. He was normally a rough urgent man, never stopping long enough to relish in any moment.

But now, the world seemed to stop with only the river flowing continually near their feet. They explored each other's mouths as their lips parted. Her mouth tasted like sweet grapes, and he instantly felt ashamed of his cigarette breath. It didn't seem to bother her, but for once in his life, it bothered him.

Laszlo pulled her into him tighter, and she naturally wound her thigh over him to close the gap. She smelled of flowers, sweat and grass. He loved it. Her earthy way of just being herself was so genuine and wholesome.

He hugged her tighter and then broke the kiss, laying his chin on her head. Laszlo didn't want to have this moment spin out of control. They were obviously very attracted to each other, but she was a married woman, after all. He had no intention of having an affair.

Elona immediately buried her face into his chest.

Laszlo murmured and kissed her hair. "What is it?" he said.

"I feel ashamed," she mumbled into his shirt. "I am married."

"Yes," he said. "I know. We will stop." He ran his hand over her matted hair and smoothed it lovingly.

"I have fallen out of love with him," she said abruptly, gazing up at Laszlo.

"How do you know?" he replied.

"I no longer want to sleep with him," she said. "Every ounce of my body screams to be as far away as possible from him." She swallowed hard, squeezed her eyes shut momentarily, then slowly reopened them. "I believe that I made a mistake marrying him."

"Are you getting a divorce?" he asked curiously.

The word divorce hit her suddenly. She had never even uttered it before. Elona was young and didn't even know where to begin. She just wanted to leave Ferenc. "I want to leave him, yes," she answered. Elona instantly realized this was the first time she had spoken the words aloud. "I have known in my heart that it is something I must do for the past few months." She stammered. "I guess I just have no idea where to start. I have never left a man before."

Laszlo felt sad for her. It must be a difficult thing to walk away willingly from someone you used to love.

"Have you ever had a divorce?" she asked innocently.

"No, I have not," he replied. "I was only in love once, and she was taken from me."

"You stayed alone all these years?"

"Yes," he replied, his heart feeling cold at the thought.

"You never wanted to fall in love again?" she asked.

"I don't think it was that," he replied. "I just think it hit me so hard that I turned my heartbreak into war and anger. I never really thought about finding a wife. My life was about the army."

"Is it still?" Elona asked.

Laszlo paused, trying to answer the question honestly but without revealing his political misgivings. "The army is in my blood," he said, smoothing her hair. "It is as much a part of me as journalism is a part of you." He kissed her forehead. "But I am not the angry man I once was. I have grown softer over the years." Laszlo knew in his heart that he could trust her a bit. "The recent political upheavals have shown me the true face of the government. I don't care to be used as a puppet for the most current fashion of politics."

Elona nodded, encouraging him to continue.

"I cannot speak much more of this," he ended. "It is my job as a lieutenant to keep morale high. If my morale sinks, my comrades can feel it too."

"I understand," Elona replied. "Don't feel compelled to tell me what you feel uncomfortable expressing." She kissed his cheek softly. "Just know that I would never utter a word of what we speak in confidence."

"Thank you," Laszlo said, grateful to hear her say this. "If my personal political preferences support any leader no longer in power, I can be arrested and executed for treason. I hope you can understand this."

"Would you really be killed?"

"Yes."

Silence filled the air around them. Elona laid her head gently on his chest and snuggled into him. His muscular right arm encircled her shoulders and pulled her in warmly. They embraced like this for several minutes, just enjoying the warmth. Birds chirped a delightful chorus as the waves of the river continued on their endless journey. Laszlo breathed in and felt his world was suddenly changing. Something inside of him yearned for the unknown. Elona had awakened an emotion.

He closed his eyes and wondered if he could love again. Laszlo always felt he could but never put any effort into achieving this goal. Maybe his heart was irreparably broken, and he had just smothered the pain in the military. His heart beat wildly in his chest. He liked this woman, he realized.

"I like you, Laszlo," Elona said as if on cue.

Laszlo smiled. "I like you too," he said. "We will figure things out. Wherever the future will take us and all of Hungary, I am willing to follow that. Anything will be better than what Hungary has now."

"This is the truth," she replied.

Laszlo had dropped Elona off a few blocks away from home. He hugged her and patted her knee, feeling uncertain. "Will we see each other again?" he asked.

"Yes," she replied. "I work at the Corvin Cinema every Thursday and Friday night."

"Well, then," Laszlo said warmly. "I will stop by this week then. Until then, please keep yourself safe, my dear."

"I will," Elona responded. "I will." She repeated and opened the car door, stepping out. A moment of indecision streaked across her face, and she leapt back in, kissing him on the cheek, then leapt back out, slamming the door. "Bye!" Elona skipped happily down the street, her heart soaring into the cloudy sky. She walked home quickly under the swirling rain clouds when the first raindrops started falling. Then she ran the rest of the way home with a silly grin on her face.

Chapter 5

Today was like any other day, but Elona felt a glow on her cheeks and a spring in her step. She knew, of course, what had changed. It was Laszlo. His presence in her life had renewed her hope for the future.

Ferenc was gone to work, and she was glad that she didn't need to see him today. The wheels of change were filling her mind with all sorts of possibilities.

The idea of leaving her husband was forming in her mind. Elona started realizing how miserable she had been for such a long time. She was young and lacked experience with ending relationships. Elona had no clue where to start.

She heard the floorboards creak as Anyu made her way to the bathroom. Elona poured herself a strong coffee and inhaled the delicious scent of the fresh coffee. She tapped her toe to a happy tune in her head and smiled.

The bathroom door creaked open and then shut. "What are you so happy about?" Anyu said jokingly.

"No reason," Elona said, smiling. "Can I not be happy?"

"I suppose so," Anyu said suspiciously. "It is just unusual for anybody in this country to be happy lately."

Elona didn't want to tell anyone about her thoughts of leaving Ferenc, at least until she had come up with a sound plan.

Anyu would become too insistent and try to influence her plans. She needed time to figure out a way.

"You're deep in thought," Anyu said. "What has gotten into you lately?"

Elona sipped the hot coffee and almost chuckled. "Oh, nothing," she said nonchalantly. "It's just work. Lots of cleaning to do at the cinema this week. I am thinking it may take three nights instead of two."

"You shouldn't work so much," Anyu responded, blowing on her coffee to cool it down. "We can survive better on Ferenc's pay now that he is working."

"I have never relied on Ferenc's pay," Elona said. "And I won't start now."

"Good," Anyu said smartly. "That's my girl. Don't ever rely on anyone except yourself."

Elona stood and hugged her mother unexpectedly. "I am a strong Hungarian, just like you, Anyu," she said. "Thank you for being a good mom."

Laszlo couldn't get Elona out of his mind. The entire week crept by slowly. Training new recruits came and went as the days dragged on. His mind was not focused on work anymore, which was strange because his entire life for the past ten years was about defending his country.

Now, out of the blue, a woman has slipped into his consciousness.

And he can't seem to get her out of his brain now.

Tomorrow was Thursday, and Laszlo was going to see her at the cinema. He contemplated several different scenarios in his head about what they could do at 4 am but still came up with nothing. His mind was jumbled with thoughts of seeing her naked, and he struggled to think straight.

He knew it was his testosterone because his penis was stiff several times a day now, without reason. It was frustrating and disrupting to have his body reacting in such an adolescent way every day. It was like she had flipped a switch in his brain, and now his entire existence was about getting his penis inside of her.

He was a gentleman, of course, so he wouldn't be doing any such thing, but his physical body argued otherwise.

Laszlo pulled his socks off and removed his pants. He removed every other article of clothing until he was only in his undershirt and shorts. Laszlo lay down on his bed, staring at the ceiling. His hand fluttered to his groin, and felt the hard ridge poking up. He rolled to his side, trying to ignore the insistent body part vying for his attention. Laszlo closed his eyes and willed himself to sleep. He thought of his accordion and watching sunrises, then Elona filtered into his thoughts. The curve of her slender hips and her hypnotic green eyes filled his mind. He grunted and rolled onto his other side. Her laugh filtered into his ears somehow, and he saw her smile in his mind's eye.

Laszlo finally gave in and grabbed his penis, making a quick job of sexual relief so he could sleep.

Elona lay in bed, quietly listening to the calm night from her open bedroom window. Ferenc lay beside her, fast asleep. She was astonished that he wasn't snoring tonight. Normally, he would snore for hours, keeping her awake, but tonight he didn't.

But she was still awake. Too many worries were on her mind.

All week she had thought of plans to leave Ferenc. She almost went to her brother's place to tell him about her plans and ask if he would let her stay with him until they found some-place to live.

Tomorrow was Thursday, and she was excited about seeing Laszlo again. Her breasts swelled and felt tender to the touch. She found herself thinking about Laszlo obsessively. The way he walked, his muscular shoulders and his throaty laugh. Elona knew that she was immensely attracted to him, but she also knew that she would never commit adultery. Elona was a mon-ogamous committed partner. If she wanted to be with Laszlo, she would have to leave her husband first. This she knew.

But today was different. Something unexpected had hap-pened. Elona rolled onto her side, clutching her shoulders, trying to hug herself. It was actually something that had not happened that disturbed her deeply.

Her plans for leaving Ferenc may be washed away into the sewer because of this one happenstance incident. Elona peered out the window and saw a few bright stars shining back at her. She put her hands together in prayer.

"Please guide me," she whispered to the stars, pleading for guidance.

CHAPTER 6

It was a cleaning day like any other. She never had enough time to finish cleaning the entire cinema on her own. Elona would have to tell management that she could begin spreading the cleaning job over three nights to do a more thorough job. They would be more than happy with the work. They knew Elona was a hard worker and meticulously clean.

Elona reached over her head, sticking more bobby pins in her hair after several strands had fallen from the loose bun. Her hair was always wild, wavy and unmanageable, it seemed. When she was working, it became even more unruly.

And this is how Laszlo would see her after almost an entire week of absence.

She hadn't heard from him since meeting at the riverside. He said he would meet her on Thursday or Friday. Maybe he had changed his mind. Elona tried to push the insecurities out of her mind. Perhaps he would show up, or maybe he wouldn't. It didn't matter anyways. She shook her head despondently as she ran a wet cloth over the bathroom countertops.

Elona looked briefly into the mirror and saw her haggard reflection staring back. Elona smiled weakly at herself. She wasn't a beautiful woman, her nose was too pointy, and her face was square. She was more handsome than pretty. But her eyes made up for her lack of feminine facial features.

A sudden urge to urinate sent her running to the toilet, and she fumbled with her pants. Hope soared in her heart that her body would tell her some good news.

She looked down at her panties and sighed. Her menstrual pad was clear. Elona exhaled heavily. Never before in her life had she wished for her monthly period to come so badly.

Elona finished in the bathroom stall and returned to the sink, immersing her rag into a small bucket of cleaning solution. She scrubbed the sinks with the damp rag until they were sparkling clean. Elona leaned her buttocks on the counter, content with the cleanliness and stared out at the bathroom walls in deep thought.

Elona couldn't believe her bad luck. If it were true, she would be having Ferenc's baby.

She squinted her eyes shut and prayed silently.

Maybe her period would come tomorrow. It was only a day or two late, she thought wistfully.

It was 3:50 am when Elona placed her mop and pail into the cleaning closet. She unlocked the door and checked her hair one more time in the large wall mirror by the front entrance. She removed the bun and ran her fingers through her strands, trying to comb it down to no avail. Frustrated, she searched in her pockets for the keys and opened the door, locking it behind her.

Elona's eyes instantly searched the shadows for movement, anything indicating that Laszlo was here waiting for her.

The dark night air was still.

She sighed. He wasn't going to show up tonight, Elona thought wearily. She leaned back onto the locked front entrance and looked at her watch. She was ten minutes early. Elona would wait until 4:10 am then she would go home.

Laszlo stepped out into the dark night and mounted the two-wheeler bicycle. It was an old bicycle that he had shared with his brother growing up. Tibor had kept it and maintained the bike meticulously. His brother was only a private in the army and didn't have any vehicle assigned to him yet. Only the higher-ranking officers were given such luxuries.

Laszlo stepped on the bicycle pedals and swerved down the street. The cinema was not too far away from the barracks, and the riverside was only a twenty-minute bike ride. He was a bit late and worried that she might leave for home. He pumped the pedals faster, trying to race against time.

The wind blew in his face as he pedalled hard. Laszlo didn't want to take the Mercedes because it had a loud engine, and at 4 am, it would definitely awaken everyone. Laszlo didn't need to explain to everyone why he was meeting a cleaning lady at the cinema at 4 am.

He veered the bicycle around the corner, almost losing control because of the long empty back end. The cinema came into view, but he couldn't see anybody waiting. He squinted into the dark. He was only five minutes late, he guessed. Maybe she wasn't the type of girl who waited, or worse, maybe she didn't think he was coming at all.

Laszlo slowed the bicycle and smiled with relief when he saw her shadow leaning against the front door of the cinema.

"Hello, beautiful," he said, braking the bicycle to a full stop. "Sorry, I'm a bit late. Thanks for waiting."

"Nice bike. Where did you get that?" Elona said, smiling in surprise.

"It was our old bike when my brother and I were growing up," Laszlo said. "Hop on; it seats two."

Elona smiled broadly. "Sure!" she said eagerly.

Laszlo tilted the bike so she could climb on. "Sorry, it might be a bit too high. I lowered the seat as far as it could go. Can you reach the pedals?"

Elona swung her leg over the bicycle and sat on the seat, her left foot reaching the lower pedal. "I can reach," she said, giggling gleefully.

"Great!" he said. "We are going to the riverside to watch the sunrise!"

"That's wonderful!" she said. "I have never been there in the early morning before."

"I couldn't think of anything else to do at 4 am," Laszlo said, laughing. "Okay, when we start moving, hang on to the bars as if only you are steering and pedal the same as normal." He looked back to ensure she was securely on the bike, then started moving forward. "The riverside is a twenty-minute bicycle ride from here. It's a bit wobbly at first riding a tandem bike, but you'll get the hang of it."

Elona started pedalling and felt the wobble immediately, she grabbed the bars, but of course, it was only for balance, so she couldn't steer. She felt the bike lean to the right, then the left, as Laszlo adjusted his balance. Her hands were extremely close to his buttocks as his seat was almost right between her bars. Elona inhaled his manly scent and felt a rush of endorphins coursing through her body.

"Are you okay?" he asked in the wind. "Everything alright back there?"

"Yes!" Elona shouted, straining her voice to be heard over the wind. "Keep going. I'm pedalling!" She had never ridden a tandem bicycle before. Elona giggled to herself. She enjoyed being with Laszlo. It was refreshing and added light to her dismal days.

"Great, we are going to travel along the river path soon," he said. "I don't like cycling on the road too much at night."

Elona nodded. He was a smart, careful man who paid attention to small details. She wouldn't have even thought about cycling when it was too dark.

The skies were beginning to lighten slowly. A dark purplish hue graced the clouds as the coming sun lightened the skies. The smell of wet grass filtered into their nostrils as the wheels of the tandem bicycle hit the riverside dirt path. They jostled over the bumps and laughed when they had to brake for a small rodent. The animal scurried away, frightful of the human intrusion at such an early hour.

Elona held the bars steady on either side of his buttocks, yearning to touch him. His backside was most likely strong and muscular from the military, she concluded. Elona imagined how he would look naked, and her cheeks flushed at the sudden thought.

"We are getting closer!" Laszlo shouted. "Hold on! There's a slight hill coming up. We need to pedal faster to get up the incline. Pedal hard, my beautiful!"

Elona pumped her small legs with all her might. A bead of sweat formed on her hairline as they struggled up the incline.

Laszlo worked his quad muscles harder as they crested the small hill. "We did it!" he shouted. "Only a bit longer, and we should be there."

Elona didn't care how long it took. She was enjoying herself. Elona giggled to herself and thought back to her memories of a happy time. Did she ever feel this gleeful? Elona thought not.

After several minutes, the bicycle slowed near the bushes, and the path narrowed. Laszlo steered into the bushes as the scenery disappeared in a disarray of shrubs. "Watch out for the branches!" he instructed. "Duck your head."

Laszlo slowed the bike even more until they were almost walking and straddling the bike. "I think this is about as far as we can safely ride," he said. "We can walk the bike the rest of the way." He dismounted the bike and held it steady for Elona to dismount. He watched as she swung her slender right leg off. "Good," he said. "How are you doing?"

"That was fun!" she said gaily. "I've never rode a tandem bike before!"

"Well, you rode it like an expert!" Laszlo cheerfully said as he patted her forearm lightly. A bolt of electricity shot up his arm from the physical contact. He was amazed at how instantly he reacted to her. Laszlo hadn't reacted so strongly to a woman in his entire life. He briefly wondered what made her different. Maybe it was because he couldn't have her, a small voice in his head said cruelly. Laszlo grimaced momentarily, then looked up at the skies. "The sunrise should be upon us soon. We will venture to the same clearing if we can find it. I have only ever driven here."

"I have cycled here many times," Elona said. "We are not far. There will be a rocky outcropping in a few meters, then a five-minute walk from there."

Laszlo smiled. "You are a perceptive woman," he said.

"Sometimes," she replied, laughing with pride as they both started walking the bike through the bushes.

The night was slowly turning to day as the darkness took on a lightening bluish haze. Laszlo turned to glance briefly at Elona. "I think you are more perceptive than people give you credit for. A definite sign of intelligence," Laszlo said absent-mindedly. He looked up, browsing the skies. "The sun is preparing to rise. The skies are getting lighter."

"Yes, it is quite lovely," she said softly. "And thank you. Not many men pay attention to the intelligence of women these days."

It was true, especially in Hungary, Laszlo thought. Many men treated their wives as nothing more than child-rearing cooks. But not all men, he noted. There were some men, like himself, that didn't conform to society's standards. He treated his fiancé very well and encouraged her to learn right up to the day she was taken away. The harsh memory slammed into his gut and made him involuntarily grind his teeth.

He held onto the bike as they pushed it through the bushes. Moments later, they passed by the rocky outcropping, and Laszlo remembered all the Jewish people just like his fiancé, who had been killed for nothing along this river. It was a terrible dark moment in Europe, and the world had noticed, sending the American and Canadian infantries onto the western shores of Europe to fight against the Germans. The Russians fought from the northeast, and Laszlo was secretly one of them. It was easier than he had originally thought to start spying for the Russians. An old war veteran from his father's WWI days had asked him if he could help turn the war against the Germans, and Laszlo had keenly accepted. It wasn't long before he was reporting the German's movements to the Red Army.

"Are you okay?" Elona asked, interrupting the silence. "You got really quiet."

Laszlo looked behind him. "Oh yes," he said. "I'm fine, just remembering."

Elona grimaced. Memories in Hungary weren't pleasant for most people. "Well," she said. "You can put all that aside; look at the skies!" She pointed ahead near the river. "We're nearly there, and the sun is coming up fast."

The bushes parted into a clearing. It was the very same spot they had kissed each other a week ago. The skies were turning a lighter shade of purple. An orange glow streaked through a few clouds, creating the start of a beautiful sunrise like she had never seen before. Elona smiled and touched his arm as they laid the bike onto the grassy hill.

"We can watch the sunrise perfectly from here!" Laszlo said. "Come." He grabbed her hand and walked with her up to the top of the grassy hill to get a better view. Once he found a suitable spot, Laszlo sat down on the grass, pulling her with him. As she sat down, he wrapped his arms around her waist, shuffling her in front of him. He held her warmly as they silently watched the sun rising.

The only sounds were the waves along the river and their own breathing. Even the birds weren't up this early, he thought.

The clouds formed into several long thin cottony strings, one on top of the other. The kaleidoscope of colours reflected upon the lower edges of the thin clouds. Reds, oranges, blues and purples streaked across the clouds and reflected back against the darkish backdrop of the descending night sky. It was the most beautiful thing Elona had ever witnessed. There were no words to be spoken. It was breathtaking. She relaxed back into Laszlo's embrace as they both stared wondrously into the lightening skies, awed by the beauty before them.

Elona felt at peace in his arms, almost as if she was meant to be with him. Her rational mind told her that was impossible because she was still married and possibly pregnant. The possibility of being happy with Laszlo was a distant dream, not a reality, she told herself. Laszlo's arms tightened around her shoulders, giving her an affectionate squeeze. It was like he knew what her mind was thinking, and he was here to reassure her that everything would be alright.

But everything wasn't alright, Elona thought. The happiness she so craved was such a distant possibility that it almost felt futile.

Laszlo kissed her hair, and Elona's concerns vanished into the early dawn. She could feel his breath on her head, and it somehow felt calming. Elona relished in the moment. She was allowed this small joy, she told herself. The special moments in life were all that mattered in this crazy world. All the wars, deaths and oppression were heavy in this land. She ran her fingers idly through the grass.

"I enjoy these moments with you," Elona said abruptly, putting words to her thoughts. "And I don't feel guilty. Sometimes all you need in life is special moments like this to remember forever."

"Never feel guilty, Elona," Laszlo said, kissing her head again. "We are only two human beings enjoying each other's company on a beautiful morning. Right now, nothing else exists but this." He rested his chin lightly on her head and gazed at the lightening skies. "I can sit here all day with you and be happy. Just doing this. It's like we're on a different planet."

"I was thinking the same," Elona said. "I don't know if I have ever felt so content in anyone's arms before."

Laszlo shifted his buttocks. "I'm glad you feel comfortable with me," he said, his heart skipping a beat at the emotions stirring inside him.

Elona turned her head and kissed his shoulder. "I do feel comfortable," she confirmed.

They watched for several more minutes as the lazy sun rose until, finally, it peaked above the horizon of shrubs and trees. The yellow glow glared directly at them, and they had to look away from the intense light.

"Don't look directly into the sun," Laszlo stated, shielding her eyes with his arm stretched out.

She turned her face away and shifted her body to face him. They gazed at each other like this for several moments, frozen in time. Then Elona bent forward and kissed him. He accepted her kiss eagerly and savoured the moment passionately. Her tongue was urgent but gentle. Laszlo kissed her back intimately.

She pulled away gently and looked into his eyes. Her hand fluttered to his clean-shaven face. Elona's fingers traced a line down his jawline, sensually cradling his cheek in her hands. "You're so handsome," she murmured absentmindedly.

He surged forward and kissed her again, tasting her sweet mouth. Laszlo felt inexplicably drawn to this woman, so much so that he had to question his sanity. She was married, after all. Her touch electrified him and soothed all his painful memories simultaneously. Laszlo was grateful for just being with her during these moments, but something inside of him yearned for more. A stifled ache for true happiness began to grow in his gut.

Elona broke the kiss gently. "I am still married," she said softly. Guilt streaked her face, and she looked down. Elona thought of her missed period. She couldn't tell him, not yet. What if she received her monthly curse tomorrow? Then she could try to make plans to leave Ferenc. What would she do if her period never came? Elona thought hard about this. Her motherly instincts and family-centred upbringing were strong. She would stay with her husband. Elona would have to; there was no other way. Her baby would need to be with his father. Anyu would be a grandmother, she thought. Elona gasped inwardly at the thought.

"Yes, you are married," Laszlo said wearily.

Elona snapped out of her reverie at his words. How did this affect him? He must feel the same yearning, she thought. "How do you feel about me?" she asked honestly.

Laszlo grinned. He didn't know. Laszlo wasn't a man of introspection. He was a hard, war-driven man with emotions bottled up like a volcano. Laszlo yearned to have a family of his own and fall deeply in love with an intelligent woman, someone just like Elona. How could he ever tell her this? The tough man he showed to the world could never succumb to such emotional words of the heart. In that deep spot of his heart was a mixed rage of injustice like none other and a constant pain for change. She would never understand. How could he explain how he felt about her? "I don't know," he said simply. "I like you." Laszlo laid his hands on top of her palms and wondered if she would ever leave her husband. The thought made him ill to his stomach. "I enjoy our times together, but I am not a marriage destroyer. Nor was it ever my intention to be such a man."

Elona felt her heart sink. He didn't feel the same, she thought. His words rang in her ears. Laszlo didn't know how he felt about her. He didn't want her to leave her husband. Elona swallowed hard and continued looking down.

Laszlo felt strange like he had said something wrong. "Are you okay?" he asked.

"Yes," she responded. "I'm fine."

"Look at me," Laszlo said, pulling her chin up. Her eyes were moist with tears. "What's wrong?"

"Nothing and everything," she mumbled, her words overcome with emotion. Elona struggled to keep the tears inside of her until she could somehow smother the desperate yearning she had for Laszlo. "I am a faithful woman. And I like you too."

Laszlo hugged her warmly. "Don't feel bad," he said in a low husky voice. "We won't kiss anymore. We can just enjoy each other's company, and that's all."

Elona wanted so much more than that. She could never tell him. He would never understand. "Okay," she replied simply, swallowing back her tears.

Laszlo kept her in his arms, enveloping her in his warmth. He still felt odd, like something was not right. He didn't know what to do or say, so he did nothing. Laszlo felt close to Elona but yet so far away. The moments they spent together were like a fairy tale in the midst of a cruel world. He didn't want to lose these little moments of happiness, but he also didn't want to force her to leave her husband. Laszlo didn't know what to do.

Elona's mind swirled with all the conclusions that he didn't offer and all the horrible endings that she might encounter. What if he was only with her to have sex? This would destroy her marriage and her entire life. She didn't think Laszlo was that kind of man, but it was a possibility. He was a hardened man of war. What did she expect of him? She could expect nothing but companionship.

They stayed like this for several minutes, hugging each other while the sun beamed its hot rays of sunshine on their bodies. Finally, Laszlo broke the embrace. "I will take you home," he said, a note of sadness in his voice. "I want to see you again. The moments we spend together are special to me. I don't want to lose that."

Elona blinked. He was being sincere. Her mind swirled in confusion. "Okay, let's go," Elona said. She couldn't form any more words. Elona would decide what to do when her period came. And if it never did, she'd do the right thing.

CHAPTER 7

A week had passed by, and Elona felt weary. Her body was tired and utterly exhausted. Her abdomen felt bloated and tiny tinges of pain shot into her breasts, making them ache. She knew she was pregnant. Her monthly curse had never come. It was now a week and two days late. A missed period for a twenty-one-year-old woman could mean nothing else. She had all the signs of pregnancy. Elona even started feeling nauseous today.

She stared blankly at the wall in the kitchen. How could this be happening now? Every time they had sex, Ferenc had always pulled out in time. Right after the marriage, they spoke about children, and Elona had wanted to wait for a few years until they had more money. Ferenc wanted a baby right away but had held back for Elona. It wasn't a highly successful type of birth control, but it had worked for the past two years. Within the past year, she didn't want to have a baby with him at all. Elona avoided him as best as she could, except for that one night when he was insistent. She had closed her eyes in disgust, and he had pulled out in time. Why was she pregnant now?

Elona held her head wearily in her hands, deep in thought. It was bad timing, she concluded. Sometimes life is like that.

"Sweetheart?" Anyu's voice lilted through the hallway. "Are you awake?"

"Yes," Elona answered.

"It is early," Anyu said. "Why are you up? Don't you have to work tonight?"

"I'm not going to work tonight," Elona replied.

"Why not?" Anyu responded worriedly. "You don't want to lose this job. The pay is good enough to keep us fed."

"I know," Elona replied. "It is a good job. Don't worry. I will work hard every week." Elona looked up as her mother poured a coffee. She smiled weakly. If the truth was to be told, Elona didn't want to face Laszlo. Not today. Her heart was breaking for him already. She needed another day to formulate the words she would need to tell him. "I called in sick," she said. It was true. Her stomach was grossly nauseous. "I must be coming down with a summer cold."

"You don't sound like you have a cold," Anyu countered.

Her mother was always overly perceptive, Elona thought. She would tell her mother about the pregnancy, but not today. Elona was too consumed with telling Laszlo the hurtful words. "My stomach is not feeling well," Elona said, hoping this would satisfy her mother's curiosity.

Anyu looked worriedly at her daughter and laid a hand on her forehead. "You're not running a fever," she said. "Maybe it is something you ate." Anyu rubbed Elona's shoulder gently with motherly care.

"That's what I was thinking," Elona said softly. She stood and smoothed the front of her nightgown down absentmindedly. "I think I will go back to bed now."

Anyu watched her daughter walk slowly down the hall to her bedroom. It wasn't like her daughter to be so weary. Anyu sipped her coffee and wondered what the girl was up to.

Laszlo hadn't seen Elona yesterday. He tried to calm down the rising panic in his heart. She could have just left work early, or her days could have been changed, Laszlo told himself.

But a strange twist in his gut knew that something had gone wrong. He thought back to their previous rendezvous at the river watching the sunrise. A velvet cloth of warmth fell over him as he remembered the peaceful sunrise. He had never enjoyed such serenity with another human being before, and he wanted to do it again, possibly every day. This was impossible, he knew. He was a lieutenant, after all. His week was much busier than hers. Laszlo had massive commitments with the army.

But he wanted her as his partner in life.

He had come to this startling conclusion after their visit to the riverside. Laszlo wasn't a man of many words, but he did know when his heart was telling him to pursue joy. It wasn't that she gave him happiness; it was that he enjoyed moments of pure joy with her in his presence. This was the highest feeling of contentment he could ever know. He had never met a woman whom he could be himself with. Laszlo had even sung his heart out the first time with the accordion!

Laszlo stomped across the field as the first autumn leaves crunched beneath his feet. He jingled the keys out of his pocket and flipped until he found the correct one. Laszlo inserted it into the lock, and it sprang free. He opened the shed door and stared at the tandem bike. He would try again this morning. This time he was early. It was 3:30 am. He couldn't sleep. Something inside of him begged for answers. Laszlo grimaced. The thought of Elona leaving her husband had his heart soaring, and the thought of her staying with him punched him in the chest. Laszlo would ask her today. He would tell her his feelings. Laszlo would tell her that he would take care of her and marry her once the divorce was final.

His heart beat crazily at the thought of saying such words, but Laszlo knew he needed to. There was something about their last conversation that was left hanging. He had to make his intentions clear.

Laszlo pushed the shed door closed and locked it. He took a deep breath and swung his leg over the tandem bike.

As soon as he began pedalling, the wind rushed in his face. It was a cool morning with a hint of frost in the air. He pumped his legs faster until the bike gained momentum. Laszlo cruised through the streets and steered this way and that, through the quiet deserted streets. He loved his country so much. All of his life, it seemed, he had fought for Hungary's independence. But it never came. Hungary was continually taken over by one country or the next. Laszlo hoped one day, all of his efforts would not be wasted, and a new government would form, spearheading Hungary into the great country that it once was. Laszlo began to realize that more and more Hungarians thought the same ever since Imre Nagy showed them it was possible. Nagy had been the beacon of hope in Hungarians' hearts. But now they were all back to square one with Rákosi.

Laszlo grimaced. But now, something had changed inside him. His spirit had given up on Hungary, and now a woman had stolen his heart. He wanted a family and a safe place to raise children. Laszlo wanted a good woman like Elona. After all these years, the old familiar feelings of yearning and love were slowly creeping back into his soul. Little by little, his heart was opening up.

He steered around the last corner and braked to a halt at the door to the cinema. It was dark, but he could see that she was not there. It was early, of course. He looked at his watch. It was 3:45 am. He would wait.

Laszlo pulled his bike from the street and propped it against the stone exterior of the cinema. He felt the strange tug in his heart again. What if she wasn't here again? What if she was avoiding him?

He would go to her house then, he thought. Laszlo would not let her escape from him so easily. He needed answers, at the very least.

No, he would not do any such thing, he told himself. He lit a cigarette and blew the plume out toward the sky. Laszlo would find a way to contact her if she wasn't here again.

Hundreds of thoughts swirled in his mind, drawing joyful and horrible conclusions. Laszlo inhaled the smoke, drawing deeply from the cigarette and blew it out forcefully. He had started cutting down on the number of cigarettes he smoked per day. Laszlo didn't want her kissing a chimney all the time. One day, he would throw the cigarettes away for good and never smoke again.

Laszlo took another puff from his cigarette and stopped short. He heard a noise from inside the cinema. His heart hammered in his chest immediately. Was it her? Laszlo laid his ear to the door and listened intently. He heard rummaging inside, like someone was getting ready to open the door. Laszlo stood back and tried to appear casual, but his heart was beating loudly in his ears. He stamped out the cigarette butt on the sidewalk and bent a knee casually, trying to appear as if he had just arrived.

Elona opened the door and looked up in shock at Laszlo standing near the door. He was early, she thought. "Hi!" she said sincerely, rattling out her prepared response quickly. "Sorry,

I missed you yesterday. I was feeling ill, so I had called in sick." She tried to force a happy smile, then immediately noticed that Laszlo looked quite handsome this morning. He had slicked his hair back like the first time she had met him. He was quite a handsome gentleman, she thought.

"Are you okay?" Laszlo asked. "What kind of sickness? I hope it's not anything serious. Many people are getting the summer cold this year, especially now that it is growing colder outside." He took two steps towards her, concern written all over his face.

Elona opened her mouth and then closed it. She would have to tell him sooner or later. There was no use in making it a drawn-out conclusion. "Actually, it is serious," Elona said, trying to keep her chin up. She looked at him, and tears instantly started forming. She tried her best to retain her composure. "Not what you may expect, though."

"What is it?" Laszlo asked, a confused look clouding over his face.

"I don't know how to say this," Elona stammered.

"Say what?" Laszlo asked, a bubble of apprehension rising in his throat.

"Something's happened," Elona started.

"Just tell me!" Laszlo responded a bit too loudly.

Elona shifted from one foot to the other. "I'm pregnant," Elona said bluntly. An immediate deep silence fell over both of them. Elona turned to busy herself with closing the door. She jiggled the keys in the lock and then turned around to face him again. Laszlo stood straight. His knee was no longer bent, and his face was set in stone.

"Ferenc's child," Laszlo said firmly. He knew that he shouldn't be jealous, but he was.

"Yes," Elona said simply. "It was weeks before we had met by the riverside." She shuffled uncomfortably, trying her best to explain. "It's not what I had wanted. I am married, and I didn't want to, but he was insistent. I couldn't say no to him. It happened before I met you. I didn't know." Tears threatened to fill her eyes before she could finish. "I just found out a few days ago. I have all the signs of pregnancy."

Laszlo felt the anger bubble into his chest and something else, a strange sort of hurt. Laszlo looked away down the street, trying to calm the volcano threatening to erupt. She was right. Elona was married, and he was a fool to think she wanted him. And to think that he was about to spill his heart to her today and ask for her hand in marriage! He frowned and bit his tongue.

"You're not saying anything," Elona said sadly.

"What is there to say?" Laszlo said cruelly.

"I'm sorry, Laszlo," she replied quietly.

The words hit him like a knife slicing into his chest.

"I am staying with my husband," Elona stated. The tears began filling her eyes again. She could feel his heart breaking, and Elona hated every word she had to say. "I cannot leave the father of my baby, no matter how miserable I am. My future is no longer just about me. I am raised to be a good mother and a good wife." Elona let the tears fall freely down her face now. There was no use pretending. "I wanted to be with you so badly, but I can't now. This is not my decision. This is in God's hands."

Laszlo felt cold. Ice seeped into his heart and kept him frozen to the spot. His intuition was right. Something had gone terribly wrong, and now he knew. A heaviness formed over his head. He felt like an imaginary dark cloak had fallen over his shoulders. His head felt strangely heavy, as if it was a tremendous task just to keep his chin up. But he was strong, Laszlo reminded himself. Stronger than Elona could ever know. He was a Hungarian soldier. He'd seen the worst of humans and lived. Laszlo Vadas would survive this.

Laszlo turned on his heel and grabbed his bike. He swung his leg over and mounted it. Laszlo finally looked back once. "Goodbye," he muttered angrily. Then he was gone, racing down the dark streets like an animal in search of blood.

Elona cried in pain from the spear in her heart. She watched Laszlo careen crazily away on the tandem bike and felt the world crumble at her feet. Once he steered around the corner and was out of sight, Elona fell to her knees. She sat and hugged herself on the street, letting the tears fall where they may. She felt like she had lost the only man whom she had ever felt strongly for. Laszlo was gone, and now Elona was going to be a mother. She rocked herself gently and cried in anguish for an eternity, it seemed. All the years of oppression and doing what everybody else wanted from her were crushing her shoulders like an anvil.

Elona looked up at the lightening skies and whispered. "I will be the best mother ever," she cried softly. "Because I have nothing left." Elona ran her palms over her eyes and stood strongly, accepting her fate.

PART II

REVOLUTION

CHAPTER 8

After a year of Rákosi as prime minister again, Hungary had fallen back to a hardened Soviet state. Rákosi had repealed every single one of Nagy's reforms, plunging the country back in time. Imre Nagy was even stripped of his Party membership.

But the winds of change could not be held back. Turmoil existed within Moscow as well. Nikita Khrushchev rose as the new leader in the Kremlin, and in February 1956, he voiced his opinion in a scathing attack on Stalin at the 20th Communist Party Congress in Moscow. Many delegates were in shock at his harsh words, even though most knew what Khrushchev said was true. There was laughter and applause, but there were also some delegates who became quite ill and had to be removed from the hall. Reports of several heart attacks after the event and even some suicides were circulated to be only rumours, but some found it to be the truth. Khrushchev had denounced Stalin's actions as plain murders and criticized the ensuing personality cults.

In addition to the mounting pressure on Stalinist policies, Poland was also in a state of change. It would only be a matter of time before a revolution would overtake Poland.

This dramatic shift in politics affected Hungary and fueled internal tensions. By May, Rákosi was barely hanging onto his position as Prime Minister. Hungarians could feel the winds of change blowing hard now. Students from the Technical University were stunned when only a month into the spring semester, they learned that the history of the Soviet Communist Party would be dropped in the Marxism-Leninism class because the material had to be re-evaluated. An odd communist practice was in place again; the past had to be reconstructed.

Many of the students were from workers' and peasants' families. Almost seventy percent of the students were raised by communist-controlled parents who struggled in their meagre jobs or toiled to meet the quota of compulsory produce on their small lots of land. These students were mostly the first generation within their families to receive higher education. They were affected profoundly by the denunciation of Stalin, more so than anyone else. Unsurprisingly, these students were the first to stand up for reform.

Gizella had just recently become aware of a group that was forming to start debating about sensitive reform with the student assembly. They were keeping it private for now, but Gizella felt she could confide in her best friend, Elona.

She would be going to Elona's home tomorrow to help prepare for the birth, but she couldn't keep it a secret much longer.

Gizella had been dating Tibor for almost a year now, and she never spoke to him about any of the student movements. It wasn't that she didn't trust him. She knew that he was bound by military doctrine and didn't want to disturb the balance. Gizella couldn't take a chance, not yet.

But her best friend would be an excellent confidant.

⤳

Laszlo lived his life just like before. Nothing changed for him. Every day was the same in the army, one drill after another, followed by training exercises. The schedule of drills had steadily increased. Laszlo suspected it had something to do with the political upheaval within the Soviet Union. It felt like the military was preparing for something.

Laszlo didn't care which way things went anymore. He was lost. His heart had been inexplicably broken. Elona was out of his life. She had never spoken to him again. The smallest bit of happiness he had fostered with her was dead.

His brother, Tibor, was happy. At least there was something positive happening from all this. Gizella was a wonderful girlfriend, and Tibor was even contemplating asking for her hand in marriage. Furthermore, Laszlo wasn't at all surprised that her political leanings had rubbed off on Tibor. His brother often spoke of destalinization and other sensitive reform issues. Laszlo only nodded his head. His heart was numb, and his ears were deaf.

Laszlo had seen Elona once at the market just two months ago. Her belly was swollen, and she was with her mother. His heart flipped in shock when he saw her, but he shielded himself in the crowd so she couldn't see him.

His reaction upon seeing her surprised him the most. Laszlo wasn't angry anymore, nor was he jealous or hurt. He was just genuinely happy for her pregnancy and her expected baby. Laszlo understood now that he wanted the best for her. She was a woman of integrity, and the decision Elona made was not an easy one, but one that she made out of her strong family values. When Laszlo looked inside himself, he asked if he would have made the same decision if the tables were turned, and the answer was yes.

It was admirable, and he had the utmost respect for her.

Laszlo looked down at his desk, shoving a pile of documents to the side. He blinked and wondered if that meant he truly loved her. Laszlo placed both hands on his small desk and exhaled.

It probably did.

"You look so radiant!" Béláné squealed in delight.

"No, I don't!" Elona cried. "I am fat! Look at this fat on my thighs!" She squeezed her sides.

"You are nine months pregnant, my dear!" Béláné replied. "What did you think happens when you are close to having a child?"

They both chuckled with laughter.

Elona was grateful for her friend's help. Béláné had cleaned for her at the cinema during the past month. Elona could not bend forward too well anymore. Her belly swelled abnormally large in front of her, and her legs felt like cement blocks when she walked.

Béláné patted Elona's shoulder. "But seriously," she said, the warmth in her voice evident. "How are you feeling?"

"I'm okay," Elona replied. "I keep getting this annoying bloody nose and a bit of dizziness, but other than that, I'm okay."

"Did you talk to the doctor about it?"

"No," Elona responded. "It just started a few days ago."

"Are you all ready to go to the hospital when the contractions start?" Béláné asked.

"Yes," Elona replied, pointing to her overnight bag on the floor. "I'm all ready."

"Good," Béláné said softly. "You are certain your mother will send word when it's time? I don't live far. I can be over in twenty minutes."

"Yes, Anyu will contact you."

A comfortable silence fell over them.

Elona remembered something. "Oh," she said. "I forgot to tell you. Gizella said she would visit today as well. She should be here at any moment."

"I like her," Béláné responded, nodding her head. "Her ideas of reform are interesting."

"She talked to you?" Elona asked, surprised.

At that moment, a knock on the door interrupted them. Elona looked at the door and back at Béláné, surprisingly. "That is her now," Elona said as she began to push herself off the sofa chair with her elbows, wrestling her pregnant belly to a standing position.

"No, no," Béláné said hurriedly. "I will get the door." She ran to the door, thankful for the interruption. She didn't want to get into a lengthy discussion of how she had befriended Gizella and the long discussions they had regarding the governmental reforms needed. Béláné opened the door and smiled. "Gizella! How have you been?" The two women quickly hugged and closed the door behind them.

Elona tilted her head to the side, wondering what those two had been up to. "Gizella!" she said, grunting with effort as she stood. Elona instantly noticed her friend's stylish university clothing. "You are always so smartly dressed! I love that skirt!" Elona waddled over heavily and picked at the fabric skirt. "It's wool!"

"Yes!" Gizella smiled proudly. "My father bought it for me on my birthday last month."

"I'm sorry that I couldn't make it," Elona said, hugging her. "I have gained so much weight that it is too dangerous for me to ride my bike now. I can't work anymore, either. Béláné has been gracious enough to take over the cleaning until I deliver this baby."

"Oh, my dear, don't you worry about that," Gizella replied. "I am here to help you with this baby. Whatever you need, just ask."

Elona smiled. They were both such good friends. She motioned them both to the kitchen. "Let's have coffee. I will put some on."

The women sat at the kitchen table and shared the latest news, laughing at themselves and frowning when politics came up.

"I shouldn't say much about this, but I will tell you both because I trust you," Gizella said, lowering her voice to a whisper and leaning across the table. "There is a movement going on at the university. That's all I can say for now. I will know more in the next few months."

"What kind of movement?" Béláné asked.

"Governmental reform," Gizella said quietly. She looked around as if the walls had ears. "Is your husband home?" she asked.

"No, he's at work," Elona answered. "And Anyu is at the market today. There's nobody here but us."

"Good," Gizella replied. "As I said before, I can't say any more than that until I know what will transpire in the coming months, but things will definitely start to change."

Elona and Béláné both inhaled sharply and covered their mouths in shock. "Could it be true?" Elona shrieked in a hushed tone. "Could Hungary finally recover from these dismal years?"

"Yes, it is possible," Gizella said. "Anything is possible." She lifted the coffee mug to her mouth and took a sip. Her delicate fingers gripped the handle as a small diamond ring on her finger shone against the sun rays filtering into the room.

Elona's eyes widened in disbelief. She pointed at the engagement ring on Gizella's finger. "Gizella! You never told us!" Elona shrieked. "Did Tibor ask you to marry him?"

Gizella's face beamed, and her blue eyes twinkled in the sun. "Yes! He did!" she exclaimed happily. "We are going to get married!"

Béláné jumped from her seat in excitement and hugged her friend. "I'm so happy for you!" she said. "Tibor is a good man."

Elona squeezed Gizella's hand from across the table. "I am so excited for you, Gizella," she said. "You deserve a good man." Elona smiled and felt her heart wither inside. Tibor was Laszlo's brother. Elona would undoubtedly see him at the wedding. She didn't know if her heart could handle the pain of seeing Laszlo again. Elona was convinced that she loved him more and more as the months passed. Her eyes lowered to the table. "When is the wedding?"

Gizella understood her friend's heartbreak. Ferenc was not a good husband. "It won't be for another six months," she said. "We were thinking maybe in October or November. You will have the baby by then and should be healed enough to attend. I could not get married without my best friend at my wedding!"

The women all shrieked together and kissed each other on the cheeks in joy. Elona was so thrilled for her friend. Tibor was a handsome man with a great future in the military. This felt slightly odd to Elona because Gizella was completely against governmental powers. Elona knew that sometimes love was stronger than any political boundaries. She smiled and stared at the ceiling, knowing that it was true because her feelings for Laszlo had proven it so.

"Have you said anything about the movement you speak of to Tibor?" Béláné whispered in a conspiratorial tone.

Gizella grinned sadly. "No, I have not," she said. "He is not your average soldier. He does believe in reform. We have had discussions about politics several times, but I am hesitant to say anything more at this point. Maybe in the future, when I know more about where things are heading."

Elona nodded. Gizella was a smart woman. It was not a discussion to be leaked to the Hungarian Army. "I would do the same," Elona said quietly. "Best to keep things quiet and away from the Army."

"Exactly," Gizella said. "At least for now." She sipped her coffee again and felt the delicious warm brew coat her throat. She swallowed and looked across at Elona. "Enough about me. How exciting is it that you are having your first baby! Tell me what day this little child will be born!"

Elona smiled sincerely. She truly felt a warm love for the baby inside her. "Any day now," she said, smoothing her dress around her round belly. "The doctor said maybe one or two more weeks, and the baby will be born."

Gizella grasped her hand and squeezed it. "Tell Anyu to contact me, and I will meet you at the hospital."

"Tell her to contact me too," Béláné interrupted. "I will be there as well."

Elona rubbed her belly gently and smiled. She looked forward to the baby being born. Elona could hug and rock the baby with all the love in her heart. "You are both the best friends," she said. "I am so grateful."

CHAPTER 9

I mre Nagy had listened to the entire speech over and over again. Nikita Khrushchev had described the murders of many innocent citizens for simply not following orders or expressing opinions not strictly within the sphere of Stalinization.

The Secret Speech was no longer secret at all. Copies of the speech were sent to all the Eastern European delegates, and by the end of March, an official translation had been sent to Poland. The Polish people printed 12,000 copies of the speech, and now, in early June, the West had copies of the speech also. Khrushchev's son had even remarked that his father wished for millions to hear the speech.

Imre Nagy ran his hand over his almost bald head. His hair had been receding so much that he now only had hair on the sides and back of his head. A small tuff sat on the back of his crown, but that was also receding farther and farther with every year that passed.

He listened to the tape again and heard the voice of Khrushchev fill the small room of his study:

'It is here that Stalin showed in a whole series of cases his tolerance, his brutality, and his abuse of power ... he often chose the path of repression and physical annihilation, not

*only against actual enemies but also against individuals who
had not committed any crimes against the party or the Soviet
Government.'* [1]

Imre felt the words burn in his heart. He felt the truth in
those words as clearly as if it had been done to him. He stood at
his desk and straightened his tie. He would soon become Prime
Minister of Hungary again. A position that he still refused to
accept he lost.

He was Hungary's Prime Minister, and Rákosi would soon
be a bad relic of the past.

꒡

It was early June, and Elona was worried. Ferenc was always at
work, and Anyu was urging her to go to the hospital.

The birthing cramps had not started like they were supposed to. She had regular small contractions, but they had
stopped a few days ago. She was two weeks past her due date.
The nurses said it was common to have a late birth. Often the
date of conception was wrong, one of them said.

Elona rose to her feet slowly and felt her head swim in a
cloud of dizziness. She rested her side on the door frame as her
mother rushed with her belongings to the door.

"The ambulance will be here soon, my dear," Anyu said in
a gentle tone.

"But I'm not getting the contractions," Elona said worriedly.

"It is okay," Anyu said. "It is time. That baby can't stay in
your belly forever. The doctor will find a way to get it out.
Don't worry."

---

1   **New York Times 1956-05-06**

Elona nodded and trusted her mother's words to be true. Anyu had several successful pregnancies and only one stillbirth. Her mother really did know best, Elona thought.

"I will carry your bag," Anyu said, gently urging her daughter to the front step.

As the door opened, Elona felt a rush of blood spurt from her nose and reached up with her hand in terror, trying to stop the sudden flow.

"Oh my!" Anyu cried. "Hold on. I will get a rag for your nose." She ran back inside and returned with a cloth, stuffing it towards Elona's bloody nose. "Hold it there," Anyu shouted. "Squeeze your nose to stop the flow."

Elona did as she was told, tilting her head back slightly. A wave of dizziness assaulted her balance, and she teetered.

Anyu held her strongly from behind as the ambulance pulled up on the street. The men jumped out of the emergency vehicle and grasped Elona's arms, leading her safely into the ambulance. Anyu followed and stepped into the van with them. "I am going with my daughter," she said strongly, with a look that threatened them to defy her.

"Alright," one man said. "Stay in the back with your daughter. We will get to the hospital soon."

The ambulance doors slammed shut, and the vehicle sped away to the hospital, careening around corners and stopping abruptly.

Elona was soon wheeled into the hospital with her mother walking worriedly behind. The dark look on Anyu's face scared her, and Elona felt her body shudder.

When they arrived in front of a doctor, he helped lay her down on a small hospital bed. He removed his stethoscope and placed it on her protruding belly. He gently placed the earpieces in his ears and listened. He focused briefly and frowned. Then he placed the stethoscope on another spot. He frowned with a strange look on his face. The doctor moved the stethoscope yet again and again. Placing it in as many spots as possible.

Finally, he straightened and took a deep inhale.

Elona shivered. "Is something wrong?" she asked, her heart hammering in her chest.

The doctor looked at her with sympathy in his eyes. "The baby's heartbeat," he said slowly.

"What's wrong with my baby's heartbeat?" Elona cried with anxiety. She shuffled her arms up and suddenly felt an awful pain in her belly. A strong contraction gripped her, and she cried out.

"I will call the nurses to prepare you to deliver your child," the doctor said quickly, exiting the room.

"Anyu!" Elona cried. "What is going on?"

"I don't know, sweetie," Anyu replied, but her face belied her words.

"Is the baby dead?" Elona shouted, clutching her belly. "He can't be! Why won't the doctor talk to me?"

Anyu smoothed Elona's hair. "Shh, don't get yourself more upset than you already are," she said.

"You heard the doctor!" Elona screeched. "He said something's wrong with the baby's heartbeat!"

"It could be a weak heartbeat," Anyu said sympathetically, but yet again, her face failed to support her words. Anyu had been through a stillbirth before. She knew what it was like. Her second baby was stillborn. Anyu stared hopelessly at her daughter's large belly.

A nurse appeared with another nurse in tow. "We're taking you to the birthing room," she said hurriedly and began wheeling the bed to another area of the hospital.

The white walls passed by one after another as Elona's eyes began to moisten. She felt like she was in a tunnel of white walls, being led toward a very dark place. All the whiteness was only here to fool her.

Elona felt sadness rip through her veins, and like any mother, she knew something was terribly wrong with her baby. Elona's nose squirted blood again, and a nurse stopped suddenly and grabbed Elona's nose, pinching the ends.

"Stay strong, my dear," one of the nurses said.

Elona's eyes darted wildly in response.

"Don't worry, we're almost there," the taller nurse said, resuming the urgent push to get Elona to the maternity department. She patted Elona's hand reassuringly and wheeled the cart in a hurried fashion into a quiet ward.

The walls were painted an off-yellow colour here, but it still felt like nothing had changed. Elona's heart fell into her stomach as another contraction gripped her abdomen. She lurched forward and grabbed her belly.

"Hold on, we're almost there," the tall nurse said. "Just give us a few more minutes!"

Elona's breathing started getting heavier and heavier. Hope flitted in her mind. Maybe the baby just had a weak heartbeat, and the emergency delivery would save him. "Hurry," Elona mumbled weakly.

Anyu chased after the nurses and her daughter, panic rising in her throat. She wanted to wrap her daughter in her arms and take away all her pain and suffering, but it was, of course, not possible. Life would happen the way it was intended to, she knew.

"Okay, we're here," the shorter nurse said in a calm voice. "We will deliver your baby now." The nurses wheeled Elona into a white birthing room. The room was nicer than the rest, with a soft chair and some art on the walls, but it was still a hospital room.

They transferred Elona to a long bed with a birthing end and footholds. She crouched forward as another cramp seized her abdomen. Elona groaned as the pain radiated throughout her back. The nurses were working quickly, grabbing towels, blankets and a wash basin.

Finally, the tall nurse crouched at the end of Elona's bent legs. She laid a thin sheet over Elona's knees and looked underneath. "The cervix is ready," she said, positioning herself to pull the baby out, if necessary.

"We need you to start pushing, dear," the other nurse said caringly. She swiped a gentle hand across Elona's forehead.

Elona pushed hard and felt a satisfying movement in her belly. Hope rose in her throat as she bared down again, pushing with all her might. She noticed Anyu in the corner of the room with a worried look on her face.

"One more push," the taller nurse said as she placed her hands on the baby's crown. "The baby's head is coming. Push, dear, push!"

Elona groaned loudly as she squeezed her pelvic muscles, thrusting the baby out. "Oh my God! It hurts!" she shrieked as a stinging pain ripped through her vagina.

"The baby is out," the nurse said loudly. "Gentle push, one more. The shoulders are coming, yes, that's perfect." The nurse held the top of the unmoving baby's body as it slid slowly out of Elona's body. "One more push."

Elona pushed again and felt the baby slide out of her body. Tears gathered in her eyes from the pain of the delivery but also from something else. Her motherly instinct knew something was terribly wrong. The baby wasn't crying. Elona's heart hammered in her chest.

The nurse inspected the baby. She washed his face gently and wrapped the infant in a tight bundle. "It is a stillborn baby boy," she said solemnly. She looked up over the sheet at the mother. "Would you like to hold your baby before we take him away to the chapel?"

Elona burst into tears. She felt overwhelmed with sadness, like a wave of emotion was overtaking her body. No words would come to her mouth, so she simply nodded.

As the nurse handed her the tiny bundle, Elona extended her arms and held her baby. She gazed down through tear-filled eyes and saw that her son's eyes were closed. He looked peacefully asleep.

At the same moment, Anyu rushed over to her side. She ran a gentle palm over the baby's head. "I'm so sorry, sweetheart," she said in a choked-up voice. "He is with God now."

Upon hearing those words, Elona broke down completely and kissed the baby on the forehead. "Goodbye, Mathias," she mumbled quietly.

With this, the nurses took the baby, whisking him away, leaving mother and daughter alone in the white-walled hospital room.

CHAPTER 10

The hospital sent Elona and her mother home the next day. They had a brief funeral service set up for Monday, so Ferenc and their relatives could attend. Elona was beyond upset; she was devastated. Every day just blended into the next, and her heart felt inexplicably shattered.

Gizella had arranged to have Tibor and Laszlo escort them to the funeral service. Elona didn't know how to feel about this but accepted it as the only transportation to the chapel. The family did not have much money to spend on an elaborate funeral, so it would have to do.

Ferenc was upset. He thought maybe Elona had slept wrong or eaten something to upset the baby in her womb. Anyu spoke loudly, drowning out his ridiculous accusations. Ferenc narrowed his eyes and wondered how such things happen.

Gizella grabbed Elona's arm gently and guided her to the car. Elona had recovered physically from the birth, but her emotions were overtaking her body. She was bent forward in a permanent position of torment, her eyes not able to look up or even see through the tears.

Laszlo held the back car door open as the trio sat in the back. Gizella squeezed in as Laszlo and Tibor seated themselves in the front. The car started and sped away.

Elona felt the hot tears course down her face and wanted desperately to just be left alone. No number of hugs or condolences made the pain better. She barely noticed Laszlo, but Elona did notice her husband wasn't offering his arm or any kind of affection. Her brain snapped awake at this realization, and a tendril of anger weaved its way into her heart. Elona would never forgive her husband for his treatment in her time of need. Never, she thought. Elona glared a spiteful look at her husband as he stared out of the window, watching the scenery speed by.

"Is everyone alright back there?" Laszlo asked as he drove, weaving through the streets to the church.

No one spoke for several seconds. Anyu was crying, and Elona was still as a statue. "We are alright," Gizella replied with a look of concern at her best friend. "Béláné is meeting us there along with your brothers and sisters." She patted Elona's arm.

Elona only nodded, her eyes red and swollen. She had tried many times to speak, but her throat was hoarse from the prolonged sobbing. But today, she tried to swallow her tears, and a small voice croaked out. "Thank you," she said to Gizella.

"I am here for you, always," Gizella responded, hugging her with one arm. "We will all be here to help you through this."

Laszlo peered through the rear-view mirror and caught a glimpse of Elona's grief-stricken face. He was happy to see her again, but he knew it was not the moment to reflect on such things. She was going through a very difficult time, and the least he could do was drive them all to the funeral of her dead child.

The church loomed in the distance, and Laszlo braked slowly as they approached. Two other vehicles were parked there, along with a large group of people standing in black clothing chatting solemnly. Laszlo drew to a complete stop. "We're here," he said, stating the obvious.

Elona looked up for the first time and caught his eye in the rear-view mirror. She immediately looked away and shuffled to exit the vehicle. His eyes had bored right through her soul with sympathy like no one else had, not even her own husband. Elona gently straightened out of the car with Gizella's help. Anyu was just as upset, not able to contain her own tears.

The family rushed over and hugged Elona and Anyu. Her brother, Frank, wrapped his strong arms around her, squeezing her tightly, nuzzling her face into his shoulder. "Everything will be alright, Elona," he whispered sincerely. "Anything you need, just call."

With this outpouring of sympathy, Elona couldn't help but cry again. All her friends and relatives were so helpful, kind and compassionate.

Béláné stepped forward next and hugged Elona warmly. "It's so terrible," she said. "I'm so sorry, Elona."

Elona hugged her back and sobbed openly now.

After several minutes of emotional interactions, the small crowd filed into the church slowly, their heads down, accepting the fate of an unborn child, a life unfilled.

After the service, Laszlo drove them all back home and then dropped off Gizella. Tibor was the only one left in the car. Tibor was immensely supportive, and Laszlo couldn't be prouder. He braked and stopped the car, parking it in his usual spot. As Laszlo pulled the key out of the ignition, Tibor cleared his throat.

"You care for her," Tibor said.

"What?" Laszlo replied.

"You care for Elona," he repeated. "I can see it in the way you look at her."

Laszlo shuffled nervously. Nobody knew about the many times Elona, and Laszlo had kissed. They had both kept it a secret. Only Jozsef knew about his feelings for Elona. "Yes," he admitted. "I care for her."

"Is it more than just friendly caring?" Tibor asked, concern washing over his face. "She is married."

"She's married to a terrible man," Laszlo responded. "But yes, I care deeply for that woman. She's been through a lot."

Tibor thought calmly about the declaration. He opened his mouth to voice his opinion and then closed it, thinking it may be wise to say nothing further. After several moments of silence in the car, he noticed Laszlo staring out the front windshield in deep thought. Tibor finally opened the passenger door. "Well, we did a good thing for them today," he said, straightening and shoving his hands in his trouser pockets. "It's time we got back."

Laszlo didn't move, his eyes still transfixed on the late afternoon sun, his mind racing with compassion for Elona's future.

Tibor ducked his head back into the car. "Are you okay?"

Laszlo blinked and turned to his brother. "Yes, I'm alright," he said as he shuffled out of the car, slamming the door. "Let's get back to our jobs."

Tibor frowned worriedly. That was the first time Laszlo had called their military careers a job.

Several weeks later, news of the Polish uprising in Poznań reached Hungary. Gizella had been spending so much time with Elona that she hadn't been as involved with politics as she normally would. The uprising was encouraging, and a few members of the inner circle at Budapest Technical University sat together in a private room, including Gizella. Only eight people were present, and they debated the future of Poland and the ramifications it had on Hungary's political future. Amongst the eight people were members of the Union of Working Youth, or DISZ, a youth organization that published a daily newspaper with political leanings towards Imre Nagy and his reforms. Gizella was delighted and honoured to be invited.

"The Poznań protest is gaining movement," a third-year engineering student said to her left. "It is not over yet, but reports have shown consistent victories. The strike started at 6 am yesterday morning at the Joseph Stalin Metal factory. An impressive eighty percent of workers took to the streets, marching towards the city centre! Workers at other plants and other industries joined the procession, including many university students, just like us." He shuffled in his chair, the passion rising in his voice. "By 9 am, approximately 100,000 people had arrived in front of the Imperial Castle at Adam Mickiewicz Square! The square itself is home to several governmental buildings, the city and police headquarters. Many brave people there." He paused for the information to sink into each and every Hungarian at the table. "They are demanding lower food prices, wage increases and revocation of laws that degrade working conditions. The very same things Hungarians should be demanding!" With this, he stood and slammed his open palm onto the table.

Gizella jumped slightly from the physical display of emotion. Her heart burst at the possibilities of a reformed Hungary, free of Stalinization. "Are they winning, Marcell?" she asked, leaning into the table. "What is the current news? What is the government's reaction?"

"Incredibly," Marcell said, still standing. "There were reports that some local police had joined the people's protest!"

With this, all the people stood in joy. "Yes!" Gizella shouted. "Finally, some progress!"

"Furthermore," another DISZ member interjected. "The reports stated that those local units of police could not contain the crowd. It became violent. The protestors stormed the prison and released many of the delegates who were being held there! Hundreds, and I mean, hundreds of prisoners were released!"

Marcell, the engineering student, sat back down worriedly. "An hour later, the arms depot at the prison was seized, and demonstrators are now armed."

Gizella's eyes widened as she kept standing. "But that is good news!"

"Yes, it is," Marcell said. "But with every victory is a looming threat to the Stalinized Polish government."

"How can you say that?" shouted another woman. "I heard that the government had sent in numerous tanks and armoured vehicles! And there were no shots fired! The military personnel were actually conversing with the protestors. Some reports stated that a few tanks were seized and disarmed!"

The DISZ member stood standing, shaking his fist. "The people are winning!" he shouted. "The crowd had ransacked the Communist Party's headquarters, several local police stations, a military school, and the list goes on!"

Marcell calmly continued among the interruptions. "But with every violent insurgence comes a violent response," he said. "I fear what the Soviet General is preparing. Rokossovsky is a brutal man. I hope for the best! Poland deserves it! We deserve it."

"What are you suggesting then?" a shorter man asked, a look of confusion on his face.

"I suggest," Marcell said, clearing his throat, nervousness crawling up his spine. "That Hungarians do it better. No violence. Send out a table of reforms. We, students, are the intelligence of our nation. We have the power!" He looked at each individual sharply. "We do it with integrity and style."

"We'd need arms to defeat the government," Gizella stated.

"Maybe, maybe not," Marcell said.

The shorter man sat down. "Let's wait and see what happens in Poland tonight. We will meet again tomorrow to discuss our plan of action."

The engineering student exhaled calmly. "That is the best rational response I've heard yet," Marcell said. "If we are to overthrow this Russian government, then we must learn how to become a government."

Gizella smiled. He was right, she thought. A warm feeling of joy spread throughout her body. Reform was within their grasp. Several students stood, and the meeting unofficially adjourned for the night. They could do no more until they heard more news.

Gizella stood and bid farewell to everyone until tomorrow. "Let's hope the Polish uprising is successful in the long term," she said, her heart hammering with hope. "It gives Hungarians hope."

They all nodded and filtered out of the small makeshift room, intent on meeting again.

CHAPTER 11

The sun filtered into her bedroom and warmed the blankets at her feet. Elona's feet had been so cold for weeks. She couldn't understand why. But she couldn't understand much of her life lately, it seemed. Everything had ceased to make rational sense.

Her mother was able to get a small job as a seamstress at an alteration shop. She was happy for her mother, and it was good for the family because Elona hadn't gone back to work yet. She just laid in bed every day, barely able to get up. Elona ate but not much. She barely cooked for anyone anymore, and this angered her husband, which angered Elona even more.

Elona swung the blanket off and inspected her cold feet. They looked fine. It was all in her mind, the doctor had said. She was supposedly experiencing a mental disorder from the birth of her dead baby.

Elona stared up at the ceiling and wondered why some people had so much to deal with in life, and others expected everything to be served to them on a silver platter. She shook her head and contemplated getting out of bed. Elona looked back at the empty spot beside her. Ferenc was at work, and so was Anyu. She was alone in the house.

Elona fell back onto her pillow and cradled another pillow on her side. "My baby boy is dead," she whispered. "Why did he have to die?" she asked the universe.

The silence in the house was deafening as her heart yearned for answers.

She pulled the blankets back on top of her and stayed in the warmth of her bed. There was not much to look forward to now. She was in a loveless marriage with a terrible man, childless and the one man whom she felt genuine love for she had pushed away.

Elona snuggled her face into the pillow. All she had ever wanted was love and peace. She had never gotten a real chance to get either. Maybe it was because she didn't work hard enough, or maybe she was being punished by some evil spirit. She sighed.

She needed something, someone, to hold onto. Something to help her believe again, to realize the purpose of living.

Then she started sobbing because Elona didn't believe that she would ever find such a thing.

Laszlo was in shock. They had all heard about the Polish uprising in Poznań. It had been only a few days since the protests had started, and already the government had begun squashing it with brutal force.

Rokossovsky had commissioned his deputy, the Polish-Soviet General Stanislav Poplavsky, to crush the protest in typical Russian standards. Soviet officers arrived at Lawica Airport with special troops north of Poznan. Laszlo heard rumours that the troops were being told the demonstrators were German provocateurs. At first, this angered Laszlo until he found conflicting reports of the mass demonstration being held by simple steel workers wanting better working conditions. The Germans had nothing to do with it.

Laszlo stared at his friend and wondered what impact all these demonstrations would have on Hungary's politics and their commands here.

"I have to get back home soon," Jozsef said abruptly. "My kids are a handful for Marika. Ever since the baby came, it's been hellish. Grandma doesn't come on Saturdays."

"Alright," Laszlo replied. "Keep your ears open about the Poles. It may affect our military position here in Hungary."

"Do you think the behaviour will spill over into Hungary?" Jozsef asked.

"I think Hungary has been on the path to reform for the past three years," Laszlo said. "Whether the government likes it or not, it's coming."

Jozsef stared in shock at his best friend. It was highly unusual for Laszlo to speak politics. "The reports I heard were not good for the protestors in Poznan," Jozsef stated. "Just yesterday, four army divisions and even the Internal Security Corps had entered Poznan. An impressive show of 10,000 troops!"

"Yes, I heard," Laszlo replied. "Hundreds of protestors were detained and sent to Lawica Airport." Laszlo lit a cigarette slowly, contemplating his next words. "I heard of vicious interrogations."

Jozsef swallowed hard. "It's that bad?" he asked.

"The Polish Prime Minister even stated on the radio," Laszlo said, inhaling and exhaling a plume of smoke into the air. "Any lunatic caught raising his hand against the government will have it cut off."

Jozsef stared at his friend in disbelief. "Did they actually say that on radio?" he asked.

"Yes," Laszlo stated solemnly, staring up into the darkening sky. What this meant for Hungary was peculiar, Laszlo thought. He had heard rumours that secret meetings had begun taking place at the university. He hadn't told his captain. Laszlo chose to keep this information to himself. He couldn't even tell his best friend, even though every fibre of his body wanted to. "So far, the Russians have stopped the protestors. I don't know for how long or what this protest will mean for the rest of Europe, but I have a feeling it will spread. Be ready; that's all I'm saying."

"Do you think the workers were right to protest?" Jozsef asked hesitantly, looking down at his shoes.

Laszlo grimaced and crushed his cigarette butt under his foot. "I can't comment on that," he said admirably. "It's not my job. I'm just a lieutenant."

"An important lieutenant at that," Jozsef said.

"Maybe," Laszlo said, stuffing his hands in his trousers. "But one thing I know is that I will never do anything morally wrong to my own people." Laszlo's blue eyes turned a lighter shade of ice, and he nodded to Jozsef's police car. "You should go home now. Take care of your family and your wife. They're important in this world."

"Yes, definitely." Jozsef nodded and walked away, entering the police cruiser and slowly driving away.

Laszlo watched the taillights of his friend's vehicle for several minutes, then started his Mercedes and drove back to the barracks.

7

Gizella's eyes were shining as the ladies spoke about the Polish uprising. Elona couldn't understand why Gizella was so excited. There were many reports of the uprising being stopped viciously by the Russian forces. Then they had heard nothing after that. It was as if an information ban had occurred or something. No news of anything from Poland other than the demonstrators were detained and threatened publicly. How was this good for Hungary? Elona couldn't understand.

But Gizella was bursting with pride and hope. "I can't say too much," she said. "But I know of a group of people meeting to discuss reform in Hungary. They are calling themselves the Petőfi Circle." Gizella blinked, knowingly omitting that she was an active participant in the Petőfi Circle. It was better to keep some things private, she knew.

"Discussing reform?" Béláné asked, surprised.

"Well, they debate about reform," Gizella said. She spread her long fingers in a tent above her nose, wondering how much she should reveal. "It is an important development, regardless if we are just a bunch of students."

"We?" Elona asked incredulously. "You are part of the debates?"

Gizella frowned. She was trying to keep this quiet, but the hope in her heart couldn't be silenced. "Yes and no," she lied. "I have only been to one debate." Gizella pursed her lips, hoping the lie would hold for now. On the contrary, Gizella had attended every single debate and meeting of the Petőfi Circle. In fact, she was increasingly becoming a prominent figure in the group.

Elona reached over and held Gizella's hand thoughtfully. "Please don't put yourself at risk," Elona said softly.

"On the contrary!" Gizella said in a burst of passion. "We must all do what is necessary!"

Elona and Béláné looked at each other in surprise from the outburst.

"Don't look at me like this," Gizella said warmly. "Don't be afraid." She smiled and sipped her coffee, calming down the passion in her heart. "I am just one woman like you. Man or woman, it doesn't matter. But together, we can force change, and that's what matters."

Elona nodded. "I know you are right," she said. "But my spirit has been so broken. I am not sure if I can even get out of bed some mornings."

Gizella wrapped her left arm around Elona's shoulders. "Your heart will heal. It just takes time."

"I hope so," Elona said, smiling weakly. She stood unsteadily and grabbed her summer shawl, wrapping it around her head and shoulders. "I have to go now. Ferenc and Anyu will be home soon."

"I will walk you home," Béláné said, standing on the grassy hill. "I live so close to you."

Gizella looked at Elona with concern. "I will visit you again next week, my dear," she said. "Please stay well and drink lots of fluids. Your body has been through a lot."

"I will," Elona said, hugging and kissing Gizella goodbye.

Gizella jumped on her bicycle and waved, riding back to the university, leaving Elona and Béláné alone.

The two women walked down the grassy hill towards a wooded path alongside the Danube. Elona's eyes glazed over at the memories. She listened intently to the birds as a comfortable silence fell over them. She could hear a distant accordion, similar to the music that Laszlo played so well. Elona strained her eyes through the bushes, a bubbling hope in her heart. "Did you hear that?" she said in wonderment.

Béláné squinted her eyes in the bushes. "What? You mean the birds?"

Elona shook her head in dismay. Her mind was playing tricks on her. It was only the birds singing their afternoon melody. No accordion music and no Laszlo. "Yes," she lied. "The birds sound like music today."

Béláné smiled and hugged Elona's shoulder lightly. "Yes, the birds are singing songs of hope."

After bidding Béláné goodbye, Elona stepped into the house. Ferenc was sitting at the table with his glasses on, reading the newspaper. Her mother was washing her hands in the sink, preparing the ground pork for goulash. Ferenc looked up as Elona closed the back door behind her. She took off her worn boots tiredly and then walked into the kitchen, hugging her mother.

"You made it home finally," Ferenc said with a sneer.

Anyu shot a mean stare at Ferenc. "How was your day, my darling?" she asked Elona sweetly. "Did it help seeing your friends again?"

Elona responded to Anyu, ignoring her husband altogether. "Yes, it felt nice to just chat with them. They are good friends."

"Don't ignore me when I'm speaking to you," Ferenc said loudly.

Elona turned and glared at her husband. "It is okay for you to come home late every night," she said strongly. "But if I am a little late coming home, then I get questioned? Of course, I will ignore you when you make comments like this towards me."

Ferenc stood up, his face turning a slightly red colour. "How dare you speak to your husband like that!"

Anyu pulled the hot spoon from the colander and angrily waved it at Ferenc. "Don't you speak to my daughter like that!"

she yelled protectively. "She has been through a lot. She doesn't need you to make things harder for her."

Elona stood strongly beside her mother. The anger in her heart gave her more strength every day. The fear she previously had for her husband melted away in her subconscious with every new day. Each morning and each night, Ferenc became more and more of a monster in her eyes. Elona had no words for her husband. She just glared at Ferenc with hatred in her eyes.

Ferenc grinned and tossed his head back, chuckling. "I am leaving then," he said decisively. "I don't need to be in a hen house. I am going to the beer hall." He turned on his heel and headed for the back door. Ferenc zippered his boots on and pulled on a light suit jacket. He stood, glaring at Elona. "Don't wait up for me." Then he slammed the door, and he was gone.

CHAPTER 12

In July 1956, Rákosi was finally forced from power by the Kremlin. He was ordered to Moscow, where he dutifully fled. Gizella's hopes flew high in her heart. The other twelve members smiled happily as she entered the room with a guest.

Nagy was not reinstated as Prime Minister as everyone had hoped. It was a blow to the Petőfi Circle. Instead of Imre Nagy, Ernő Gerő was appointed as Rákosi's successor. This cosmetic move only fueled more public dissatisfaction.

"Do not dismay!" Marcell, the engineering student, proclaimed loudly over the chatter. "This is good news! It is fueling more people to realize the weakness and ineptitude of our government. We will continue, and our cause will become greater with every step!"

A member of DISZ stood up. "We still need to reinstate Imre Nagy!"

Several students agreed, yelling and shouting.

Marcell sat down, shaking his head.

Gizella stood and cleared her voice. "I brought with me today a former member of MEFESZ from Szeged University," she said loudly, motioning the slim man to stand as the entire room quieted eerily. MEFESZ was a democratic student organization that was established in 1945 but was quickly dissolved

by the communists in 1948. It was rare to find anyone associ-
ated with MEFESZ because all the former leaders had been
jailed by the Communist government. "I am confident you all
know of MEFESZ. Wonderful, now that I have your attention,
let him speak." Gizella sat down.

"I am not one of the former leaders or anything," he started.
"I am Sandor, and I am only one man whose beliefs reside in
Hungary, the true Hungarians. I support our country and the
people who are at our core, not the communists." The slim man
glared at the members of DISZ and then continued following
his gaze toward everyone. A few people grumbled their discontent, and a few shouts sounded from the DISZ members. "Hold
on," the slim man said. "I understand there are Imre Nagy supporters here, and I'm not saying it is wrong. He was the man
who started reform in Hungary!"

Several nods of approval and shouts of agreement sounded
in the small packed room. An oval table stood in the center
with sixteen chairs, only twelve of them occupied.

Sandor continued. "I am here to speak on behalf of
Hungarians. We deserve so much better than what we have had
to deal with in the past ten years. Hungarians need to reclaim
their country. Please keep your minds open to all possibilities."

Marcell nodded thoughtfully. "This man speaks the truth,"
he said. "Reform takes time. We are only at the beginning
stages. We need to take Poznan as a lesson. Communism will
not disappear overnight."

Several DISZ members stood angrily and shouted.

Gizella wondered if it wasn't such a good idea to bring
Sandor into the meeting today or not. She stood with uncer-
tainty sitting in her heart. "Everyone, stop shouting!" she yelled
in a high-pitched female voice.

The entire room quieted. "Look, I would love to write some articles for DISZ one day and have even discussed this with some members here today!" she said loudly. "But I also want to see all aspects of reform, not just the ones defined by our government. Because we all know that governments lie!" She paused for a moment and started again. "We, as Hungarians, need our country back, as Sandor said. But we need to do it together. A force united as one is mightier than a force divided."

The room fell silent.

Gizella wasn't sure if she had said something wrong or not. She stood strongly in the face of the oncoming criticism.

Marcell stood and started clapping. Several others stood in turn, clapping slowly. Finally, the DISZ members stood as well, clapping until the entire room was applauding and shouting loudly as one.

Imre Nagy sat at his desk, mulling over the recent events. Ernő Gerő was no better than Rákosi himself. Ernő would not be able to reform Hungary like he could. He was still displeased about being forced from his party and his position. He truly had a vision for Hungary, and the country needed him. Nagy tapped his glasses up and glanced at the man across the desk. His name was Miklós, and he was a friend of his daughter. Miklós was an average-looking Hungarian man with a high forehead and an upper lip that was thinner than his bottom lip. Miklós was a well-respected journalist from DISZ and Magyar Radio. He had served in Imre Nagy's government between 1953-1955 as the government's press secretary. Imre trusted him.

"What is the Petőfi Circle up to nowadays?" Imre asked his friend.

"After the Poznan uprising," Miklós started. "The circle was solidified with many of your supporters. The Polish protest has given many people renewed hope for reform in Hungary." Miklós rubbed his high forehead as if deciding on his next words.

"Go on," Imre replied, tapping his fingers on the desk.

"Well, some unsettling news," Miklós said. "Sad to report."

"What is it?" Imre moved closer to his desk, leaning over it.

"A former member of MEFESZ was a guest at the meeting last week," Miklós reported quietly.

"What!" Imre shouted. "That democratic gang of misfits was dismantled and jailed! There is no MEFESZ anymore!"

"That's correct, Nagy," Miklós said calmly, waving his hands to calm the ex-Prime Minister down. "He was an ex-member, as I said before."

"Were you at the meeting?" Imre asked.

"Yes, I was," Miklós replied. "I stood for the Nagy government. I loudly protested any influence from the MEFESZ chain of democratic thought."

"Who brought this man into the meeting?" Imre said loudly. "Did you get the name of this man?"

"A woman brought him," Miklós replied quickly. "And the man said his name was Sandor."

"A woman brought him?"

"Yes, a journalist student at Technical University," Miklós responded, spilling the words out. "Her name is Gizella."

"Do you know any more about her?"

"Only that she is engaged to a young Hungarian soldier," Miklós said.

"Then she should be sympathetic to communist reform," Imre said slowly, rubbing his clean-shaven chin.

"People admire her, Nagy," Miklós pointed out. "She's an attractive, smart woman."

"Then you must talk to her," Imre said abruptly.

Miklós sat back in his chair, staring over the top of Imre's head, deep in thought. "What do you suggest that I say to her?" Miklós replied in frustration. He could not just walk up to her and demand that she supports DISZ. "It is a complicated matter, Imre."

Imre Nagy stood and walked casually over to the large second-story window, looking down onto the street. He shifted his feet and tilted his eyeglasses several times on his nose, thinking of a good strategy.

Almost five minutes of silence had passed before he turned around in exaltation. Imre pointed his finger hard in the air. "I have the solution!" he shouted exuberantly. "You will offer her a job at the DISZ newspaper!"

Elona agreed to resume working at the cinema after Béláné's insistence. It was her first night, and Béláné had offered to help during the first few nights. Returning to work was a sudden decision, and Elona hadn't even told anyone at home. She felt a burning desire to get out of the toxic house she shared with her husband.

Béláné had faithfully covered all of her cleaning shifts since her late stages of pregnancy. Elona knew that her friend had started working at a lamp factory and sorely needed the extra sleep. She felt so blessed to have such a wonderful friend.

Béláné looked up. The skies were still light. At 9 pm, the sun still had not set, although the skies were displaying purplish and pink hues from the sun dipping so low on the horizon. It was a busy Friday night, and Béláné looked exhausted.

Several groups of people were walking along the streets, most leaving restaurants and beer halls, then returning to their homes. Some were loud and raucous. It annoyed Elona for some reason. She was never a heavy drinker and couldn't understand the preoccupation Hungarians had for their alcoholic spirits.

Béláné removed the large key ring from her trousers and jingled them into the lock at the side door to the cinema as Elona watched the revellers. "They're having a good time, it seems," Béláné said softly, chuckling.

"Yes, it appears that way," Elona replied, staring out at the group of people.

Béláné jiggled the lock, but it wouldn't open. "Wrong key," she said, giggling. "I still have not gotten used to all these keys." She searched for the correct key as Elona continued staring at the crowd of people. "I found it," Béláné said and turned the lock with the large key ring jangling on the end. The large door creaked open.

Béláné stood holding the door open, but Elona was still staring out into the crowd of people. Béláné poked her head out. "Do you see someone you know?" she asked in confusion.

"I think so," Elona said slowly, transfixed to the spot. Her body froze like a statue, and then her blood began to pump loudly in her ears.

Béláné looked at Elona's line of vision and saw several couples dancing in the streets, obviously inebriated. "Is it one of them?" Béláné asked, pointing.

"No, it's that couple in the back of the crowd," Elona said slowly, her teeth grinding against each other.

Béláné squinted, trying to see the couple in the back as they danced in a circle, farther away.

Elona tilted her head to see around the throng of people in front. She stepped to the side. "Hold on," she said. "I need to be sure."

"What is it, Elona?" Béláné asked worriedly, the hairs raising on her head from the cold look of stone on Elona's face.

The couple danced closer, circling the crowd. The man swung the young lady, almost dropping her. They laughed happily as he grasped her by the waist just in time. The couple kissed passionately, then swayed into another dance right in front of the crowd now, directly in their point of view.

Béláné's mouth dropped open when she realized who the man was.

"That's my husband, Béláné," Elona said, her teeth clenching in a tight embrace. Good thing they were far enough away, or she would have slapped her husband's face. Elona turned to Béláné and smiled viciously. "That's Ferenc."

"Oh my God, Elona," Béláné cried, pulling Elona into the safety of the Cinema. "I'm so sorry, dear."

"Frank, you need to come get Anyu and me," Elona said into the phone calmly, her teeth still clenching. They had finished cleaning all night and returned home in the morning. Ferenc was already gone to work.

"You are finally leaving that husband of yours?" Frank said. "Good. You should have never married that man."

"I am a family woman," Elona responded in her defence. "I pledged myself to my husband for the rest of my life. He's the one that broke that agreement."

"What did he do now?"

Elona wondered if she should get into all the details now or later, but part of her heart didn't want to speak of it at all. "I have realized that it was a mistake marrying him," Elona said. "He proved it to me many times over. It just took this long for me to finally release my obligation to him. He broke a vow of our marriage, and that's all I care to say right now."

Frank cupped the phone to his ear. "I understand," he said. "It is a difficult decision, but it had to be made. Better sooner rather than in ten years from now."

"Yes," she said slowly, sipping a fresh cup of coffee to keep herself awake. "Béláné is helping me pack our things. Hopefully, I can have most of it ready to go before he gets back from work."

"Where's Anyu?" Frank asked.

"You will need to go to her work and tell her," Elona said pleadingly. "I want to focus on getting as much stuff out of this home as possible."

"I can do that," Frank replied. "I will go see Anyu right away. When do you want me over to move your stuff?"

"Five o'clock," she said.

"Isn't that when Ferenc comes home?" Frank replied, astonished.

"I am a woman of integrity," Elona said, her voice steady with a tone of steel determination. "I will tell him to his face that I am leaving him. I would like you to be there when I do."

"I will be there for you, my little sister," Frank said. "Always."

CHAPTER 13

Gizella calmly removed the curlers from her hair in the mirror and smiled. Tibor was coming to pick her up for dinner tonight, and she couldn't be happier. She loved that man with all her heart and soul, but Gizella knew it was time for her to let him know more about her political leanings. She was marrying the man, after all.

Gizella stood back and ran her fingers lightly through her released curly waves. She teased it this way and that, finally content with the result.

She leaned over the sink and applied some red lipstick, smacking her lips together. Gizella smiled and felt an uneasiness come over her gut. She was well aware of the possibility that Tibor may cancel the wedding or even report her to authorities. But something in her gut told her that he wouldn't. Something told her that he might even agree with her political theories. But it was still a risk that she had to take, especially now.

Gizella had been offered an important position at DISZ's newspaper. She had gladly accepted the position, and they were oddly accommodating. They would allow her to continue her studies in the fall. She would only work on Saturdays during the school term and full-time in the summers. In fact, she was starting tomorrow as a political columnist.

Gizella was thrilled and elated. But she knew now that she must tell Tibor. It was better to tell him now rather than have him find out based on a reform article she had written.

The doorbell rang, interrupting her thoughts.

Gizella shrieked and ran to the door, swinging it open.

Tibor stood there with a boyish grin on his face and a bouquet of flowers.

She hugged him fiercely and pulled him into the room, kissing him fully on the lips. "Thank you, my sweet!" she said gaily, snatching the flowers and putting them in a vase with water.

"Are you ready to go, beautiful?" he asked, touching her waist gently.

"Yes, yes," she replied, wondering when she should bring up her new job. "Do you have a car?"

"Yes, Laszlo gave me the Mercedes for tonight," he said proudly.

"Wonderful, let's go!"

They walked hand in hand out of the dorm onto the street. They looked like a fine couple, Gizella thought. A handsome young man in uniform with an intelligent woman of determination. As they approached the vehicle, she crossed her fingers silently that he would stay by her side. He opened her door and waited until she was seated comfortably, then shut the door, going around to the driver's door. He opened the door, sat down and turned the ignition, starting the car.

The Mercedes roared to life with a satisfying rumble. Gizella smiled at his handsome face and wondered if this was the right time. "Sweetheart," she said softly. "I have something to tell you. I want you to keep an open mind."

"What is it?" Tibor asked, a look of confusion on his face.

"I love you, Tibor," she explained quietly. "Please know that I will do anything for you."

Tibor frowned worriedly.

"I have accepted a position at DISZ newspaper," she blurted out. "I start tomorrow." Gizella smoothed her skirt down on her lap, awaiting his response. Her heart felt caged inside her chest, and her breathing felt like it had stopped altogether.

Tibor looked at her with relief and laid his hand on hers. "Is that all?" he laughed reassuringly, patting her hand. "You know I will support you with any position at any newspaper. Imre Nagy's newspaper is just as important to this country as my position in the Hungarian Army is. I'm happy for you!"

Gizella straightened proudly. "Thank you, my dear," she said, a feeling of warm relief spreading through her body.

"Thank you for what?" he asked.

"For being the man who you are," she answered demurely, kissing him on the cheek. She would give him more details on her political thoughts as the days grew closer to their wedding in November. She would not make the same mistake Elona made, marrying the wrong man. Gizella would know for certain in a few months' time.

"Anyu," Frank said. "You must take everything you need today. We will come back tomorrow to get more."

Elona walked into the room with another box, placing it at Frank's feet. "I think that is it for my things," she said.

"Alright," he said, picking up two boxes. Frank stomped outside and handed the boxes to several of his friends filling up the moving van. They were a good crew and were sorely needed with such short notice. Elona needed the help, and they were happy to oblige.

He thanked a few men and calmly walked back into the house with another friend when they heard the bicycle tires clink on the gravel driveway. Frank turned and watched Ferenc dismount with a look of utter astonishment on his face.

"What is going on?" Ferenc asked Frank.

"You need to ask Elona that question," Frank answered firmly.

Ferenc stared angrily at the front door and stomped towards the house, with Frank following closely behind.

"Elona!" Ferenc shouted into the house.

Anyu stood with her hands across her chest. "She's grabbing one of my boxes," she said angrily. "It's about time Elona has come to her senses."

"What are you talking about?" Ferenc asked, his eyes wild.

Elona appeared in the hallway. "I'm leaving you," she stated firmly.

"Why?" Ferenc cried. "What have I done now?"

"You know what you did last night," Elona said stonily. "If you wish for me to let everyone here know, then so be it."

Ferenc glared behind him at Frank and his burly friends, then forward at Anyu and Elona. "Please don't leave," he pleaded, his voice echoing with an odd ring of insincerity.

Elona smiled. "You think you're sly," she said. "But you're not." Elona balanced the box on the table to relieve the weight while she talked. "I know where you were and who you were with last night. I saw it with my own eyes. And so did Béláné."

Ferenc's face flushed pink, and he looked momentarily down. "It was a mistake," he said briefly, unsure of how much she saw.

"You were kissing that woman with a lot of passion," Elona said with a glare of hatred brewing in her eyes. "It didn't look like a mistake to me."

Ferenc stood rooted to the spot with his mouth slightly agape. No words came to his mouth.

Elona shifted the box back into her arms and walked straight towards Ferenc. "If you'll excuse me," she said. "I have a lot of moving to do. We will return tomorrow for the rest of my stuff. I'm sure you'll be very happy with your new girlfriend." With that, she lightly bumped Ferenc's shoulder on the way out.

Laszlo awoke with a start in the darkness. He didn't know what had awakened him, but whatever it was, his heart was racing. He blinked and sat up in bed. The room was dark except for the refracted light of the barracks filtering into the room at odd angles.

His trained instincts told him to check, even though he knew that no civilians could access the barrack housing units. It was safer than any place in Budapest. Laszlo stood and padded to the small kitchen, pouring himself a glass of water. He added a splash of vodka to calm his nerves so he could sleep. It was strange that he would feel anxiety because nothing unusual had happened at the barracks lately.

The general political climate of Hungary was changing, though. This made him think about where his country was headed, and his mind was constantly filling with questions about where he, as a man and a soldier, stood with all of it. He had recently read intelligence reports of the Petőfi Circle holding meetings during the summer. DISZ was putting out newspapers on a daily basis, supporting Imre Nagy. Along with a general discontent at the lack of reform, Laszlo felt something momentous was about to occur within the Russian-controlled country he called home.

Laszlo sipped the strong water and grimaced as the alcohol slipped down his throat. He lit a cigarette and blew out the smoke towards the small window.

Ever since he had last seen Elona, he had thought about her every day. It was just silly thoughts, like how she was doing, what she was doing, whether she was working at the Cinema again or staying home to heal.

It had been almost two months since he saw her last. Laszlo guzzled the rest of the water quickly and felt the alcohol run through his system, a calming wave coursing throughout his blood. Laszlo placed the glass down on the counter and gazed out at the barracks.

It was quiet. Nobody was awake; only the barrack guards were at their stations. Laszlo enjoyed the night sometimes. It gave him time to think.

He wondered when he would see Elona again.

He shook his head. Laszlo found his continued preoccupation with Elona troublesome. He had not found any other women attractive since. In fact, he hadn't found anyone attractive for the past ten years until Elona had walked into his life.

Laszlo wondered what he should do with this internal information.

He settled with knowing there was nothing he could do. Laszlo was a firm believer in letting the world take care of events beyond his control, and when he was called for action, he would stand with integrity.

Maybe one day, he would somehow be reunited with Elona, he thought.

Laszlo padded gently back to bed, rolled onto his side and closed his eyes. Everything eventually happens for a reason, he mused. Laszlo closed his eyes and allowed sleep to overtake his thoughts.

CHAPTER 14

Elona turned the mop in the pail, squeezing out the remaining moisture. She had been working alone for over a month now. Béláné had started working overtime hours at the lamp factory and was quite happy. The Cinema was Elona's only cleaning job, and she missed Béláné's nightly companionship and help. She stopped briefly to rest and mused about her life.

She still lived with Frank and his family. Her brother was trying to find a suitable home for her and their mother. He was a good brother, Elona decided. Frank was always there for her, and that was like finding gold in this volatile world.

News of Gizella getting a prominent job at DISZ was exhilarating. Maybe there was hope after all for this country, she thought.

But for her life, Elona couldn't see much of anything positive. Her mental state had deteriorated so much that some mornings she felt like nothing more than a zombie. She slept, awoke and worked. Sometimes she talked to her friends, but mostly she existed quietly on her own.

There wasn't much to be hopeful about. Her baby was dead, her ex-husband was a cheater, and her country was in a constant state of instability.

Elona sat down on a bench and cupped her hands onto her forehead, looking down between her small feet. What was she going to do now when she had lost everything? What was the reason for her existence? She had been raised to be a mother and a wife. She had a dream of being a journalist like Gizella, but life always seemed to have other plans for her. Elona was slightly envious but mostly overjoyed that Gizella was working for a newspaper. However, it made Elona question her own purpose in life.

If not to be a wife, mother or journalist, then what purpose did she have? She doubted that God had created her simply to be a cleaner at Corvin Cinema for the rest of her life.

Elona clasped her hands in prayer and looked up at the dark ceiling.

"Give me purpose," she whispered into the dark recesses of the Cinema. As soon as she uttered the words, a pain hit her gut. Not a physical pain but an emotional one. She had always repressed her purpose for everyone else. Elona never realized until now that she was nothing but a whisp of her former self, her essence given away to please others.

Her eyes moistened at the thought.

Several tears dropped onto her knees, and she cried for her future. Elona had no idea where her path was anymore. The sombre thought made her sob even harder until the empty dark corners of the Cinema reverberated her cries for help right back to her.

He had found out from Tibor that Elona had left Ferenc several weeks ago. Laszlo wasn't sure what to do with this information. His heart jumped with joy, then just as promptly crashed at his feet. It was heartbreaking for any person to end their marriage, no matter the longevity or instability of the union. He knew this.

Jozsef nudged him out of his reverie. "So what are you going to do?" he asked.

"I don't know," Laszlo replied.

"What?" Jozsef cried. "You know what to do! You must talk to that woman!"

"It's easy for you to say," Laszlo replied. "You've been married for six years! What do you know about winning a woman over again?"

"True," Jozsef chuckled. "My wife is an angel sent from God." Jozsef tapped his fingers on the coffee table. "But I do know love when I see it."

Laszlo looked up in shock. He opened his mouth and then closed it.

"You are in love with Elona, aren't you?"

"I don't know," Laszlo replied.

Jozsef frowned. "When was the last time you thought about her?" he asked.

Laszlo pulled another cigarette out of his package. "Yesterday," he lied.

"That's a lie," Jozsef said, stating the obvious. "We wouldn't be talking about her then."

"True," Laszlo replied. "Well, the last time before today, then."

"So you think of her every day then," Jozsef stated.

Laszlo exhaled a heavy breath and then took a moment to inhale from his cigarette, blowing the plume of smoke into the air. He stared at the ceiling without making eye contact with his friend. "If the truth must be told, then yes," he admitted.

Jozsef grinned. "Then you must find her and talk to her, Lieutenant," he said. "And that's an order."

Laszlo chuckled. "Is that so?"

"Yes," Jozsef said, plucking the cigarette from Laszlo's mouth and throwing it on the ground, crushing it with his foot. "Stop those cigarettes. You've been smoking way too much."

Laszlo stood, a bit of anger rising in him, then calmed at the look of concern on Jozsef's face. He felt his arms loosen at his sides and exhaled heavily. "Alright," he said. "I will try to talk to her."

⌐

"Gizella!" Miklós shouted into the hallway.

She stood abruptly in the small room where she worked for DISZ. "What is it?" she asked, fear rising in her gut. She loved the job so much that she had a constant fear of expulsion.

"There you are!" Miklós exalted.

Gizella smiled her prettiest grin and nodded her head. "Miklós!" she said eagerly. "What brings you here today?"

Miklós hugged her and kissed her cheek. "I just wanted to tell you how much I value your work!" he said energetically. "Your last column in DISZ detailing all the reforms Imre Nagy had instituted in the past was brilliant! You are reminding every single Hungarian the high cost of the decisions to repel these reforms."

Gizella smiled proudly. Her cheeks blushed lightly, and her back straightened fully. "Oh, thank you!" she exclaimed.

"Keep up the good work!" Miklós said. "You have been a light in these dark days. Communism is the answer, but it must be done with the proper amount of reforms to fit our beautiful country."

Gizella nodded. She was beginning to believe this more and more every day. The amount of positive feedback she was receiving from the people at DISZ was furthering her cause. She felt like a true journalist now, spreading the word of reform to Hungarians. "I am so glad!" she said joyfully. "I truly love working for DISZ, Miklós. Thank you again for offering me the job. I cannot express my gratitude enough."

"No thanks needed," he said. "It is I who needs to be thankful to you for being on our team." He patted her arm. "Will you be at the Petőfi meeting tonight?"

"I will definitely be there," she replied, smiling.

Miklós walked into the room quickly and sat down. "I don't have much time," he said abruptly.

Imre Nagy swung his chair towards Miklós. The chair's wheels creaked and sent a shiver through Nagy's body. Imre pushed the eyeglasses up onto his nose and wondered why he was feeling so dreadful lately. Everything was beginning to come to a resolution. Hungary was heading to true communist reform. He splayed his hands down onto the desk. "How is the newspaper? Have you heard anything more about Hungarian discontent?" he asked.

"Yes, the newspaper has grown in popularity, and I can almost assure you that the moment of communist reform is close at hand," Miklós said, moving his hands confidently back and forth along the arms of the chair.

"What has been happening in the Petőfi Circle? Have you seen Gizella again?" Imre asked. "I read her last column, and it was very well written."

"I thought so, too," Miklós replied. "And I told her as such." Miklós uncrossed his legs and leaned forward. "She is much better than we could have ever expected. Everyone loves her. She is pragmatic, outspoken and a truly beautiful woman inside and out. People like listening to her ideas."

"That's wonderful news," Imre Nagy said, his smile abruptly not carrying to his eyes.

"But you don't seem as happy as I would have thought," Miklós said, a crease forming in his eyebrow. "Are you alright, Imre?"

"I am fine," Nagy responded, trying to hide the uneasiness in his gut. "Just the jitters, I suppose. What are some of this woman's ideas?"

"Well," Miklós replied. "In yesterday's meeting, she proposed detailing a new list of reforms. Some of them were very good. I will go through it in more detail when I have time. I need to get back soon before the daily paper comes out tonight." He stood and smoothed down his trousers. "Don't worry, her ideas are very much in line with your previous reforms. We are getting closer, Nagy." Miklós waved quickly and left the office.

Imre Nagy stood looking at the door as it closed. He knew deep in his soul that going against the Russians was a risky endeavour. Nagy had lived a quiet existence and had escaped the wrath of his comrades so far.

Hungary deserved so much better, though. His reforms have worked and will work again. He stood and placed his hands in his pockets firmly, looking out the window. The benefits were far greater than the risks. If not Imre Nagy to save Hungary, then whom?

He would have to be the pillar of strength Hungarians were looking for, Imre thought.

Elona closed the door to the cinema and jangled the keys to lock the door firmly. The lock stuck again, and she cursed silently until, finally, the sticky lock clicked into place. She turned and gazed down the street towards home. The skies were lightening up with dawn slower than usual, indicating autumn was here. Elona felt the familiar melancholy settle in her heart. She had still not found her purpose, but Gizella and Béláné now routinely met with her at the market. They both filled her head with politics and renewed hope for Hungary.

She believed it was possible, and this small glimmer of hope was the only thing that warmed her heart. Even if it was only a tiny spark, it was just what she needed. If her country could become whole again, then maybe she could as well. It filled the empty void, and she was like a sponge soaking up every drop. Elona supposed many other Hungarians felt the same way. After years of repression and stagnancy, any human being would wonder about the purpose of living. Hungary had its fair share of suffering, and so did she.

Elona was no different than every other Hungarian, except she had lost her child and her husband. She gazed up at the lightening clouds. She didn't have anything else to lose. That single thought settled in her heart for a long moment. Elona could make something of herself with this kind of selflessness. She could serve her country and help make it great again.

Elona inhaled the crisp morning air and shuffled towards the street with her bicycle, her heart warming with the thought of a better country and a better life. Her mind drifted to the possibilities as her right foot tapped against the pedal. The early morning was calm and deserted as it was every morning.

She heard a shuffle and glanced up. A man in a long coat was walking on the other side of the street. At first, she was alarmed. Not many people were out in the streets at this time. Then she noticed the man's gait. It was familiar.

Elona stood motionless on her bicycle, waiting for the man to approach. The figure took deliberate steps in her direction, obviously intent on meeting with her. She waited patiently until the man had cleared the darker corners of the street and the street lights shone above, illuminating his thin head of hair. He had a handsome, confident stride, quite unmistakable, actually. It was a walk of an important soldier. It was the walk of a lieutenant.

"Good morning, Lieutenant Laszlo," she said, smiling.

"Good morning, Elona," Laszlo replied back, stopping in front of her.

"What brings you here on such an early morning?" she asked.

"I need to talk to you," Laszlo said.

"About what?"

"About us," he replied.

Elona stood frozen on her bike. "Oh?"

"I heard you left your husband," he said solemnly.

Elona frowned. "Yes, I did," she replied, gripping the bicycle steering bars tightly. "It doesn't mean I am free." She looked down. "I am trapped in my own mind. An evermoving merry go round of thoughts."

"I realize that," Laszlo responded. "I just wanted to talk to you."

Elona shuffled her feet nervously as a moment of silence descended upon them. "Thank you for driving me and my family to my baby's funeral," she said sincerely. "I never really got the chance to express my gratitude."

"You are welcome, Elona," Laszlo said. "My condolences about your child's death. It shouldn't have happened. Babies shouldn't die." He reached out and hugged her briefly.

Elona felt his sincere warmth on her skin and inside her heart. He truly cared, she thought. She instantly felt her eyes moisten at his expression of sympathy. Elona swallowed back the tears. Too many tears had been shed this summer. She would have no more of it. "Thank you, Laszlo," she said quietly, her voice muffled into his collar.

He hugged her for a few more seconds, then respectfully let go. Laszlo pulled himself away from her bicycle and inspected her ragged appearance. Her hair was unkempt as usual, but her clothes were dirty, and her eyes had somehow lost their shine. "How have you been?" he asked, concern ladened in his voice.

"I have been surviving," she replied. "Nothing more to do than work, sleep and eat. Maybe one day, time will heal everything, including this country."

Laszlo nodded. "Time has a way of bringing people closer and sometimes further apart," he said. "It does heal all wounds, eventually."

"True," she agreed.

A brief gust of warm summer air blew around them, and they both just inhaled its scent. The early morning dawn was starting to rise, and they stood together, just appreciating its glow. Laszlo shuffled his feet, trying to break the silence. "Look," Laszlo said nervously. "I wanted to know if we could go to the river again and just talk." He looked down at his shoes. "I missed you."

Elona looked up at his face and felt her heart flutter. She shuffled off her bike and propped it against the wall. Elona could think of a million reasons why she should say yes and immediately go running off to their magical place. But something stopped her. A strange tug in her heart spoke loudly, as if time had wizened her, giving her thoughts to reflect upon instead of always doing spontaneous actions. "I missed you too, Laszlo," she said sincerely.

He finally looked up, and their eyes met. Elona could sense the longing in his blue eyes and felt it inside herself as well. She inhaled and hugged him fully this time, feeling his warmth and caring permeate her being. They stood for several moments, just embracing on the street with only the early morning birds chirping. No other sounds or movements surrounded them. They just existed in the void together for these lovely few moments.

A random thought snapped Elona out of the moment. She could not be with him, not right now. What if he was a cheater as well? It was more than her damaged heart could take. She needed to heal herself first before accepting love again. Elona pulled him away and held him at arm's length. "I would love to go to our special spot one day," she said softly. "But I just can't right now. I need time to heal. My heart is too broken." Her voice trailed off unexpectedly.

Laszlo held her arms, looking into her sad eyes. "I'm so sorry for everything that you've been through."

"Thank you," she said. "I appreciate that." She stepped back one step, trying to create distance between them. He was an incredibly handsome, strong man. She wanted to kiss him and sing songs by the river with him. Elona wanted to remove his clothing one by one and delight in his naked body. She wanted to make love with him for endless days. Her passion burned wild for this man and only him. But he also worked for the government, and that was troublesome. "I don't know if I could be with a man who supports and protects this government," she blurted out.

"Who said that I support this government?" Laszlo replied, one eyebrow lifting up. He leaned back. "Say yes," he urged. "Come with me to the river, maybe not today, but someday soon. I want you in my life, Elona. The politics of Hungary are in a state of flux, but I am a man of integrity, and I will always do the right thing."

Elona smiled and felt a warm tingle in her heart. "Yes," Elona said. "One day soon. Give me some time. I have to heal myself before I love another person again." She let her arms fall to her sides. "I know it's not what you wished to hear, but it is my situation at the moment." She smiled weakly. "I have to find out who Elona is again."

Laszlo grinned gently, his head tilting to the side. "You are Elona," he said. "And you are beautiful, inside and out. You will find this out one day." He stepped back. "I will be here when that happens." He waved gently. "Be gentle on yourself, sweetheart." Laszlo walked away into the dark street, turning back one more time and waving.

Elona waved back and felt the tears trying to moisten her eyes. She swallowed back the sobs and grabbed her bike. Elona mounted her bicycle and rode towards home, her heart heavy but somehow feeling marginally lighter.

CHAPTER 15

Gizella held Tibor's hand as they crossed the bridge into Pest. She loved this man with all her heart and soul. She swung his hand in hers as they walked near the river while several other students crossed into Pest.

"Did you set everything up for the wedding? Is there anything you need me to help with?" Tibor asked.

"I think everything has been taken care of," she said proudly. "My mother and my friends are helping with the food. At the moment, it will be a small celebration in the community hall in Buda, as we discussed. Too much is going on with work, our country and, of course, school. We will have to accept it as a simple ceremony." Gizella smiled and paused, searching his eyes. "It doesn't matter to me how many people attend or how extravagant it is. What matters to me is that I'm marrying a wonderful man, and, most importantly, that man is you."

Tibor stopped and kissed her immediately. He held her chin gently as he tasted her lips. He pulled back momentarily. "You are the best woman I could ever be blessed with," he said. "I don't know what I did to deserve such a gift."

Gizella smiled, looked back at the students and kissed him back. She was not ashamed and felt the intense love pouring from her heart again. It was a common occurrence when she was with him. Her heart loved this man so much that it almost ached. When they were together, she felt so happy that she felt like crying. Gizella had never experienced such love before. This wonderful feeling was solid confirmation to her that Tibor was indeed the man she was meant to marry.

"You are the best man I could have ever met," Gizella murmured between kisses. His affection, his smell, his love and his support were everything she needed. Gizella felt like she was the luckiest girl alive.

"I can't wait to call you my wife," Tibor said slowly, kissing her gently on the chin. He looked behind her at the two groups of students. Several of the men started chuckling. "We are being watched," Tibor said, smiling.

Gizella giggled. "I know," she replied. "We will be married soon, sweetheart."

"November 15 is the day I will never forget, my dear." Tibor cupped her chin gently and kissed her lips again. "I will finally be married to the love of my life."

Gizella's heart gushed with love as she kissed him back passionately. Several students whistled as Gizella broke the kiss, laughing. "We should keep walking," she said. "Some of the students have become bothersome since Rákosi was replaced with that stand-in, Ernő Gerő. I am fearful some days that violence may erupt at the university."

Tibor grabbed her waist and led her protectively away from the other students. They walked down the street towards the quieter government building district. The students veered towards the busier markets. They heard some shouts and laughter from the students as they ambled farther away.

"Is it really getting unsafe at the university?" Tibor asked. "Maybe we should get you moved into our new home earlier if I can arrange it."

"It would be nice," Gizella said. "But I don't think it's necessary. Most students know who I am now from my popular columns in the DISZ newspaper. Many students are very positive towards the movement supporting Imre's reforms."

Tibor tilted his head to the side. "Do you think Nagy will be brought back into power?" he asked.

"It's very possible," she replied slowly. The moment of truth was here, and she needed to let Tibor know where she stood, for better or worse. Her throat constricted, and then she exhaled out. "The student unions have a powerful voice in politics. The louder they yell, the more that the powers in government will start listening." She slowed down her walk and looked thoughtfully down at her shoes as they clicked on the pavement. "The only problem is how much louder do we have to yell?"

Tibor nodded. "True, my love," he replied, squeezing her hand. A thought suddenly occurred to him. He wondered how extreme her political views stretched. He knew that his own political views had been tested in the past few months, almost to the breaking point. Tibor cleared his throat momentarily. "Would you march with them if there was a protest?"

Gizella had never thought of that before, so the question took her by surprise. "I guess I might," she answered nervously. "I am very passionate about Hungary returning to a much better country. If it meant that I would walk with a few hundred students, I suppose I would do that." She stopped as her heart pounded with the truth. "Does that bother you?"

"No," Tibor replied immediately.

Gizella's shoulders relaxed visibly.

"I am concerned for your well-being, though," he added. "I don't want you to be hurt."

"Oh, I doubt any harm would come to me," she replied. "I am only doing what is necessary to get Hungary back to the country we once loved. There is some heroism in my veins, but I don't think I would stay if it became violent." She smiled, wondering if this was the truth. "I do believe that we all need to muster our strength and come together to rise as one. Change will happen, but it rests with us all, not just our leaders."

Tibor nodded slowly, absorbing her words. "I suppose you are right, my sweetheart," he said, squeezing her hand. "My main concern is for your safety, that's all. We will be together soon and hopefully start building a family after you complete your studies."

Gizella smiled broadly. "You have always supported me in everything," she said joyfully, her heart warming at his acceptance of her political views. "I love you." Gizella hugged him softly and thanked the heavens silently.

"Of course," Tibor murmured into her hair. "I love you with all my heart, Gizzy."

On October 6, the body of a prominent communist, Laszlo Rajk, who was executed in Rákosi's show trials in 1949, was being reburied in a politically charged ceremony. Thousands and thousands of people were here, and Gizella was one of them.

She had held her head proudly as they marched from the cemetery to the centre of town, reciting poetry and joining the crowd. Many in attendance were disenchanted communists, but the two people beside her were the ones who mattered the most.

Gizella hugged Elona and Béláné warmly as they continued their march with the crowd. Strings of poetic verses sang from their mouths as they felt the freedom blossom within their hearts. Many crowd dwellers were happily joining together with a common purpose. They would sing poetry until they got their country back! Never before had Gizella felt such pride in her country. It was as if this was her destiny.

Elona smiled at her friend's infectious enthusiasm. "Bring the inner beauty of Hungary back!" Elona shouted as the poetic verses tumbled from her lips. "The leaves will dry, and within its crumpled pieces will form a strength of unity."

"Together we will stand," Gizella cited. "For beauty and peace. Roses will bloom again."

Béláné joined in. "With togetherness, we will rise," she sang loudly.

The three friends joined hands and sang poetry loudly, their hearts filling with pride and an infectious hope for a better future.

Elona began to feel something deep in her heart. A longing, an ache and a void were slowly being filled, little by little. It was the only thing that made sense to her right now, and this movement gave her purpose. It was exactly what she craved. She had told Laszlo that she needed to find herself again. A tingle ran up her spine, raising the hairs on her head. Maybe this was it. Maybe her true purpose was grander than just being a mother and a wife. Maybe her country needed her after all.

The crowd was much larger than any of the women had expected. There were students, workers and many DISZ members. Many of Gizella's comrades were marching in tandem with the crowd. They felt safe and protected by a common cause. It was a peaceful march and just what Hungarians needed right now.

Gizella smiled proudly, wrapped her right arm around Elona and whispered in her ear. "I'm so glad you came!" she said.

Elona chuckled. "Thank you, Gizella," she responded. "You have no idea how much I needed this."

"Watering flowers bring out the beauty of the land," Béláné shouted, raising her hands and joining the two women. "Water the soil of our souls." Béláné wrapped her right arm around Gizella as they all joined together, walking as one.

"We will grow!" Gizella shouted passionately.

"With the warmth of the sun on the roses," Elona sang as she smiled happily at Béláné, glancing to the side.

Béláné smiled back. "May the colours return to our hearts!"

The three women chanted together as the crowd moved towards the centre of town. Elona's eyes moistened as she remembered seeing Julia Rajk kneeling by her late husband's burial mound earlier this morning. Millions of emotions bubbled back into her heart. The mother of Laszlo Rajk was in attendance as well. She had cried heavily as she wailed for the loss of her son. The moving ceremony was felt by every single attendee, including Elona. It had affected her in ways she couldn't quite explain. Her entire body had convulsed, and she had broken down in a fit of tears. Gizella had lifted her up and whispered in her ear. "Everything will be alright."

Elona felt her eyes moisten with emotion again. Her heart had been so terribly shattered for so very long. Elona felt the pain of Rajk's mother. It was too close to her feelings with the loss of her baby boy. Elona was crying openly now. She couldn't stop the tears. It was a mix of sorrow, pain and renewed hope. Part of her was still terribly sad, but there was a light inside of her now, a bright light that was getting stronger with every step that she took with the crowd of supporters.

Gizella held her arm onto Elona's shoulders protectively. "Hope," she said simply. "This is all we need. Including you." Gizella smiled as more tears fell from Elona's eyes. "You deserve so much more than you have been given, Elona. The day will come when happiness will be yours. Trust me, you're a beautiful girl inside and out." Gizella hugged Elona fully and kissed her briefly on each cheek. "Believe it." She gently shook Elona's shoulders to get the message somehow into Elona's body.

Elona nodded. "Thank you," she sobbed as the crowd swirled around her.

Béláné stopped with the two women and hugged Elona too. The grief was evident on Elona's face. "We will persevere," Béláné said. "This is our destiny."

Gizella looked around at the crowd and knew instinctively that it was increasing in size. She couldn't see anything except people and more people. She had no idea how many people there were, but it appeared to be hundreds of thousands. The words of Tibor rang gently in her mind. She needed to stay safe for him and their future family. "Let's start finding our way back soon," Gizella said. "The crowd is almost to the centre of town."

Elona looked up with tears still streaming from her face. "Yes," she said. "Let's find our way back home. We have done enough for today."

"Yes, we have," Gizella said, looking up over the heads of thousands of people. "Yes, we have."

Béláné, Gizella and Elona clasped their hands together and started blending toward the outer stretches of the crowd, trying to find their way out. A few DISZ members waved at Gizella, and she waved back. They pointed towards the southeast and waved as they marched on. One shouted. "You are the best, Gizella!"

The three women weaved their way slowly through the crowd until it began thinning, and they could see the streets better. They were close to the bridge to Buda. They would be fine. Gizella exhaled with relief and a mix of joy.

↗

Laszlo's small team had been called to the town centre as approximately 100,000 people were gathering. He noticed Jozsef with his police unit there as well. There were more policemen than army units. It appeared that only Laszlo's small team had been called on the military side, but he couldn't be sure.

The crowd was pleasantly subdued with chants of poetry and reform. Some people were singing, and some were reciting odd streams of poetry. Laszlo was relieved that it was a non-violent march, but he was still apprehensive. With crowds this large, things could quickly turn into a dangerous revolt.

But something occurred that he had not expected. It didn't happen in the crowd or the event or with anything that he could pinpoint with accuracy.

It had happened in his heart.

He felt the emotion of every single Hungarian in the streets today. He felt the sorrow, the pain and the beacon of hope.

It was this light of hopefulness that caught him off guard. He stood at attention, watching the crowd thoughtfully, still doing his duties, but something was changing inside of him, and it was something powerful.

His knees felt oddly weak, and his heart pounded with admiration and pride. A smile creased his mouth as he watched so many of his fellow Hungarians seeking change for their beloved country.

The economy in Hungary was in ruins, and something needed to be done.

Laszlo felt a strong surge of pride and hope sneak into his heart. He watched Jozsef from afar to see if the emotions of the crowd had affected him too. Laszlo squinted to see in the distance.

He saw Jozsef standing with his fellow policemen, and as he tilted his head towards another man's ear, Laszlo noticed a genuine smile crease Jozsef's face. The other policemen were smiling too.

Laszlo turned his head to his fellow soldiers standing beside him. He could see the hope in every man's eyes, which glowed with something indescribable.

CHAPTER 16

Elona stepped out of the cinema and jangled her keys into the lock. She had worked all week, and it felt good. Her heart was repairing itself, and her hope was returning. For once in her life, she felt like the future was something to look forward to.

She turned to mount her bike and noticed his presence down the street before he even moved.

Laszlo was leaning against his Mercedes, almost an entire block away, smoking a cigarette.

Elona mounted her bike, rode to him and stopped suddenly, her hair a windblown mess. "Laszlo," she said gently. "You have come again." She smiled and nodded her head. "You are a determined man." She couldn't stop the smile that crept onto her lips. "I must say this is a redeeming quality."

Laszlo grinned and threw the cigarette to the ground, crushing it with his foot. "I'm going to quit these damn cigarettes, too," he said. "They're no good for me."

Elona chuckled. "Everyone I know smokes," she said. "I am used to it."

"It makes me cough," Laszlo replied. "Something about these cigarettes can't be good."

"I haven't heard they were too bad for people," she said.

Laszlo nodded, pulling his hands out of his pockets and gesturing into the air. "But that's the thing," he replied. "We are only told what we are sanctioned to hear."

Elona grinned. "Something has changed," she said thoughtfully.

"Yes," he replied slowly, measuring each word thoughtfully. "My team was called to the funeral reburial demonstration a few days ago."

"You were there?" Elona interrupted, her mouth hanging open in animated disbelief.

"Yes, my unit was instructed to attend for security," he answered, shuffling his boots. "But something about the crowd touched me. I don't know what it was, but I think it touched every single policeman and soldier there."

"I was there too," Elona interjected proudly.

"You were?" Laszlo said, his eyebrow lifting noticeably.

"Yes, it was the best thing to happen for me in a very long while," she answered. "I felt purpose." She wrung her fingers, trying to find the correct words to convey what she felt. "Seeing the faces of so many Hungarians with a common passion hit me hard. It helped me to understand that every single person has been through hardships, just as bad as mine, or sometimes worse." Elona stepped closer and held his hand. "I felt united with Hungary. I have never felt that before in my life." She smiled as her eyes watered with emotion. "And I felt hope for the future."

Laszlo felt a shiver run down his arms. He blinked. "That's exactly what I felt, too," he agreed. "It's been so many years of hopelessness in Budapest." Laszlo moved closer to her, sliding an arm around her waist. "So many years," he added.

Elona accepted his touch warmly. Her skin tingled with electricity as his male scent loomed closer. It was intoxicating.

Her mind briefly shut down, and all she could feel was his physical presence. She smiled shyly and nodded. "I agree, too many years," she added. "I have never experienced this type of hope before."

"I did, but only when I was very young," he replied. "Once I grew into an older child, much of that hope was destroyed by the fascist government and then the Germans." He held her closer and inhaled her sweet-smelling hair. They stood there frozen in time for several moments, enjoying the closeness. Finally, he broke the silence. "Your hair smells like flowers," he said absentmindedly.

Elona chuckled. "I washed it yesterday."

"Well, whatever you washed it with, it smells good," he replied, grinning.

"Thank you," she responded softly.

He kissed her head gently.

Elona felt her arms melt as his caring kiss travelled down to her toes. It had been so long since she had any sort of intimacy with a man, and her body instantly craved it. Her physical response was immediate. Her legs began to weaken, and her mouth watered. Elona wasn't sure what to do but just accept the feeling and let it ride through her. "You are a wonderful man," she said softly. "I don't know why I sent you away."

Laszlo kissed the top of her head once more. "You only did what any mother would do," he said. "It was admirable, and I am proud of you."

"How can you say that?" Elona replied. "I forced you away after so many lovely moments that we shared and for another man." She frowned, her eyebrows knitting together in pain. "A terrible man who never cared for me."

"You were pregnant," he answered, the silence falling heavy between them. He slowly wrapped his arms tighter around her small body. "A good mother would have done nothing else but invest in her family. This makes you a high-quality woman, my dear. Don't think any less of yourself."

Elona felt sudden tears escape from her eyes. She buried her face into his warm chest as the cool wind swirled around them. She had never felt so cherished in her life, and this unusual soldier, a man of integrity and steadfast determination, had somehow found the gold inside her. Elona smiled and sniffled back the tears. "You're special," she whispered.

Laszlo smiled warmly. "You're special too, my dear," he replied.

They continued hugging warmly for several moments, with a light silence floating in the air. No uncomfortableness, just acceptance of sharing each other's space. It was what they both needed, moments of physical closeness, just that, nothing else.

Elona inhaled the subtle scent of his cologne. A slight musky and woody smell drifted pleasantly into her nostrils. She smiled and kissed his chest lightly. "Do you have any time to go to the riverside today?" she asked. "I'd be happy to spend the morning with you."

Laszlo grinned, a beam of joy running through his veins. "Of course," he replied. "I would be most gracious to have your company." He pulled slightly away but kept his arm curled around her waist. His other arm stretched out towards the Mercedes. "Shall we? We can leave your bike at the cinema. I will bring you back here."

She dismounted, and Laszlo grabbed the bike, walking it back to the cinema. They secured the bicycle inside the back entrance and returned to the car. Once they were back at the Mercedes, he opened the passenger door for her, motioning for her to enter. Elona sat down on the hard leather seat as Laszlo closed the door and circled around to the driver's side. He started the car, and they drove through the streets. Elona gazed out the window, watching the night turning into day. The dawn came later in October, and the air cooled somewhat. There was no snow until January usually, but Hungary was still warmer in October than other northern countries.

The purplish skies were slowly lightening. Elona gazed in wonderment from the car window as the skies turned into lighter colours while mixing with the darker shades of blue. "It's a beautiful morning," she commented.

"Yes, it is," Laszlo replied, his hands on the steering wheel. He pointed in the distance. "Look at that purple cloud!"

Elona smiled. "I have never seen such a beautiful morning like this before."

"It is windy," Laszlo pointed out. "Maybe those are storm clouds or something."

"You're right," she agreed. "Maybe they are."

He slowed the vehicle into second gear as they neared the grassy hill by the river. Laszlo pulled alongside the bushes and parked the Mercedes, then got out to open her door.

Elona smiled gently as she swung her legs to the side, holding Laszlo's hand immediately. Instantly, the swirl of darkish clouds surrounded them. Lightish rays of pink streaked across the sky as the storm clouds receded.

"It looks so strange," he stated. "Like we just stepped onto a different planet or something."

Elona chuckled. "I was just about to say the same thing!"

"Well, whatever it is," Laszlo said. "It is mesmerizingly beautiful." He looked back at the car. "Hold on, I have to grab something."

He returned to the car and opened the trunk, removing the large accordion.

"You brought it!" Elona shrieked.

"Yes," he replied. "I needed my music today." He closed the trunk, shifted the accordion strap over his body and returned to Elona, slipping his hand into hers.

They walked together to the small hill, their hearts shining within. Elona felt like there was a wondrous cloud beneath their feet as they returned to the lovely spot they had shared over a year ago.

Laszlo squeezed her hand briefly. "It is nice coming back here with you."

"It is a beautiful feeling," Elona agreed, her face beaming brightly as they arrived at the grassy mound.

Laszlo removed the accordion and his long trench coat. He laid the coat down as a blanket. "After you, my dear," he said softly.

Elona sat down and waited for Laszlo to get settled with the accordion beside her. They smiled at each other as they clasped hands and stared into each other's eyes. Then he started to play.

The accordion music lilted into the air and rushed into Elona's heart like a forceful tide. Her skin tingled as his deep voice joined the melody.

The song was a new one. She hadn't heard it before.

Laszlo sang passionately along with the music.

Emerald eyes shooting into my soul
Longing, longing, longing
Knowing it to be true
A dream, so close but so far away
Longing to touch her one more time
Longing, longing, longing

Elona felt her heart soar and crash with every word. It was evident that she had caused him so much pain. Her eyes watered, and she touched his knee as he performed the remainder of the song. His voice rose to a crescendo as the passion in his eyes lit up. Laszlo played the accordion fiercely and let out one last croon before the song slowly faded to the end.

"It was about me," Elona stated finally, with tears in her eyes.

"Yes," he replied, looking away. "I wrote it after I saw you pregnant at the market with your mom."

"You saw me at the market?"

"Yes," he replied.

"You didn't say hi," she stated.

"No, I didn't want to intrude."

"I understand," she said softly.

"You looked radiant."

"I did?" she asked.

"Yes, you did."

Elona looked down at her fingers on his lap. "I'm sorry that I caused you so much pain," she said. "I wanted to be with you. I was preparing in my mind to leave Ferenc. Then I found out I was pregnant." She looked up at the purple skies with tears in her eyes. "It was the hardest decision I have ever made. I wanted that child to be yours, not Ferenc's."

Laszlo calmly pulled the accordion off his lap and set it aside. "I think sometimes life works in mysterious ways," he said slowly, entwining his fingers into hers. "I am just glad to be here with you once again. Whatever journey it took to get here, I'd gladly do it over and over again just to be with you, Elona." Laszlo squeezed her hand warmly.

Elona hugged him instantly and kissed his cheek. His words consoled her heart. Her throat felt constricted with emotions, and she tried valiantly to stop the flow of tears. Elona swallowed and inhaled his scent as the scenery around them continued to dance in an array of colours.

Laszlo hugged her tightly and felt his heart rupture open. It was painful but yet so very delightful at the same time. After several moments, he kissed her forehead and looked down at her face buried in his chest. "Are you okay?" he asked.

She sniffled. "I'm fine," she answered. "I'm just so happy we found each other again." Elona pulled away slightly, looking up at him. Her eyes shined a deep emerald green, and Laszlo's glittered an icy blue but with a ring of darker blue around the iris.

"Your eyes have changed," she said. "You have a ring of darker blue around the lighter colour." She smiled, gazing into his eyes languidly.

"They do change sometimes," he replied. "Usually with my moods. When I'm angry at work, they turn a very pale ice blue. Some people say it is the wolf in my veins." He chuckled and laid his palm along her cheek, leaning closer. "When I am relaxed, there can be some darker rings of blue."

"What is your mood right now?" she asked.

"I want to love you," he blurted out. Laszlo leaned in and kissed her lips softly. The electricity between them sparked like fire. "I want to give you everything you've never had before."

Elona kissed him back passionately. An instant fire started in her abdomen. She was suddenly restless and fidgety. Her desire for him enflamed her senses, and an urgency took over. Elona felt if she could jump inside his clothes, she would do just that.

Laszlo grabbed her buttocks and shifted her entirely onto his lap, with them facing each other as they kissed. They didn't lose the kiss, instead leaning in towards each other with the movement, both keenly aware of staying connected.

She could feel his desire meeting hers. Elona felt an urgency like none other, as if this moment was one to be cherished forever, and it was imperative that it must continue to its fruition. She moaned as his tongue met hers, and they kissed in the open air almost feverishly now.

Laszlo pulled her backwards and laid on his back as Elona splayed on top of him, still kissing passionately. He wrapped his long arms around her and splayed his large hands on her buttocks. Her butt cheeks were small but round and very pliable, like dough. He squeezed them both as she suddenly moaned into his mouth. Laszlo slid his tongue deeper into her mouth and squeezed her buttocks again.

Elona moaned deeply again, her body on fire with an insatiable desire to make love. Her legs quivered, and her arms felt rubbery as she kissed him back with everything she had. Elona could feel his hard penis poking into her abdomen. She wanted to touch it so badly that it ached for her to remain a lady. She bit her lip and willed her desire to cool down.

Laszlo ran his left hand along her side, brushing the edge of her breast and then back down to her buttock. He squeezed her right buttock in tandem with the light caresses on her opposite side.

She moaned so deeply this time that her body shuddered.

Laszlo's hands moved on their own accord now, working in conjunction with every moan and kiss. Her responses were his starting and ending points. He brushed her upper leg with his right hand, and she was quiet, so he didn't do that anymore. Laszlo's hands moved higher alongside her breasts, again another groan resounding into his mouth as she kissed him. He could feel her entire body shuddering from his touch as if there was an electric beam connecting the two of them, and he was only the messenger.

"You're so beautiful," he whispered.

Elona groaned again as her eyes fluttered closed. His hands moved all over her body, touching places that she had never been touched before. Her heart pounded in her chest as the need for him escalated past any rational thought.

The wind blew at her back, but she was oblivious. Her skin was on fire, and her heart needed Laszlo. There was a powerful necessity within her deepest feelings that she couldn't quite understand or fathom at all. Elona felt drawn into his strength, his desire and his love. She realized now that he probably loved her. The realization made her head swim. She pulled back and looked into his hooded sexy eyes.

"It's like we never left each other," she murmured. "Like time didn't stop between us. We are just picking up where we left off."

"Yes," he said, his words tangling in his brain.

Elona looked deeply into his eyes, then glanced down at the hard ridge in his pants. "Can I touch him?"

Laszlo felt his penis twitch. "Yes," he said in a throaty reply.

Elona's hand fluttered down to his groin as her small fingers pressed against the fabric of his pants. She cupped her hand over his width and slid her fingers up and down.

Laszlo groaned heavily as her urgency permeated his pants and throughout his entire being. He licked her ear urgently as she gazed down at his rigid penis, working her fingers over his groin. Laszlo found her earlobe and sucked on it, pulling the sweet tissue into his mouth gently, biting it softly.

Elona moaned as her body fired responses to his touches. She no longer thought with her mind. Only her physical responses were doing the thinking. Each movement, each moan, each kiss was a thought of its own, and each thought became a sentence and rolled into a physical love story.

Elona felt Laszlo's hands unzipping his pants as she ventured further and further into his being, his soul. Finally, his penis was freed, and she wrapped her slim fingers around the tip, then slid down to the base, the girth thickening here. She delighted in the feel of his warm penis in her hand. Elona slid her fingers back up to the tip and back down, rhythmically moving within the music of desire.

Laszlo groaned loudly as she stroked his penis with her tiny fingers. He could feel her heart hammering against his chest, and he looked down, found her neck and kissed her there. She moaned heavily. He kissed her again, delighting with the delicious feminine slope of her neck and shoulder. She trembled and moaned again. Laszlo felt compelled to this spot and began sucking it with vigour.

Elona stretched her neck out, giving him complete access to her shoulder as waves of pleasure coursed throughout her body. Sparks of electricity danced along her nerves, her skin and her hair. Every suckle on her shoulder sent a new wave of desire throughout her body, liquifying her muscles.

Laszlo sucked harder on the sensitive spot until he could take it no longer. His penis was on fire, and he needed her right now. He grasped onto her and gently rolled with her until she was on her back. He leaned in and kissed her gently, pulling back briefly to look into her eyes.

Elona's eyes were wild with desire. The dark emerald green irises shone against the lightening skies. Her hair was splayed all over his coat, and she reached up urgently to kiss him again. She was like an animal beneath him, and it was all he could do to stop himself from taming her. Laszlo pushed his groin into hers instinctively. Elona closed her eyes, and her head flopped to one side as a steady moan released from her mouth. She exhaled rapidly and clenched her fists onto his shirt.

Laszlo fumbled with her clothes until he found her pants, sliding them quickly down to her knees along with her underwear. He didn't bother to remove them completely. There was no time. Everything was a very urgent necessity now.

Laszlo centred his hips above her open vagina and grasped his penis. He locked eyes with Elona as they kissed softly, much more gently this time. He released the kiss as Elona panted heavily.

"Please," she begged.

Laszlo guided his penis to her opening and felt the flaps of her vulva encircle him warmly. The wetness was hot and slick as his penis throbbed against her tight entrance. He shifted his hips between hers to try to widen her legs. Her knees were still joined with her pants. In the back of his mind, he thought he should remove her pants. His penis didn't agree, and he somehow wriggled his way between her inner thighs. Her wetness called to him like a beacon, urging him to penetrate her, claiming her as his own.

Her legs wiggled apart to allow him more room.

He shifted one more time, then slid easily into her wet vagina.

They both groaned in unison. Elona lightly bit onto his shoulder as he gently rocked his full length into her. He stopped once when he reached her cervix. Laszlo panted on her like a teenager. His mind was swirling with ways he could avoid ejaculating too quickly. He raised himself on his palms and looked down at her.

She was a beautiful hormonal mess. Her hair was pointing out in all directions now, her cheeks were flushed, and her lips swollen. Laszlo smiled. "You look so lovely right now," he murmured.

She inhaled. "Laszlo," she breathed. "I've been waiting for this for so long."

Laszlo felt his eyelids close momentarily as his penis throbbed inside of her. He held himself frozen as a statue, afraid that even the tiniest movement would trigger an ejaculation. He calmed his breathing and focused just on his breath. He couldn't even open his eyes because one look at her enchanting face would surely send him over the cliff of desire.

Elona was pinned beneath him, and her entire body felt immobilized by a will of its own. She intuitively knew that he needed a rest from the intensity. Her head swam with dizziness from the lack of blood flow, and her mouth felt raw, but her vagina was pulsating on its own without her consent. His penis stretched her vagina to the limit, her moisture slicking his base. She wanted this precious moment to be suspended in time forever. Nothing she had ever experienced before in her life compared to this feeling. His love filling the void inside her felt like the thing that was necessary to balance her life right now.

She craned her neck up and kissed his jawline. "Laszlo," she breathed. "If I could capture this moment, I would."

Laszlo slid his penis slowly outwards, then moved back into her, prompting another groan from her. He squeezed his eyes shut and willed his penis to behave. Laszlo slid himself outwards, then inwards again. Finally, he felt his penis relax slightly, and the throbbing diminish. Laszlo exhaled in relief and continued his slow rhythm into and out of her body. She moaned and twisted beneath him as he continued his steady movements. He could feel her vagina begin to crest slowly, the pulses getting stronger and stronger with each sliding motion of his penis. He was not sure how much longer he could hold out for.

Elona's moans intensified and steadily got deeper and deeper. Her legs began to shudder involuntarily as every muscle in her body tensed with an unstoppable energy. Finally, her body convulsed into itself, and her vagina gripped him in a fierce throbbing hold. Elona cried out.

Laszlo's stamina was no match against the intense grip of her vagina. She pulsated wildly around his penis, and he could hold back no longer. He pushed one more time, and as if her vagina had milked him of everything, he ejaculated forcefully into her womb, one stream after another. His heart beat wildly in his chest as all the pent up love from the past year flooded out of his body and into hers. Laszlo collapsed clumsily onto her, barely catching himself on his elbows. His heavy breathing caressed her shoulder as his body drained every ounce of energy it had once contained.

Elona felt his semen fill her vagina, and it was the most heartwarming sensation she had ever experienced. She realized that she loved this man. She had always loved Laszlo. Elona just never allowed the thought to settle in her mind because she had been married. But now she realized with the heavy dawn of understanding that this was the man she was meant to be with.

She circled her arms tightly around his flaccid form and smoothed her hands under his shirt on his back. Elona massaged his skin lightly until the intensity of the moment finally passed. The morning air blanketed their bodies as the sun tentatively rose over the horizon, splaying rays of orange into the skies.

He raised himself tentatively onto his palms, gazed briefly at the rising sun and then looked thoughtfully into her eyes. "I hope you know that I love you," Laszlo murmured with a thick deep voice.

"I know," Elona replied, with emotion wetting her eyes. "I love you too, my dear." She hugged him warmly and kissed his shoulder as the sun scattered its warmth onto their embrace.

Chapter 17

Nagy kept his eyes glued to Miklós as his friend explained where things were heading. The movement was growing but not as Nagy would have liked. It was reform. It was necessary, but it was no longer in his control, he realized.

"There was an urgent meeting tonight at the Petőfi Circle," Miklós said. "The students are actively discussing reform now, pinning it down to several points. Some are clear, and some are not."

"What are the reforms being discussed?" Nagy asked as he sipped a small cup of coffee. "Is it centred on student issues and educational reform?"

Miklós shook his head and pursed his lips. "No. Surprisingly, there has not been a single discussion of student issues. They are mostly political, social and economic concerns. These students are intelligent and passionately involved now."

Nagy set the small ceramic cup down and placed an index finger on the bridge of his nose in thought. "This sounds like something that is reaching out of our control," he said slowly. "Or is there some way?"

"I can only influence the meetings," Miklós said, shifting in his chair confidently. "But don't fear. The meetings are still going in our favour. Many in attendance are your supporters."

"Did we hear from that man from MEFESZ again?" Nagy asked.

"No," Miklós answered. "Not since that last time."

"Have they discussed democratic reform?"

"Not really," Miklós replied. "Most of the discussions are centred on communist reform, but there are a few discussions that have led out of that realm."

"MEFESZ must not be allowed at these meetings," Nagy said. "Hungary cannot be led in this direction. It is a recipe for disaster."

Miklós shifted uncomfortably. "Every time discussions start straying to democracy, I do intervene," he said. "I try to steer the debate back to communist reforms and the reforms you instituted when you were in power. They were working, and it only serves to prove that this is the right way." Miklós stood and brushed his pants smoothly. "But I am only one man," he said slowly. "These meetings are growing larger and larger in size. Last night, I would guess there were almost one hundred people. I am one of the key people there, but it is still difficult."

"Well, thank you for all that you are doing for Hungary," Nagy asked. "My gratitude is immeasurable." Nagy stood and placed his hands firmly on the desk, with emotion in his eyes. "We need more people like you."

"There are many of us, Nagy," Miklós said as he walked to the door, opening it. "I assure you, we all want the same thing. We want Hungary to govern as its own country someday. The path to this ultimate goal is through communist reform. We all know that. I have to go now, but I will keep you updated." Miklós waved and disappeared into the stairwell as the floors creaked with his retreating steps.

Imre Nagy watched his receding form and willed himself to believe what Miklós was saying. Nagy listened as every step Miklós took creaked the stairs. Then he heard the door slam shut.

Something was tightening in his chest, a strange evil in the pit of his stomach. Nagy sat down heavily and accidentally brushed his empty cup of coffee. He jerked forward as the cup teetered off the desk, trying to catch it. But it was too late. The ceramic cup hit the floor hard and shattered into several pieces. Nagy cursed and picked up the largest piece, staring at it. He could maybe fix the cup, but he wasn't sure. He leaned back in the chair and exhaled heavily.

⁊

Elona finished washing the dishes when there was a knock on the door.

Her brother looked up. "Are you expecting anyone?" he asked.

"No," she said. "Are you?"

"No, I'm not," Frank replied. "I will get the door." Frank walked confidently to the front entrance and pulled it open. A man was standing nervously on the other side.

"Oh, hello," Frank said, surprised.

"Is Elona here?" Laszlo asked, shifting his feet uncertainly. "I'd like a word with her."

Frank smiled. "Of course, come in," he said. "She has told me much about you. You are Laszlo, right? The man who drove her to the baby's funeral."

"Yes," Laszlo replied.

"That was a nice thing to do," Frank added.

"It was what anyone with a heart would do," Laszlo said.

Frank nodded and gestured the lieutenant into the house. "Elona!" he shouted towards the kitchen. "Someone is here to see you."

Elona quickly dried her hands and removed her apron. "Who is it?" she shouted back.

"It's Lieutenant Laszlo," Frank answered back, walking into the kitchen with Laszlo behind him.

Elona's heart skipped a beat, and her face flushed warmly as she saw Laszlo walk into the dining area.

"Oh, hi!" Elona said, her cheeks turning a light pink.

"Elona," Laszlo said, a slight grin on his face. "I'm sorry to interrupt you on a Sunday. I just thought I would stop by. I don't have a lot of time during the week." He reached into his pocket. "I brought these for you. Gizella gave it to Tibor and asked me to drop it off."

"What is it?" Elona asked, curiously peering into his hand.

"It looks like seeds," Laszlo said confounded.

Elona grasped the small bag and peered inside. She smelled it. It didn't smell like anything. "Why would Gizella give me seeds?" she laughed. "It's October. I could only plant them inside."

"I don't know," Laszlo said. "There wasn't a message other than she was planning to visit you on Wednesday." He stared down at her small palm, holding the bag of seeds. "Maybe you should plant them. Maybe it is a much-needed vegetable."

"That would be nice!" Elona said. "Yes, I will plant them." She smiled at Laszlo and placed the seeds on the table.

Frank coughed nervously. "I was just on my way to the market with Anyu and the kids," he said. "I will be back. Maybe we can chat some more, Laszlo." Frank patted him on the back and disappeared into the hallway. Muffled voices sounded from the bedrooms as the family shuffled to leave.

Elona smiled at Laszlo once they were alone. "You're here," she said.

"I am here," Laszlo responded.

"You just came to drop off the seeds?" she asked.

"No," he said. "I came to see you."

"Oh," Elona said softly. Her eyes twinkled with delight.

Laszlo stepped closer and grasped her hands. "Of course, I missed you," he said. "It's been two long days since I saw you last."

Elona smiled. "Two days?" she laughed.

"Yes," he chuckled. "Two days is a long time."

Elona laughed. "No, it isn't," she said with a twinkle in her eye. "Two days is only 48 hours. There were times when I didn't even see my mother for 48 hours because of my night cleaning job."

Laszlo stepped forward and wrapped his arms around her waist gently. He bent his head down to look into her eyes. "Two days is an eternity when I finally have the woman I've always wanted." He kissed her forehead gently.

A pleasant warmth spread through her body, sending loving sensations to her heart and her gut. She had never felt such feelings before and wondered what it was. Laszlo's arms gently pulled her closer, and he kissed her head one more time.

"You make me feel warm," she said, snuggling her nose against his chest.

"I'm glad," he answered.

"You actually make my body feel warm inside," she said. "I've never felt that before."

"You always feel cold?" he asked, chuckling.

"No," Elona replied. "I just never had another person's presence make me feel warm inside like that."

"Oh, I see," Laszlo said. He ran his hand over her hair, smoothing it down to her shoulders. "Maybe you feel my love, and that's the warmth you describe. You can feel that someone absolutely adores you."

Emotions quickly bubbled up to the surface upon hearing his words. It was true. She had lived her entire life feeling cold and unloved. Now, out of all the people in the world, a lieutenant in the army gave her this truest form of love. Elona struggled to hold back the tears. She sniffled involuntarily.

Laszlo immediately smoothed her hair again, knowing he had somehow hit a deep emotional nerve. "Don't worry," he said quietly. "Maybe everything that has happened to this point was for a purpose. Maybe we were always meant to be together. Who knows?"

"Do you believe that?" she asked. "I would have never dreamed that I would fall in love with an army lieutenant."

"I have to believe in something," Laszlo replied. "Or else my life and my work would be a waste."

"Do you believe in this government?" she asked suddenly, unsure of his position. "Do you believe that you should be protecting this Russian puppet regime?"

Laszlo exhaled and mused over his response. He wasn't sure that he even understood his own beliefs at the moment. Every day seemed to chip away another block at his old beliefs. "I am a soldier, Elona," he said slowly. "But I am also human. I see the suffering, the passion and the hope. I have a job to protect our country, and I will do that, regardless of the government in power."

Elona exhaled in relief. She loved this man and didn't want to lose him, but she had to know where he stood. "I support the old government," she stated. "I support the things that Nagy was doing to help Hungary. The economic reforms were working, but now we are plunged back to where we were with Rákosi, just a different name." Elona pulled back briefly and placed her hand on his jaw. "I don't want to lose you ever again. But you must know I feel passionate about change in this country. I will join another protest if there is one. I will fight, if I have to, for our country. I have never felt anything stronger in my soul, my purpose or my life."

Laszlo cupped her chin. "I understand, Elona," he said.

"Do you really?" she asked, her eyes searching his for the truth.

The shuffling in the back bedroom grew louder suddenly as several people spilled into the hallway.

Laszlo pulled away from embracing Elona and simply held her hand as her family slowly appeared one by one in the dining room.

"Laszlo!" Anyu cried. "You are here."

"Yes," he said. "I came to see your daughter."

"You did?"

"Yes, we have been friends for awhile now," Laszlo said.

Anyu looked at their joined hands and looked back to his face. "It looks like you are more than just friends," she said.

"Anyu!" Elona cried in disbelief. "We have been friends for over a year now. Nothing happened between us while I was married."

"You are still married," Frank pointed out.

"Not for long," Elona said, holding her head up high.

"Good, I'm glad," Frank said. "That Ferenc was a useless husband."

Anyu grabbed one of the kid's hands, shuffling the small boy onto her lap as she sat down to put the child's boots on. She peered up at her daughter and Laszlo. "I'm happy for you," she said sincerely. "I really am. Elona has had her fair share of misery. She deserves to have some happiness in her life."

"Thank you, Anyu," Elona replied. "That means a lot to me."

"But if you don't treat her right," Anyu said, pointing. "I swear, I don't trust what I might do to you."

"Anyu!" Elona cried out in embarrassment.

Laszlo and Frank laughed. "Not to worry," Laszlo said, slipping his arm around Elona's waist. "I will have her best interests at heart."

"I will hold you to that," Anyu said, smiling. She placed her small grandson down and grasped his hand. "Let's go. We need to get some food in this house."

Laszlo and Elona watched as the caravan of relatives left the house. He turned to Elona and cupped her chin, tilting her face up to his. Gently, he bent down and kissed her lips slowly and lovingly. "I will always stand beside you, Elona," he stated firmly. "Never forget that I am a Hungarian too."

Gizella smiled and tapped her hand. "The seeds are a mixture of vegetables," she said. "You can grow them inside until they are ready to be planted in your garden."

"Well, thank you so much, Gizella," Elona said, a frown creasing her eyebrows. "But why send seeds to me? I don't understand. It is a little strange."

Gizella leaned forward. "They are not just seeds," she said. "They are the seeds of change. We are handing them out to everyone close to our hearts. The Petőfi Circle is growing in numbers every day. The meetings are so crowded now, and my heart is overfilling with hope. Those seeds," she said, pointing.

"Those are the seeds of change in our hearts. We will form our own future. A beautiful one that no one can take away from us."

Elona felt hope bubble to the surface. "Do you really think the people can do this?"

Gizella leaned over and hugged Elona warmly. "Yes," she said. "We can. I can feel the hope every morning when I awake."

A smile creased Elona's cheek. "We will have a better future?"

"Yes, if we believe it to be so," Gizella answered. She released Elona and smiled, gesturing in the air with her fine-boned fingers. "The Petőfi Circle is putting together some ideas for reform. I believe the people will have more power soon."

"What do you mean?" Elona asked. "I thought this was all to get Imre Nagy back in power."

"It's much more than that, Elona," Gizella said, putting her hand inside Elona's and squeezing it tight. "The people are coming together. Every Hungarian is joining together to plant the seeds of change. Together the people of Hungary will rule as one."

"But how?"

"We have to show the government that we are serious and that we'll never give up," Gizella said. "The logistics are still unclear, but we stand for a newly improved Imre Nagy government. If he doesn't produce the reforms we need, the people will run the government."

"What if it gets dangerous for us?" Elona said. "Is it possible that there might be violence?"

"Anything is possible," Gizella said in a quiet voice, almost a whisper. "But we must never back down. Freedom is only achieved through determination."

Elona blinked and swallowed hard. "I am here with you, Gizella," she said. "For Hungary!"

CHAPTER 18

Miklós walked into the Technical University Aula on October 22, 1956. The auditorium was packed with thousands of people, more than he had ever seen before. DISZ had called the general meeting for this day at all universities. They were attempting to pre-empt other challenging initiatives like the one at Szeged University just last week. Students at Szeged came together and dangerously set up the MEFESZ organization again, resurrecting it out of the ashes of 1948. It was a worrisome development, and DISZ felt pressured to position itself firmly as the official youth organization.

Miklós was walking alongside Gizella but had somehow lost her in the thick crowd. The din of mass conversation and debate was overpowering. Miklós felt slightly unbalanced, and his ears were ringing from the noise. He searched for Gizella in the crowd, but it was futile. He assumed that she would find her way to the front. Both of them were speaking today, and he felt a strange chill, like something important was happening.

Miklós stopped to talk to people he knew as he worked his way through the crowd to the front, where a podium had been set up for people to speak at. He was nervous, and he didn't know why. It was most likely due to the overwhelming amount of people who had showed up for the general meeting.

He hadn't seen this many people attend a DISZ meeting ever before. He was amazed and grateful for the support, but something felt wrong.

He finally arrived at the podium and found Gizella talking quietly to a young student. She gestured passionately, using her arms to encircle the entire auditorium. Gizella glanced to the side and caught Miklós's eye. She waved at him, gesturing for him to join them. Miklós walked up to the small group and introduced himself.

"Gizella, I finally found you," he said, hugging her gently.

"Miklós! I am exhilarated to be here today!" she exclaimed joyfully. "Change is in the air, and we have such a large crowd showing up. It speaks to the magnitude of Hungarians and what we all collectively feel in our hearts."

"Yes, it is an important day," Miklós said. "To witness such common goals is heartwarming and conducive to communist reform. Once Nagy returns to power, we can step on the path for hope and a better future."

Gizella pursed her lips, words forming at her mouth, but she decided to swallow them. Things would unfold as the crowd wanted, she thought. "Yes, Miklós," she said. "Reform is necessary now. Hungary cannot grow without it." Gizella grinned. "In fact, there is no future without reform."

Miklós raised one eyebrow. Gizella was one of the most passionate advocates of reform. He should expect nothing less. But something about her stance was different. He watched her gestures and the man who she had been talking to. The young man looked at her with admiration. It was something that worried him, and it felt like Gizella had changed. "Yes," Miklós agreed slowly. "Communist reform is no longer a want now. It is a necessity."

Gizella smiled sweetly. "Come, let's get ready," she said. "The meeting should be starting soon."

Miklós nodded and followed Gizella to the podium that had been set up. Several other key members of DISZ were there, many members of the Petőfi Circle and two other people he did not know. He stopped beside Gizella as she hugged and introduced herself to the people who didn't already know her. As he was watching Gizella interact with others, he realized what it was about her changed behaviour that he had detected. And it chilled him to the bone. A shiver ran up his spine and settled in his sparse hair near the back of his head.

Gizella was acting like a revolutionary. She was no longer the passionate journalist or the patriotic Hungarian wanting good for all her fellow citizens. She was ready to fight.

Miklós swallowed as he turned around and assessed his fellow comrades. Most of the DISZ members were like him. Somewhat surprised by the size of the crowd and a tiny bit unsettled. Miklós opened his mouth and thought better of it. He searched his brain for a clue, something she had said that was irritating him. It was something subtle, almost as if it was something she had not said.

Gizella hugged one of the newcomers that Miklós had never seen before. "Tamás!" she exclaimed. "I'm so glad you came!"

"I wouldn't miss it for anything," Tamás said strongly as he lightly kissed one of her cheeks.

A loud tap of an old microphone sounded in the distance, and they all took two steps closer to the makeshift podium. The microphone was obviously old and borrowed from the Radio Station in Pest. It was one of those old circular broadcast-type microphones. Gizella smiled and was thankful that someone had brought it. Anything would do at this point.

Miklós stepped forward as one of the DISZ members began to speak.

"Hello, everyone and thank you for coming to this important meeting!"

The crowd cheered.

"We have much to discuss. Hungary is at a breaking point, and we must pave the way to a country of communist reform and a brighter future for all of us." The man looked down at his scripted notes. "We have many guests speaking today, and I urge you all to stay as late as needed until we all come to an agreement on several points of reform."

There were numerous nods from people in the crowd, but some looked blank-faced and almost angry like something he had said was being construed differently. Then it dawned on Miklós what Gizella had said or, rather, what she omitted from her conversations earlier. Not once did Gizella mention communist reform. She often talked about reform but never used the word communist in front of it. Miklós felt another chill run down his body. He was afraid that he may have underestimated the woman. Gizella was much loved by all her peers, and Miklós could do little now to influence her. He tilted his head to the side and regretted not noticing this in the beginning.

"The meeting will be conducted in the classic style of the Petőfi Circle meetings. Each guest will come up in order and have the opportunity to speak."

A commotion was happening to the right of the podium where Gizella and Tamás were. Miklós immediately tried to move closer, but the crowd had wedged him several throngs of people away.

"Oh," the DISZ member said into the microphone. "Wait, we have an unanticipated guest."

Suddenly Gizella and Tamás walked onto the podium. Gizella grabbed the microphone sweetly, smiling at the DISZ member and spoke into the mic at the crowd. "I would like to introduce an important guest from Szeged University."

The crowd murmured loudly.

Gizella pulled the microphone closer to her lips to be heard. "His name is Tamás Kiss. He is one of the founders of the Szeged MEFESZ."

The crowd erupted in cheers and boos at the same time. Gizella gave the microphone to Tamás, but it was quickly snatched out of his hands by the DISZ member. Miklós pushed his way to the podium in panic. This couldn't be happening, he thought.

There was a brief struggle, and the DISZ member won. He straightened his collar and spoke into the microphone. "This is a DISZ meeting," he said strongly to the crowd, his voice booming across the auditorium. "I would kindly ask that the MEFESZ members leave the aula."

The crowd erupted in angry boos, and the DISZ member could barely be heard, even with the microphone.

Several people began to shout. "Let's hear what he has to say!"

"Open speech!"

"Democracy!"

"Hungarians unite! No division!"

Gizella stepped forward again and nodded to take the microphone. She tapped it to calm the crowd so they could speak. Gizella smiled at the passionately fuelled assembly. "Let's hear what Tamás Kiss has to say," she shouted into the microphone. "Let's not silence reform and accept whatever shape it may take!"

The crowd cheered and raised their arms in the air. "Yes! Yes! Yes!"

The DISZ members shook their heads. Miklós finally reached the podium and huddled with his fellow members. "We cannot allow this," he said, slightly out of breath.

The University Party Secretariat and staff of the Marxism-Leninism Department filtered through the crowd to the DISZ members. They were red-faced and angry. "This will not be happening here tonight! Szeged MEFESZ members at our meeting! Blasphemy!" a member shouted, waving his arms angrily.

"We cannot have a free open meeting of anarchy!" Miklós agreed. "It must follow our strict scripts as it always does!"

Gizella bowed to the audience and glanced briefly at Miklós before speaking into the microphone again. "The crowd has spoken!" she shouted, smiling broadly. "Tamás Kiss will speak to all Hungarians regardless of political stripes. We are gathered here as one!"

She bowed again and passed the mic to Tamás.

Miklós and his comrades looked on in complete and utter shock as the audience quieted to listen to Tamas's speech. "Nonsense is being spewed into the minds of our university students!" Miklós shrieked.

"I agree!" a professor from the Marxism-Leninism Department shouted. "We are leaving! I advise you to join us." He pointed angrily at the podium. "Unless you want to be part of the anarchy we are witnessing today!"

Miklós looked at his DISZ comrades, and they all nodded in agreement. "We all leave then. Right now!" he said.

The large group pushed their way out of the crowd as Tamás paused at the podium. "It looks like we are losing some communist members of this open free speech meeting." He looked up and smiled. "No matter, the people who stay will be the strong Hungarians! The people who actually care about Hungary will fight for reform. The future of our country is in our hands!"

Gizella smiled and felt a glow of hope stretch from her head all the way through to her toes.

By midnight, after many gruelling hours of the open meeting, the students had formulated several points of reform. They had collectively narrowed it down to 14 points of political, social and economical reform. Not a single point had anything to do with student or college life. This was serious now. The students openly discussed ways of communicating the 14 points to all of Hungary. A few ideas circulated, but nothing was completely agreed upon.

Toward the end of the meeting, several students began shouting slogans. One, in particular, hit home for most Hungarians.

People in the crowd hugged and sang in a jolly spirit. Except one slogan was met with fists in the air and cries from the very pits of their stomachs.

"Russians, go home!" the crowd yelled in unison.

Gizella joined the chant with several MEFESZ members. "Russians, go home!" she shouted.

The crowd eventually dispersed with no clear plans to table the points to the government, except one.

A march was planned in sympathy for the Polish workers in the morning. They would hand out the points of reform to as many people in the crowd as possible and figure out what to do afterwards.

Chapter 19

On the morning of October 23, 1956, the entire student population of Budapest, all universities combined, joined in the sympathy march for Polish workers, gathering at the statue of General József Bem. The General was a Polish hero in the Hungarian uprising of 1848-1849, and the crowd was pleasant and upbeat.

Gizella, Elona and Béláné were all together once again, happy to be a part of a hopeful future. "This is a wonderful day," Gizella smiled broadly as she passed out copies of the now 16 points of reform. "Early this morning, we added two more points of reform and printed off the pamphlets. It's been a long night but well worth it." Gizella grinned. "One day soon, people will be writing this down into our history books."

Elona and Béláné each had a stack of papers to hand out as well. The women zealously handed out the points to each person that passed them, smiling and even hugging sometimes.

As the large crowd settled in front of the statue, Marcell, the engineering student, climbed up onto the base of the monument, grasping Gizella's hand. She smiled and clambered up, handing him the list of 16 points.

He was an intelligent, loyal student and had a loud, boisterous voice. Marcell shouted loudly to the crowd and began reading the 16 points.

"Number one! We demand the immediate evacuation of all Soviet troops, in conformity with the provisions of the Peace Treaty!"

The crowd cheered.

"Number two!" Marcell continued. "We demand the election by secret ballot of all Party members from top to bottom and of new officers to the lower, middle and upper echelons of the Hungarian Workers Party! These officers shall convene a Party Congress as early as possible in order to elect a Central Committee."

Gizella smiled and shouted into the crowd. "Yes!"

"Number three! A new government must be constituted under the direction of Imre Nagy!" He paused as the crowd shouted their agreement. "All criminal leaders of the Stalin-Rákosi era must be immediately dismissed!"

The crowd shouted into an even louder uproar of agreement.

Gizella smiled broadly and nodded as Marcell continued reading out all of the remaining 16 points of reform. She had never felt so hopeful before in her life. Every Hungarian present was just as passionate about change as she was. It felt like one large family finally coming together to support their mother country.

Every point read was met with cheers of support! Gizella looked down into the crowd and noticed Elona and Béláné still near the statue where she had left them. Elona had a radiant shine to her face as she raised her arm in agreement. Béláné was equally enthusiastic, whistling into the crowd. Hope was glowing on every face.

The wind was very calm, and the day was perfect. Gizella felt like this was a turning point in her country. This could be the day, she thought, as she gazed up at the clouds coming towards them slowly and methodically. The sun was quickly being obscured by the clouds that grew heavier in the distance. It was still a perfect day, Gizella thought.

After the last point was read, Gizella spread her arms up to the sky and started singing the censored anthem loudly. A large group of people near the statue began singing along with her. The crowd heard, and a ripple of chanting waved through the crowd until the National Song was being sung by tens of thousands of citizens. Gizella grasped the hands of the other students on the base of the statue and sang even louder.

When the students got to the censored part of the National Song, Gizella burst into tears of joy and sang it loudly with the crowd. "We vow, we vow, we will no longer remain slaves!"

An electric jolt of pride, hope and strength danced through the crowd, touching every person in attendance. Some people waved their hands overhead, and some were crying with patriotism like Gizella. The crowd was energized like nothing she had ever seen before.

The people all cheered at the end of the song, and every Hungarian had hope in their eyes. Gizella wiped the tears from her eyes and dismounted from the base of the statue to a flurry of hugs and kisses. Elona rushed forward and hugged Gizella firmly as Béláné joined in. The three women cried together with happy tears of hope on their cheeks.

"I have never felt anything so heartwarming in my life!" Elona said loudly.

"It is truly a day of change," Béláné said in agreement.

Elona released Gizella as the crowd began to disperse. "Where is everyone going now?" Elona asked. "We can't just go back home. We need the government to hear these 16 points. How do we do that?"

"I don't know," Gizella replied. "I was just thinking the same."

Marcell jumped back onto the base and addressed the crowd boisterously, holding a Hungarian flag. Another female student climbed onto the base and began cutting out the middle Soviet emblem. The crowd cheered loudly as a hole appeared in the centre of the flag. The two students held the flag up high between them as a loud cheer of support reverberated throughout the crowd.

"We march to Parliament!" Marcell yelled, waving the flag high. "To Parliament!"

Elona and Gizella shouted in unison. "To Parliament!"

Many other people hollered in agreement, and the crowd began to march towards Parliament. The three women walked within the crowd, handing out the remaining 16 points pamphlets.

It was a long walk in a thick mob of people. The afternoon had begun turning into evening by the time they had crossed the Danube.

A mass of steel factory workers had joined the crowd, and it suddenly swelled in numbers. Others joined as the march continued to Parliament. There were so many people, in fact, that Elona held hands with Gizella and Béláné in the hope that it would keep them from losing each other.

Several people were holding placards with several slogans scrawled on them. Elona noticed a steel worker holding a placard with bright red lettering saying, "Russians Go Home!"

The women looked at each other and smiled nervously.

"There are so many people here now!" Elona shouted anxiously.

"Yes!" Gizella shouted over the crowd noise. "Hungarians are uniting as one!"

Elona smiled uneasily as Béláné patted her back. "It will be alright," Béláné said reassuringly. "The protest is peaceful and spirited. We will achieve our points of reform in peace!"

Elona nodded, but something twisting in her gut told her to find a way out. She smiled and looked around, realizing that she was trapped in a sea of people. There was no escape now. She would have to trust Béláné's words. Elona noticed several students mixing with the steelworkers, and they did indeed look peaceful. More people began singing, and it helped relax Elona's apprehension.

As the evening descended, the crowd began to reach Parliament Square. Elona, Gizella and Béláné were still safely together with joined hands, although they were situated far into the middle left of the enormous crowd.

Gizella squeezed Elona's hand. "Don't worry," Gizella said. "It is a peaceful protest. So many people! But it is peaceful."

Imre Nagy knew he had to say something. The situation was getting out of control. His supporters were behind him one hundred percent. They had even included him as the leader in one of the 16 points.

Forty-five minutes ago, at 8 pm, Ernő Gerő had broadcasted a special message. He condemned the students' demands and called the crowd a reactionary mob. This fuelled the anger amongst the demonstrators, and the crowd was increasingly becoming inflammatory.

Imre adjusted his tie and stepped out onto the balcony as a cheer of support came from the crowd below him. He had to do something.

He motioned with his hands to quiet the people so he could speak.

Finally, after several minutes, a calmness settled upon the protestors.

"The Hungarian people have spoken loudly," Imre shouted, his voice carrying over the crowd. "We have heard your demands."

The crowd cheered wildly and passionately. Several groups of people began chanting the National Song again.

Imre Nagy waited patiently as the crowd sang the anthem, pride with a mix of fear in his heart. He was being given the impossible task of uniting this angry mob and somehow pleasing his Russian superiors at the same time. It was his wish to reform Hungary and become the best Prime Minister in the history of the country. He had to step carefully, Imre knew. He could not repeat the mistakes of the past and lose favour with his Russian comrades.

Nagy raised his hands again after the anthem was finished, appealing for the crowd to quiet down.

After several minutes, he spoke again. "Hungarians are asking for change," he shouted. "And change will happen."

The crowd cheered again.

Imre raised his hands in exasperation. "But it will not happen overnight," he shouted.

The crowd quieted down suddenly, almost eerily.

"I urge you to recognize that these conflicts need to be resolved within the Party. We are working on them!"

The demonstrators quieted down even further.

"We will come to reform within the Party."

Hardly anyone spoke a word.

Imre cleared his throat. "I urge everyone to disperse and let my government handle the reform."

Several demonstrators whispered amongst themselves as Imre stood waiting for the reaction. He bowed and heard several chants in the crowd.

"Russians, go home!"

Imre grimaced and tried to calm the crowd again, to no avail. His speech seemed to have angered them even further, he realized with trepidation.

He bowed his head and ducked back into his office as the shouting increased. Nagy wiped the sweat from his brow. He lifted his head and looked at his communist party comrades in the room. "I tried," he said.

⟩

Laszlo's unit, the Hungarian Army's 8th Tank Regiment, was called to assemble for further orders. He counted every soldier in his unit and gathered in the field beside the tanks and army truck. Laszlo walked alongside his unit soldiers and took attendance methodically, counting every one of them.

The protest had started peacefully, but the crowd was estimated to have grown to over 200,000 people now. That was definitely a concern for the government. The more people, the more chance for violence.

After Nagy's speech, the crowd had split into two groups. One large group was marching towards the Stalin monument that stood upon the old grazed church site, and the other mob was already at the Radio Station, demanding the 16 points to be broadcasted.

There were already reports of some demonstrators beginning to demolish the Stalin statue in response to Point number 13 on the demands, the removal of the statue of oppression.

Laszlo frowned as his head throbbed. He nodded as the soldiers checked their weapons and loaded the ammunition into the tanks and truck methodically. Not one soldier showed emotion. Each man had a blank stare. They were following orders.

Laszlo returned to the weapons supply shed with Tibor. He groaned and lifted a box of ammunition from one side as Tibor held the other. The brothers were one of the strongest men in the unit. Normally he would leave this to his unit soldiers, but Laszlo thought it was important to show that he was part of the team. Morale was definitely lacking, and he assumed every soldier felt as confused as he did right now.

The two brothers shuffled as they moved the heavy box together, walking towards the supply truck. Both men felt sweat form on their foreheads from the exertion.

Finally, Laszlo balanced the edge of the ammunition cart on the truck, breathing heavily, as two other men grabbed the box from inside, shifting the weight from both the brother's arms. Laszlo watched as the two men shuffled with the heavy cart, placing it along the side of the truck box for easy access.

Laszlo glanced at his brother and noticed a tendril of revolt in Tibor's face. Neither brother acknowledged the feeling that was spreading in their hearts. A deep voice of reason in Laszlo's gut told him just to do his job. He waved to his brother, and they returned to lift another ammunition box.

As Tibor bent his knees and grasped the box, he looked up and caught the familiar glance from Laszlo.

They both knew it well.

They were brothers. They would act in unison.

⌐

Elona, Gizella and Béláné had marched towards the Radio Station with the largest group, intent on getting their 16 points broadcasted to all of Hungary and the world.

"Do you think the Radio Station will do it?" Elona asked.

Béláné chuckled. "With this crowd, they'll have to," she said. "There's no other way. There are way too many people demanding it."

"They must!" Gizella added.

The crowd was wildly passionate now. Many people were shouting, and some were pushing towards the front of the crowd. Elona didn't know what was going on, but she could sense a certain rebellion in the crowd, and it seeped into her heart. She wanted to force change now. The government officials were trying to dismiss them, and it wasn't fair.

Gizella tapped a man's shoulder beside her. He had blonde hair and a strong husky build. "Do you mind if you could lift me up so I can see what's going on?" she asked.

Some people began pushing in the crowd, and several people forced their way to the front. Elona held tightly onto Béláné's hand.

The blonde-haired man smiled warmly. "Certainly," he replied. "Can you climb up onto my shoulders?"

Gizella smiled. "Yes, I can!" she replied. "Thank you."

Elona watched as the man cupped his hands together as a step, and Gizella placed her foot in his hands and swung up onto the man's shoulders.

Gizella could instantly see what was going on above the crowd. Several large groups of people were storming the Radio Station building! She squinted and witnessed several people throwing a broken door to the side as demonstrators ran into the building.

"What's happening?" Elona asked loudly. "Can you see anything?" Elona shouted the words at Gizella, sitting atop the man's shoulders.

"Yes!" Gizella shouted back, looking down at Elona. "There's a group of demonstrators that have forced their way into the building!"

"Why?" Elona asked, anxiety filling her heart.

"I don't know why!" Gizella shouted back.

"It must be that they refused to broadcast the points!" Béláné added angrily.

"Possibly!" Elona replied.

"Wait!" Gizella said loudly. "Something's happening! The AVH are there!"

A sudden rush of fear ran through Elona's body. "Get down, Gizella!" she shouted.

"No, it's fine," Gizella replied loudly. "They're just trying to control the crowd."

Suddenly, the sound of gunfire erupted. Elona panicked and pulled at Gizella's pant legs. "Let her down! Now!" she shouted at the blonde-haired man.

The man's eyes bulged out suddenly as he was thrown back from a sudden impact. Elona cried out as the man and Gizella fell back into the crowd, several people breaking their fall. Elona's heart hammered in her chest as she pushed several people away and ran to Gizella. The fallen man was struggling to get up, twisting his body out of Gizella's legs which were lopsidedly still wrapped around one part of his neck. He finally stood and looked at Elona. He had blood smeared on his face.

Elona screamed, "Are you okay?" The man looked blankly at her and ran. Elona couldn't make sense of what had happened.

Everything was occurring so quickly. Had she heard gunshots? Yes! She had heard gunshots! "Move! That's my best friend!" Elona shouted at the people. "Gizella!" she screamed as she reached her friend. Gizella's legs were crumpled in a strange direction, and her body wasn't moving.

More gunshots were fired overhead, and everyone ducked, running in different directions. Elona knelt down beside Gizella and grasped her friend's head, shaking her body slightly to try to awaken her. "Gizella, are you awake? Wake up, beautiful!"

Gizella's eyes were open, and looked right through Elona, seeing nothing. "No!" Elona screamed. "Someone, help me! You have to wake up, Gizzy!"

A woman rushed over. "I'm a nurse," she said urgently.

"Can you save her?" Elona pleaded. "Please!"

The woman knelt beside Gizella and placed her hands on Gizella's neck, feeling for a heartbeat. She shook her head slowly and opened Gizella's coat to reveal a large red blood stain growing with blood. The nurse removed several layers of clothing until she discovered the wound. "Your friend has been shot."

"No!" Elona cried, tears streaming down her face as the crowd continued to run in all directions. "Please save her! She's my closest friend! I can't lose her!"

The nurse picked up Gizella's arm and placed two fingers on Gizella's flaccid wrist. The nurse shook her head sadly and stood. "I'm sorry, Miss. Your friend is dead. You need to get out of here!" The nurse ran off into the chaos, stumbling amongst many other demonstrators. Elona sobbed openly, cradling Gizella in her arms. She partially stood and started dragging Gizella's body to an alcove in the next building, where several other people were heading.

Béláné appeared in the crowd suddenly. "Elona! Oh my God, Gizella!" Béláné grabbed Gizella's feet and helped Elona get their friend's body into the alcove. Amidst so many people pushing to get away, they stumbled a few times but finally reached the alcove.

Elona slumped against the wall, cradling Gizella's upper body. Elona's arms were stained with her friend's blood.

"What happened?" Béláné asked anxiously.

Elona opened her mouth, and the words felt smothered in thick cotton balls. "She's dead," Elona said hoarsely. "They shot her." She swallowed hard. "AVH shot her. Gizella's dead."

CHAPTER 20

Laszlo's unit arrived at the Radio Station to quell the violence. They heard shots fired from the direction of the Radio building. The tanks and supply truck were forced to stop in the street as mobs of people began running away from the Radio Station. Several other citizens were also running towards the Radio building with weapons raised. Laszlo could hear return gunfire. It sounded like a gunfight. Laszlo knew the AVH were stationed at the Radio building. He grimaced and shook his head as the situation unfolded around him.

Laszlo and Tibor opened the back of the truck and gazed out into a thick throng of people. The supply truck and tanks were no longer able to advance against the people clogging the streets. The supply truck was at the rear of the line of tanks. Several demonstrators began to form a group around the military vehicles, anger and passion in their eyes. Laszlo and Tibor stood motionless at the large opening of the truck with several of the team behind them. For several moments, time stood still. The demonstrators stared down the truck full of Hungarian soldiers.

"You are Magyar too!" one man shouted.

"Do the right thing!" another woman cried.

There was a murmur of agreement within the crowd. For the first time in his life, Laszlo felt fear, but with it came a certain type of admiration. He was proud of his fellow countrymen. Laszlo assessed the situation, wondering if the mob would attack the truck with all his soldiers in it.

"You are not Russians!" A man shouted. "Do not fight against us!"

"Do the right thing!" the woman shouted again.

Laszlo cleared his throat and raised his hand. "What would you consider to be the right thing to do?" he shouted angrily at the throng of people. The crowd was quickly gathering larger as he spoke, which simultaneously raised his fear and patriotism at the same time.

The woman looked to one of the other men as if to gain assistance in answering the question. Finally, she shook her head and replied. "Lay down your weapons," she said. "We are not the enemy."

Laszlo stood confidently and assessed the crowd. They were passionate and friendly but on the verge of extreme violence. "What happened?" Laszlo shouted. "Someone tell me. I want to hear it from the mouths of fellow Hungarians."

A man spoke. "The AVH opened fire into the crowd," he shouted angrily, waving his fist. "They killed some students."

"Why did they fire?" Laszlo asked.

"The students were trying to get inside the Radio Station to broadcast the 16 points of reform!" the woman shouted. "We all need to hear what they were demanding. Every countryman."

Laszlo bent down to Tibor as his brother whispered in his ear. "Gizella was talking to me about several points of reform they were discussing. That must be it."

"Was she part of the demonstration today?" Laszlo asked, a cold shiver running through his body.

"Yes, most likely," Tibor said softly.

"That means Elona and Béláné are probably here as well," Laszlo replied as he stared out at the crowd, trying to find a solution to the predicament and wondering if they could even find the three women in this mass of people.

After a few moments, Tibor leaned towards Laszlo. "What do we do, Lieutenant?" he asked, his voice shaky and uncertain.

Laszlo inhaled sharply and came to a conclusion. He raised his hand again. "We will not fight against the Hungarian people," he stated loudly. Laszlo paused and formulated the next questions in his mind. He must remain calm, he told himself. But something terrible was wrong, and he could feel it. "Where are the dead and injured?"

A blonde-haired man with blood splattered all over his face raised his hand and pointed. "To the right of the Radio Station!" he shouted.

"You are bleeding," Laszlo said. "Are you injured?"

"No," he replied. "I am fine, just bruised. The blood is from a young blonde-haired woman who was sitting on my shoulders at the time of the shooting. She was very beautiful." The man looked visibly shaken.

Tibor felt his blood run cold. He spoke. "Where is she?"

"She is dead, I think," the blonde husky man answered. "Her friends dragged her off of me, and I ran with the crowd. They kept shooting. It was the AVH, those bastards!"

Laszlo heard his brother's breathing turn raspy and rapid. "It's alright," Laszlo whispered reassuringly. "It may not be them."

"It was three women together," the blonde man added. "I have never seen them before. They looked like students."

Tibor moved slightly to the right, and Laszlo caught his shoulder. "We will find them," he reassured his brother.

Tibor's hands began to shake. "I will go on my own," he stated firmly.

"No, you will not!" Laszlo commanded.

Tibor straightened to attention. "Yes, Lieutenant."

Laszlo pulled out a cigarette and tried to calm his nerves. "Does anybody have a light?" he asked.

The first man in the crowd raised his hand. "I do," he said, opening the lighter and igniting the flame.

Laszlo leaned down to the proffered lighter and inhaled deeply as the cigarette glowed brightly at the end. Laszlo looked up to the sky and wondered why these decisions were only left to a select few in the world. The weight was a heavy burden to shoulder. He had felt it time and again during his military career. Now he felt it again, but this time it was crushing. The woman was right. He had to do the right thing. Laszlo could no longer serve the Russian communists in their bid to destroy everything Magyars valued. He would not. It would go against everything he was put on this earth to accomplish.

Laszlo blew out a cloud of smoke and watched the small white clouds drift into the sky. His mind was made up. He turned to face his soldiers in the truck. Tibor remained straight as a statue, his face set in stone. The other soldiers wore an expression of panic and admiration. Some had no expression at all. "Men!" Laszlo spoke loudly. "We are Magyars. We will not fight against our own people. Put down your weapons."

Several of the tank soldiers emerged from their tanks, sitting atop the heavy artillery, awaiting further orders.

The woman in the crowd spoke loudly. "If I may," she shouted. "Those weapons would be better utilized in the hands of the people. We can then fight against the Russians evenly. Some people already have weapons in the crowd from the police station. They stand with us."

Laszlo frowned and watched his brother's hands start shaking violently. "Calm yourself," Laszlo instructed. "We will both go together. The entire unit will go. Do not let your emotions control you."

Laszlo inhaled on the cigarette in silence and then threw it on the ground, stamping it out.

"So?" the woman asked politely.

"We could kill you all right now," Laszlo said firmly, looking right into the eyes of the demonstrators. "But we won't because you are right. We are Magyars too."

The crowd cheered.

"If we are to fight against the Russians," Laszlo paused as the words of what he was about to say sunk heavily into his gut. "We need to identify ourselves!" Laszlo commanded loudly. He called to a man waving a Hungarian flag with a hole in the middle. "Sir! We need that flag."

The man pushed through the crowd with the flag on a large pole.

"For now," Laszlo said. "We will each wear an armband of our country's flag." He reached for the flag as several other citizens tore pieces off.

Another woman had a flag and started ripping lengths off, waiting for instructions.

Laszlo cleared his throat. "Tear enough fabric off and tie it around your upper arm like this," he commanded. "Soldiers too!"

The soldiers snapped into attention and grabbed lengths of the flag and wore them as arm bands as well. There was a frenzy within the crowd as everyone tried to wrap the arm bands on. "What is the point of this?" a man shouted.

"So we will not be shooting at each other," Laszlo yelled into the crowd. "If you see an armband, whether it's a soldier or a fellow citizen, do not shoot!" Laszlo patted the armband on his bicep and faced the crowd again. "Is that clear?"

"Yes!" a loud uproar of agreement erupted from the mob.

Laszlo looked briefly at his brother and noticed the armband wrapped tightly around his arm too. He nodded. "We will go find Gizella and Elona now," he whispered. "We will not get shot this way."

Tibor nodded, his eyes almost bulging out from adrenaline.

"My unit is going to advance towards the Radio Station," Laszlo shouted. "We will fight against the AVH. Give us clearance! Tanks are to remain stationary!"

The crowd erupted in cheers. People waved what was remaining of their flags and shouted in agreement. Some people climbed the tanks and talked amicably with the remaining tank regiment members.

Laszlo tried to quell the noise, but it wasn't possible. He raised his hand, and nobody quieted. Laszlo jumped back onto the ledge of the truck and opened the heavy ammunition box. He moved to the next box and opened it to reveal the rifles. Laszlo removed a rifle and held it high in the air. The crowd quieted considerably.

Laszlo motioned for one of his corporals. "You and the driver will stay with the truck and hand out the weapons and ammunition to the crowd, one by one. Keep two weapons for yourself and the driver. Be careful and make sure each person who is allotted a weapon also has an armband. You got that?"

"Yes, sir!"

Laszlo turned to the ledge of the truck again and raised the rifle. "Each revolutionary will receive a weapon with ammunition, but you must wear an armband!" Laszlo shouted. "We must remain as calm as possible and only fire when it is clearly identified as the enemy."

The crowd cheered again.

"Calm!" Laszlo shouted. "Our unit will advance now, and my two corporals are in charge of distributing weapons. Be respectful!" Laszlo loaded the rifle and handed it to Tibor. He grabbed another one, loaded it and slung it across his shoulder along with an ammunition belt. Laszlo jumped off the truck and shouted to the remaining soldiers. "Attention, soldiers! We are advancing towards the Radio Station and the AVH. We are to stay together initially, then separate into two teams flanking the building on both sides. March!"

The soldiers grabbed their own weapons and jumped from the truck, advancing as a unit toward the Radio Station.

Elona cried heavily as Béláné soothed her as much as possible. Several more shots were being fired, and Elona didn't know which way they were coming from. She saw several men in civilian clothing cradling rifles. Elona watched as the scene unfolded in front of her, dazed by grief.

Béláné patted her arm suddenly. She was trying to get her attention. "Elona!" Béláné cried.

"What?" Elona replied, tears swelling her face.

"We need to get out of the open!" Béláné shouted. "Do you have the keys to the Cinema?"

Elona was momentarily confused. "Why would my cleaning job matter right now?" she mumbled. Then she followed Béláné's finger pointing to the building a block down across the street from the alcove where they rested. Elona's eyes focused, and it all made sense. "That's the Cinema! Yes, I have the keys!" she said incredulously as she finally understood where they were. They were only a block away!

"Let's get Gizella into the theatre and protect ourselves from all this shooting," Béláné said, grabbing Gizella's feet.

"That's an entire block to carry her," Elona said. "Do you think we can do it?"

"We can certainly try our best," Béláné replied as a new round of shots fired around them. Both women ducked farther into the alcove.

Elona looked around in bewilderment. "Those shots sound like they are being fired from the crowd, not at the crowd," Elona stated.

"I saw some citizens with weapons," Béláné added.

"This is a lot worse than we thought," Elona said, stating the obvious with ridiculous clarity.

Béláné laughed grimly. "That is an understatement."

Elona shook her head. "Okay, let's move her to the Cinema." Béláné and Elona lifted Gizella's body along the street, praying they wouldn't get shot. A moment of silence was in their favour as they shuffled along the road, trying to stay close to the buildings.

A man with an armband rushed to their aid. He slung a rifle across his shoulder and took the weight from Elona's hands, and whistled for help. Another man came running and relieved Béláné's hold. Elona and Béláné rushed alongside the men as they crossed the street.

Elona was in such a state of panic that she barely noticed everything that was going on at once. Behind them, a wounded person was wailing in agony as two men lifted him across the street as well. The group stopped and watched as the women and men moved Gizella's body to an obvious predetermined destination.

"Where are we moving the body to?" The lead man asked.

Elona snapped out of her brain fog and pointed to the sign that said Corvin Cinema. "The Cinema," she said plainly. "I work there."

The men nodded, and they all scuttled quickly along the street until they were in front of the doors. Elona jangled her keys with shaky hands and opened the lock, swinging the door wide open. The men shuffled inside as Elona turned on the lights, and the entire high ceiling lit up the large open area. They laid Gizella on a long table. Her body lay motionless with her eyes still open.

"The woman is dead," the lead man stated. He laid his two hands gently on Gizella's eyelids and closed them.

Elona burst into fresh tears, the stress of the day weighing heavily on her shoulders.

Outside the door, the injured man wailed. Béláné jumped and opened the door wide for them. "Come in!" she said. "It's safer in here."

The injured man was rushed in and laid on a table.

Elona watched as many other people rushed into the Cinema behind them, some bleeding and some dead.

"Come help me!" Béláné shrieked.

Elona blinked and rushed to her aid.

"This man is bleeding," Béláné said, her voice coming out in raspy breaths. "We need to tie a tourniquet on his arm above the wound."

Elona nodded. "What do you need me to do?"

"Find me a good strong piece of rope or cloth," Béláné told Elona. Then speaking to the injured man, she said, "We need to take your shirt off to see where the wound is."

The man groaned and nodded, rolling over to his side. "I can't get it off. It's stuck to me," he said.

One of the men who carried him in walked over and pulled out a knife, tearing the sleeve up to his shoulder. The wound was near his elbow, bleeding profusely. The blood began dripping onto the table and running off onto the floor.

Elona returned with a man's belt. "Is this good?"

"That's perfect," she replied, grasping the belt with both hands and shuffling it under the man's injured bare arm. Béláné calmly stopped and placed four fingers together to measure approximately two inches above the wound. She held her finger there and motioned Elona to help her position the tourniquet. "Here, above this line," she said as they prepared to pull the belt tight. She paused and spoke to the patient. "We are going to tie this tourniquet to slow the bleeding. We have to tie it very tight. It will hurt." Béláné looked at the man, trying to get his full attention. "Do you understand?" she said loudly.

The man's eyes were darting from side to side. "Yes!"

Béláné and Elona pulled on the tourniquet as tightly as possible, but they needed another hole in the leather to secure it. "Where's the guy with the knife?" Béláné shouted.

The man rushed over. "What is it? Will my friend be okay?"

"I don't know!" Béláné shouted with anxiety. "I am not a trained nurse. I only know how to do this from a safety course. I need you to poke a hole in the leather belt with your knife. I need it right here." Béláné pointed at the strap of leather.

The man pulled out his knife and worked carefully, finally piercing a small hole in the leather. "There," he said. "That should do."

Béláné nodded. "Thank you!" She grasped the belt while Elona kept the man's arm stable on the table. "Keep your weight on his arm, Elona. He may flail." Béláné positioned herself and then pulled hard on the belt, wrapping the tourniquet tight, then looping it into the hole, securing it. The man jerked and screamed as the pain shot up his arm. "It's alright," Béláné reassured him. "It's over. We got the tourniquet on. Everything is alright." She looked at the blood pooling under his arm and ripped a piece of her blouse off as a rag, pushing on his wound firmly. The man wailed again. "Shh, it's alright." Béláné inspected the rag and chose another one that Elona handed her. She pressed on the wound again, then inspected the rag. There was less blood. "It's working," she said to the injured man. "We need to find a doctor to stitch you up."

Elona looked up at the front door as many more people began walking in with wounded people, seeking shelter from the war going on outside. "Hold on," she said and walked to the front door. "Are there any doctors here?" she asked the growing collection of people.

"I'm a medical student," one man said.

"That will do!" Elona shouted. "Come here!"

The young man rushed over to the table with the injured man. He inspected the tourniquet. "Who tied this tourniquet?" he asked, looking up.

"I did," Béláné replied.

The young student said appraisingly, "Well done. We can move on to another victim. This one is stabilized for the next two hours. Write on his forehead the time of the tourniquet. I will stitch him up before two hours is up." He patted Béláné's shoulder. "You saved this man's life. Give him some water, and then come with me."

Elona rushed to the bathroom to fill a container full of water as Béláné walked behind the medical student assessing other wounded people. Elona returned a few minutes later to a group of people removing Gizella's body from the table. Elona rushed over. "That is my friend!" she shouted.

One of the women patted her arm. "We are just moving her. We need the tables to tend to injuries."

Elona's eyes fell down to the floor. "She is dead," she stated gloomily.

"I'm sorry," the woman replied. "Many people have died. We will put the wounded on the tables, and the dead we will lay on the floor by the corner. It'll keep them dignified and safely out of the way."

The men lifted Gizella's body, and Elona followed as they moved her to the opposite side of the large open hall. The men placed Gizella down gently, then left Elona alone with her.

Elona knelt down beside her friend and laid Gizella's hands down straight beside her body. She pulled a lock of Gizella's hair to the side. Her face was barely recognizable. Blood was everywhere. The right side of her face was missing. It looked like she had been shot twice. Elona exhaled, looking up to the ceiling and said a silent prayer for her friend's soul.

After several moments, Elona inhaled deeply and stood. She searched the open hall for Béláné and the medical student. Many more people had entered the Cinema, and it was quickly becoming a makeshift hospital. There were about fifty wounded people now. Some were laid down on the tables, some clutching themselves against the wall. A few were crying out in pain, but some were silent and obviously dying.

Elona gathered her courage and walked towards the commotion. She had to do what she could to help the living.

CHAPTER 21

Laszlo and his team moved along the streets toward the Radio Station. It was mayhem. Several cars and trams were overturned and were smouldering in smoke from recent flames. Several policemen were sitting in their vehicles, some handing out weapons to civilians.

A few ragged and bloody demonstrators chanted. "Death to the AVH!"

Another civilian shouted. "We need more weapons!"

Several boys, hardly over the age of twelve, were outfitting glass bottles into deadly Molotov cocktails. One of the boys stuffed a gasoline-soaked rag into the mouth of the fifth bottle and waved angrily at Laszlo and his team.

Laszlo shouted commandingly and pointed to his armband. "We stand with you!"

The group of youngsters shouted in joy. "Magyars for freedom!"

A group of policemen watched as Laszlo's team crisscrossed toward the Radio Station. They lifted their hats and saluted them. "We must stop the AVH!" a tall policeman shouted, pointing at the building and joining Laszlo's team as they passed.

The team was approximately fifty meters away now, and they had amassed a group of policemen behind them. Laszlo gestured for the other half of his unit to circle around to the left as he raced to the right with his smaller group. Following their movements, the policemen team had split to the right and left as well.

Tibor ran along Laszlo's side as they reached a blood-stained alcove. The team crouched down and assessed where the shots were being fired from.

"AVH sniper, third-floor window," Laszlo said. He ordered his unit to spread out and focus on specific targets.

"Tibor," he said. "You're staying with me."

Tibor was gazing down at the floor in deep thought.

"What is it?" Laszlo asked, confused.

Tibor slid his hands in the blood and pulled a large hair clip out. It had tiny fake diamonds on the ridge and glowed silver in the evening darkness.

Laszlo gazed at the object with a perplexed look on his face. "What is that?"

Tibor placed the hair clip in his pocket without answering and pulled his rifle out, aiming for the third-floor window.

A brief calm descended onto the street in front of the Radio building. It didn't last long, maybe only a few seconds, but Laszlo took the moment to calm the adrenaline shooting through his veins.

Then as quickly as the calm had descended, it was gone and replaced with destruction and chaos.

The group of young boys had followed the group, and now they ran directly towards the building, throwing the Molotov cocktails at the windows. Two bottles fell harmlessly against the stone wall erupting in flames, but another cocktail caught its target and smashed through a first-story window. A screech from within the building echoed throughout the flames as the AVH suddenly opened fire.

A fourth Molotov cocktail sailed through the air as bullets flew overhead. Several gurgled cries filled the area as two of the boys fell to the ground. The third boy fell dead in the street, still as a statue. The remaining boys screamed blood-curdling war cries and rushed at the building, hurling the final cocktails as Tibor crouched on one knee and opened fire from across the street.

Tibor's bullet crashed through the third-floor window, and a head ducked back in. Laszlo watched and was unsure if the bullet had made contact.

The boy's gasoline bombs had made contact with several windows, and the building was partially alight. Laszlo moved to a sheltered spot in the alcove, shooing the team to the other sides in preparation for return fire.

Laszlo aimed at the third-story window, waiting.

The young boys burst into the building, followed by several policemen. Laszlo focused on the window, breathing out heavily, trying to calm his mind.

A head and a rifle butt poked out of the window.

Laszlo sighted his eyes along his rifle in the evening darkness and fired. Several other men from his team simultaneously fired at the same moment.

The head lobbed against the window frame, and the rifle fell out of the building, clattering onto the street. The body of the bullet-ridden AVH soldier stood in a strange, grotesque manner, wedged somehow against the window frame.

Laszlo nodded to his team. "Blow out every remaining window and take out the rooftop too! Fire!"

A cascade of bullets riddled the Radio Station building from both teams, right and left, firing into the windows and rooftops.

An AVH sniper on the roof toppled and tried steadying his rifle, then looked down at the blood on his chest. He teetered in Laszlo's sights, then finally fell forward, his body falling down the building onto the street with a thud.

Several demonstrators cheered, and a mob of civilians stormed the building. Laszlo raised his hand to his team. "Cease!"

The men shouldered their weapons and awaited further instructions.

"We're going in," Laszlo said, patting his pistol on his side belt. "Take any remaining AVH as prisoners."

Laszlo rushed towards the building with his unit, and as they breached the doors, more chaos erupted. Several fires from the Molotov cocktails were being extinguished by officers as several wounded citizens were shuffled to the sides. Makeshift tables were transformed into emergency triage units for the wounded civilians. The wounded AVH officers were corralled into a corner. Laszlo witnessed some being shot.

"Halt!" Laszlo shouted. "We are the Hungarian Army 8th Tank Regiment. We stand with the people. All AVH officers wounded or surrendered will be kept on the first floor. We will move them once we have collected them all." Laszlo paused and shouted angrily. "No one, I repeat, no one, is to execute the remaining AVH officers. Do not commit war crimes, people! Be mindful of your actions!"

Some demonstrators shot angry looks at Laszlo, but most nodded their heads, and a few people murmured in agreement.

Laszlo pointed at several factory workers with weapons over their shoulders. "You and you!" Laszlo shouted. "Gather as many other like-minded strong men and scour each floor for AVH officers. My unit will assist you." He waved at the men behind him and picked out five men to assist in rounding up the AVH. Laszlo turned back to the factory workers. He was relieved when he noticed that they stood at attention. "We need to secure the building. Bring as many men with you as possible."

The men nodded and turned to the stairs with the regiment soldiers. Their heavy boots thudded up the stairs in search of the remaining AVH. A policeman on the second-floor landing was bending down to the two boys still alive, pressing a bloody rag on the younger boy's forehead.

Laszlo stepped forward. "I thought you two boys had made it," he said. "What happened?"

The policeman turned his face to Laszlo. It was Jozsef! "Comrade!" Laszlo exclaimed.

The boy looked from Laszlo to Jozsef, slightly confused. "We escaped the bullets, it is true!" the young boy said. "But we were trampled by the demonstrators getting into the building."

Jozsef nodded. "I picked up the boys before too many people had stepped on them," he said worriedly. "This crowd needs to be calmed. It is turning into pandemonium."

Laszlo patted Jozsef's back. "Good work, officer!" he smiled, and the two friends hugged briefly, with Laszlo whispering in his ear. "I am glad you are alive, brother."

"Same to you," Jozsef said.

"Where did the rest of the crowd go?" Laszlo asked. "I heard there were almost two hundred thousand demonstrators!"

"It is true," Jozsef answered. "An alarming amount of people. They stormed the police station, and we surrendered. We told them that we were Magyars too. They took many of our weapons, and we ended up joining the fight." Jozsef paused to catch his breath. "The crowd is still large around here, although many of the injured were being taken into the Corvin Cinema."

"Have you seen Elona and Gizella?" Laszlo asked.

"No, I have not," Jozsef responded. "We would be lucky to find anyone in this mob. I am surprised I found you here, my friend." Jozsef pat Laszlo's shoulder.

Tibor was suddenly by Laszlo's side, breathing heavily. "I am going to the Corvin Cinema," he said firmly. "Gizella is not here. Several people said the wounded students were taken to the theatre."

Laszlo exhaled worriedly. "Have the AVH been detained and disarmed?" he asked.

Jozsef rattled the handcuffs on his belt. "Don't worry about the AVH," he said. "We've got control of the building here." He nodded at Tibor and pointed harshly in the direction of the Cinema. "You go find your future bride and Elona. I got this."

Laszlo shifted the rifle on his back. "Okay, I will appoint a soldier in charge to stay here with my team, and I will go with Tibor," Laszlo said. "Hang tight." He patted Tibor's shoulder and left to speak with the highest-ranking officer in his unit.

Jozsef felt the fear emanating from Tibor. "You will find your fiancé," he said reassuringly.

Tibor's face was frozen like stone. There was no expression. "I hope so," he said firmly as he fingered the hairclip in his pocket.

"You will," Jozsef replied.

"Okay, let's go," Laszlo said, grabbing his brother's arm. "Thank you," he said to Jozsef, waving.

Elona slumped against the wall, exhausted. She nibbled on some bread that someone was passing around. The large clock hanging high up above the entrance showed it was almost midnight. She rolled up a jacket behind her and prepared to use it as a pillow.

Béláné lay beside her and gazed up at the high ceiling. "If I would have known upon wakening this morning," she said, pausing briefly and exhaling in exhaustion. "That we would have been in the middle of a revolution. I am certain that I still would have joined the demonstration."

Elona exhaled heavily. "I would have, too," she said. "But I would have tried to protect ourselves better, especially Gizella."

The finality of their friend's death descended upon them wearily. It was almost as if they had been in shock all night, tending to all the wounded and never had time to grieve. Elona reached over and hugged Béláné softly. "She's gone," Elona sobbed.

Béláné cried with Elona, allowing the grief to finally take them over. The clock struck its midnight chime, and several loud demonstrators entered the Cinema. Several shouted raucously. "The Stalin statue is demolished!" one man yelled. "Only the boots remain!"

Several men behind him cheered as a new wave of demonstrators pushed into the large Cinema. Among the new crowd were several Hungarian soldiers with the armbands Elona had been noticing on many civilians. One of the soldiers spoke in a commanding voice, and something about the voice was vaguely familiar. Elona stood up and peered across the large hall to see what was happening.

The soldier spoke loudly again. It was difficult to hear him. He was too far away. But something about his voice sent a chill through her body.

Elona started walking towards the entrance, past all the wounded and dead. She passed by an insurgency station of sorts, with ammunition and weapons laid out. Several citizens in this area were still alert from all the fighting and having great difficulty getting any sleep. Finally, she came closer to the soldier who was speaking.

"We are looking for a blonde-haired student by the name of Gizella!" the man shouted. "And another two women named Elona and Béláné."

Elona felt her heart burst open in relief. "That is me!" she shouted. "I am Elona!"

The man turned his eyes towards her, and in an instant, she recognized him. It was Tibor! Elona pushed through the throng of people. "I'm here!" she yelled. The crowd parted for her to get through as she nudged her way to the soldiers. Hope flooded her heart that maybe Tibor had Laszlo with him. Finally, she reached him. "Tibor!" she yelled and hugged him tightly.

"Elona!" he said. "You are alive!" Tibor choked on his words briefly, and hope soared into his heart. He had thought the worst when he had recovered Gizella's hair clip in the blood on the street. "Where's Gizella? Are you all okay?"

Suddenly, Laszlo's warmth was behind her back. She could smell him and feel his presence before she even saw him. Elona spun around and shrieked, hugging Laszlo so tightly that he might explode from the force. Laszlo grabbed her chin, and they kissed strongly in front of everyone, tears streaming down their cheeks. Several people clapped at the happy reunion, but Tibor stood transfixed to the spot.

"Elona!" he repeated firmly. "Where is Gizella?"

Elona pulled her lips away from Laszlo and turned to face Tibor. Her face instantly darkened.

Tibor knew right then. Elona didn't have to say anything. What he had feared the most had become true in that instant. "No," he said, emotions crumbling the words inside his mouth.

"I'm sorry, Tibor," Elona said, sobbing. The words flowed out of her with the speed of suppressed grief. She mumbled everything together at once. "We were at the Radio Station, and Gizella was sitting on a man's shoulders to see above the crowd, and they fired. Shots were fired. Everyone began running in all directions. It was the AVH. They fired into the crowd." Elona started crying heavily, her body heaved, and Laszlo held onto her tightly. "Gizella was shot twice." Elona's sobs almost choked off the last of her words. "She died instantly."

Tibor felt all the blood drain from his face, and his hands went cold.

Laszlo hugged Elona tightly to keep her from falling. "Oh my God," he said as he reached out with his other arm to grasp Tibor's shoulder. Tibor's skin had turned a sickly pale colour, and he was worried that his brother might collapse. "Sit down, Tibor," Laszlo stated.

Tibor's lip quivered, and his eyes moistened with an instant redness, but no tears fell. He straightened and mustered his strength. "No," he said stubbornly. "I must see her. Where is Gizella? I need to see my wife one last time." Tibor reached into his pocket and pulled out the hair clip, rolling it in his fingers.

Laszlo understood now. The hair clip was Gizella's. Tibor had known it all along. Laszlo kissed Elona's forehead. "Please take us to her body," Laszlo said, his voice heavy with emotion.

Elona nodded. "Come," she said, grasping Tibor's hand. "I'm so sorry." Elona sobbed as she led Tibor and Laszlo to the bodies. It was a large hall, and the insurgents had laid the bodies in rows alongside the wall in the far corner. There was talk about moving the bodies to the basement, but the war continued raging outside, and the living took priority. As they neared the area of the dead, a calm descended upon them. A few mourners were kneeling by their loved ones, saying prayers and crying.

Elona wiped the tears from her eyes so she could see better and began scanning the bodies. There were many more since she was here earlier. She pulled on Tibor's hand when she spotted Gizella's body. "This way," she said solemnly.

They stepped carefully between the rows of bodies until finally, they came to a small woman covered with a dark grey wool overcoat. A tuft of blonde hair stuck out from underneath the coat.

Tibor immediately fell to his knees and kissed Gizella's hair. He flung the coat off and grasped her bloody body, lifting her into his arms. Elona turned away, clutching onto Laszlo. She hugged him fiercely, burying her face into his chest. The area had begun to smell like death, and she couldn't stand to see all the dead bodies anymore. Elona felt like her heart might collapse.

Tibor sobbed heavily. His tears fell without restraint onto Gizella's clothes and her hair. Tibor felt his body start shaking and couldn't stop the tremors in his arms and legs. He just held onto her body as tightly as possible. This was his last moment with his future wife, and he would not let anything in the world come between them. The finality of the thought burst into his mind that Gizella was dead. She was no longer living, he thought incredulously. It was like the simple truth was not accepted into his being, but at the same time, it had to be. There was no going back. He could not have saved her. Tibor was helpless to have changed the events. Life suddenly felt cruel and random.

"Why couldn't it have been another student?" he whispered to himself selfishly. "Why did it have to be you, my dear?"

Tibor sat on the floor and lifted her body into his lap, curling her bloody head into the crook of his arm. He irrationally wished he could somehow bring her back to life, or she would just miraculously wake up like it was all a mistake.

But it was not so, and he knew he must accept her death. His heart split open inside his chest, and he sobbed heavily like never before. Tibor kissed her hair and smoothed down the mass of blonde locks. Finally, he remembered and fished in his pocket for the hairclip. He found it again and pulled it out, running his fingers over the fake diamonds.

Tibor inspected the hairclip and decided upon what he should do with it. He pondered the decision heavily as if it was one of the last decisions he would make in his life. Then he calmly smoothed her hair on the side of her head and clipped it into place. He inspected his work and decided to comb her hair and insert it better. He removed the clip and pulled out a comb from his pocket. Tibor gently combed her hair, pulling some knots free. He felt a soothing calm come over him as he cared for her body. She was always a pretty woman, and he knew she would want to remain as such, even in death.

He continued combing her hair, and when he was finished, he inserted the hairclip. His heart felt somehow mended, even if it was only for a second.

Laszlo turned away from Tibor and embraced Elona tightly. He was extremely grateful that Elona was alive. Laszlo felt his heart sink at the realization that his brother was not as lucky. Life was completely random, he thought. No reasons or explanations could make his brain accept these events as logical. He gazed around at the growing number of bodies as a group of insurgents laid another fatal casualty down.

A surge of revenge and anger filled his heart. His eyes watered with the intensity of the emotions he felt against his government. The very same people he had idolized in his youth. The same government that had saved them from the Germans. Only to oppress and destroy every Hungarian like this.

And why?

"Why have the Russians done this?" he asked aloud.

Elona grasped him tighter.

Laszlo blinked and looked up at the ceiling. There were no answers but the rapid beating of his heart. He grasped Elona and walked her out of the makeshift morgue. She was collapsing in his arms, and he struggled to keep her standing. Finally, he stopped and bent down, scooping her knees into the crook of his arm and lifting her up, carrying her away from the stench of the dead.

CHAPTER 22

They awoke in each other's arms, curled on the floor. Laszlo blinked and kissed Elona's head gratefully, whispering a prayer of thanks. He would not do anything to lose this woman now that he had her. He looked around, wondering where his brother was. Laszlo remembered they had left him at the morgue with Gizella. Tibor had found them later on during the night and fell asleep on the other side of Béláné.

There was a strange rumble of thunder coming from the ground, it seemed. It sounded very odd. Laszlo looked around and searched for his brother. He spotted Tibor instantly. He was inspecting the weapons with a group of armed insurgents at the front entrance. Many of the men began to talk at once, and Laszlo could barely make out what they were saying.

Tibor shouted commandingly. "The Russian tanks are coming!" he shouted over the raised voices. "Those Molotov cocktails thrown from the third-floor windows will be better than running out with guns blazing!"

The men quieted down and listened. Tibor spoke louder, pointing at several men to organize the insurgency into teams. "You men with the long rifles, get the hell upstairs now!" He turned and pointed at several youngsters with crates of Molotov cocktails. "You young men!" Tibor shouted. "We need you upstairs now! Throw the cocktails in the open pits of the APCs!" As the young teenage boys ran to the stairs, Tibor shouted after them. "Aim well!" The APCs were armoured personnel carriers with open tops vulnerable to attack.

Laszlo roused Elona and kissed her on the head. "Sweetheart," he said. "I need to go help the insurgents."

Elona murmured and then opened her eyes, momentarily confused at her surroundings. Yesterday, she had awakened at her brother's house. Her eyes focused, and then she felt the ground rumble. She sat up in a panic. "What's happening?" she asked.

"Russian tanks are rolling in," Laszlo said firmly.

Elona's eyes darted from left to right.

"I need to help Tibor organize the insurgents," he said, crouching with his hands on his knees.

Elona stared deep into his eyes. "I don't want to lose you," she said worriedly.

"You won't lose me," he replied, bending towards her and grasping her chin. "I am well trained in combat, my sweet."

"What can we do against the tanks?" she asked, her voice shaking.

"One thing you can do right now," he said firmly. "Take Béláné and yourself to a point far away from the front of the building. If the tanks are preparing to roll down the streets, they'll shoot straight into the front of the buildings."

Elona crouched as Laszlo kissed her gently on the lips. "I love you," he said. "Now get as many people as you can, towards the back, especially the medical personnel."

She stood strongly. "Okay, love," Elona stated. "I will do as you say." She awakened Béláné beside her and yelled at everyone to move towards the back. She turned and saw Laszlo rushing towards the group of insurgents. He briefly turned back for one last glance, and Elona blew him a kiss.

Laszlo was upstairs in a third-floor room. He had the rifle poised on the broken window ledge. Laszlo saw the first of the tanks round the corner and waited until they were directly overhead to give the order. "Fire!" he commanded.

Several Molotov cocktails sailed through the air. The youngsters ducked back into the windows as instructed. Several of the homemade fire bombs bounced off the tanks, but one rested on its target, and a fire erupted on the latch door of the tank. A Russian soldier scrambled to open the latch, but the flames were already igniting the entire top. He flew open the door and was greeted by bullets, his body bouncing back into the tank. A youngster saw his opportunity and flew another Molotov cocktail. It sailed right inside the pit. The explosion of the ammunition igniting inside the tank rocked the street and the building. A mass of people on the street jumped back in astonishment as the tank turned into a black smouldering carcass.

Laszlo ran quickly into the hallway and passed several rooms until he reached the furthest office at the very end. He rushed into the room as a wounded policeman with an arm-band looked groggily at him.

"I need this room," Laszlo commanded. "Out!"

The policeman shuffled hurriedly out of the room as Laszlo opened the window carefully. He balanced his rifle on the ledge and aimed for the second vehicle, which was slowing down because the first tank was still smouldering in black flames.

He had to stop the second vehicle. It was an armoured personnel carrier with five Soviet soldiers sitting in the top. Laszlo looked down the sights towards the open APC. He fired directly at the Soviet personnel. The weapon jerked in his grasp, but he held onto it expertly. Laszlo fired again and again from the rifle, riddling the open tank with bullets. The tank stopped. The men were all dead.

Several armed revolutionaries flooded the streets and started firing at the remaining tanks. More firebombs were thrown at the APCs. He watched as Tibor ran out of the building towards the Soviet tanks and armoured personnel carriers.

Laszlo cursed, wishing he had convinced his brother to stay inside the building. He knew it was impossible to reason with a grief-riddled vengeful man. Tibor had changed this morning.

His brother had sobbed so much last night that he was afraid Tibor was having a mental breakdown. However, this morning had proved otherwise. Tibor was cold, calculating and vengeful today. His brother had transformed into a captain, intent on organizing the insurgents into a powerful army and crushing the Russians.

Laszlo watched as a firebomb sailed into an open APC. He saw that the vehicle had been pulling a howitzer. Laszlo shouted from the window to the revolutionaries on the street. "Clear the area!" he screamed. "That vehicle is going to blow!"

Several insurgents looked back and ran away to the end of the street.

The open APC and howitzer exploded in a large black bang as the heavy weaponry caught fire. Laszlo cursed under his breath. "We could have used that howitzer."

Laszlo straightened as an idea formed in his mind. He had to join the action on the street. They needed to secure the other howitzer. He was certain there would be another APC with additional heavy artillery. He raced down the stairs two at a time until he reached the street level. Laszlo instructed several men to join him on a mission to secure more firepower. Four more men joined the team, nodding in agreement. The group of eight men, including Laszlo, rushed cautiously out into the street. The chaos of heavy fighting and smoke blew in their faces. The insurgents were fighting the tanks directly, setting fire to what they could and mercilessly killing Russian soldiers.

Laszlo instructed the team on the plan. They ducked through the streets until he saw what they came here for.

It was another APC with several Russian soldiers in the open top. They were farther back from the fighting and towards the end of the line of tanks. It appeared these Soviets soldiers weren't aware of the intense fighting yet and were mostly relaxed and in charge.

Laszlo crouched behind a disabled tank with the other men. "We're going to shoot each of those Russian soldiers in the APC," he said slowly. "But be careful not to start any fires! Stop any firebombs from being thrown if you can. We need to be extra careful. See that 76.2mm anti-tank gun hitched to the back of that APC? We are going to capture that anti-tank gun." Laszlo pointed his finger at each man. "This is no game. We need that weapon to win this war against the Soviets." He calmly loaded his rifle. "If a firebomb gets near that 76.2mm, it will explode. We need it intact." Laszlo looked up. "Do you all understand?"

"Yes, Lieutenant!" one man whispered loudly.

"Use tact and surprise," Laszlo said as he peered alongside the tank. "I will count to three, and we'll start taking them out."

The men scattered to the opposite side of the disabled tank as Laszlo started counting. "One, two," he commanded. He looked down his sights. "Three!"

Firepower erupted violently into the unsuspecting Soviet soldiers. The Russians scrambled to raise their weapons, but it was too late. The flurry of bullets stopped them dead. The insurgents cheered and ran towards the APC with Laszlo. They worked quickly at detaching the unit from the back of the APC. Laszlo's fingers were black with dirt. He calmed his mind to unlatch the unit. Several of his men helped him until, finally, the unit was freed. Several shots were suddenly fired from a Soviet commander on top of a tank. Laszlo ducked as a bullet grazed his shoulder. "Kurva anyját!" he swore loudly, looking down at his shoulder and seething from the instant pain.

The other men ducked behind the APC and worried about the captured howitzer's ammunition exploding.

"Let's get this weapon out of here!" Laszlo shouted angrily. "Someone take out that shooter!"

An older male insurgent with a Mosin-Nagant M44 carbine spoke. "I got him," he said calmly. The man levelled the Mosin and fired. The bullet whizzed through the air in a split second, hitting the Soviet tank commander squarely in the chest, toppling him to the ground in a heap.

"Great shot!" Laszlo said appraisingly. He grasped his wounded shoulder, pressing down to slow the blood and instructed the men on how to use the anti-tank gun. Two men grabbed the ammunition box, and the others wheeled the heavyweight anti-tank gun towards the area of intense fighting, closer to the Cinema.

Laszlo was feeling suddenly weak and knew he needed medical attention. He pressed on the wound and winced. "We need to take out as many tanks as possible with this gun," he said commandingly. "As we travel back, let's be cognizant of which ones we take out first. I need to get back to the Cinema and stop this bleeding. But first, let's take down the tank closest to the fighting."

They wheeled it in the most opportune position and aimed it towards the tank with the strongest fighting. The tank began rotating its menacing weapon towards the Corvin Cinema. Laszlo felt his heart skip a beat. Elona was in the cinema.

"Fire!" Laszlo shouted.

The 76.2mm anti-tank gun fired like a cannon, piercing into the tank armour. The stunned Soviet occupants tried rotating the turret again, but it was no longer working, and the Russian soldiers knew that the T-54 might explode with the next shot. They emerged with their hands up from the T-54 tank, surrendering.

Laszlo tapped one of the men close to him. "I'm going back to find a nurse," he said. "Keep taking out the tanks, one by one. We will win this."

The man nodded and saluted him. "Thank you, Lieutenant!"

Laszlo smiled and crouched cautiously near the buildings, escaping between the alcoves towards the rear of the cinema.

His hand was now slick with blood, but he knew he didn't have a bullet stuck in him. It did feel like a large chuck of his flesh was gone, though. He pressed on the wound as hard as he could, but his eyesight was becoming cloudy.

Laszlo blinked and saw the back door of the cinema. He hurried across the lane and pulled the door open. A rush of panicked voices greeted him. It was complete chaos. Women and men rushed up and down the stairs, some shouting orders. Others were screaming in pain.

"I need a nurse," Laszlo said to deaf ears. Nobody took notice except one young girl. She grabbed his good arm and said, "Follow me."

She guided him to the open area where he had slept last night. It had been transformed into an intense military hospital. Laszlo followed until the young girl stopped in front of a rush of women tying tourniquets, some bandaging bloody heads, and some even stitching open wounds. Laszlo looked up as a shaky weakness started spreading through his body. He leaned on a small table, and a nurse rushed to his aid.

"Sir," she said. "Are you okay?"

The voice was familiar.

Laszlo looked up into the eyes of Béláné Havrilla. "Grazed bullet left shoulder," he said. "I just need a few stitches. Where's Elona?"

"Oh my God, Laszlo," she said loudly. "Elona! Laszlo's here!"

Another man was standing beside Béláné, holding her waist lightly. He spoke quickly into her ear. She smiled and nodded at him. The young doctor smiled back at her and looked at Laszlo. "We will stitch you up, my friend," he said. "Are you sure there's no bullet?"

"I don't know," Laszlo replied. "It feels like just a bad graze."

"Let's see," the doctor said, leaning Laszlo down onto a table.

Elona pushed through the chaos and arrived at Laszlo's side. "My love," she said, a frown of worry wrinkling her brow. "You're alright, dear. We got this." She kissed him on the forehead as the doctor began cleaning out the wound. "Hold my hand, squeeze it tight. This will hurt." Elona squeezed his right hand. "We can give you a sedative. Do you want something? We only have morphine and vodka."

"I'll take the vodka," Laszlo breathed out between winces.

"It will increase bleeding," Elona stated simply.

"Is the doctor stitching me up?"

Elona looked to the young doctor as Béláné helped with cleaning out the wound. They stood side by side as if they were a doctor-nurse team. Béláné smiled at the young doctor, and he asked for a needle and thread.

The young doctor leaned over Laszlo. "There's no bullet," he said. "But there is a large chunk of flesh missing from your shoulder. We are stitching it up now. No vodka. You've lost a lot of blood. Grin and bear it, lieutenant."

Elona kissed his hand. "No vodka," she said. "You'll be alright, sweetheart. You'll make it. Just a few more minutes. Hold on, my sweet."

Laszlo squeezed her palm harshly, seething as the skin tugged with each stitch. He tried to think of a better time, a better moment in his life. The first thing he thought of was playing his accordion at the riverside, singing to Elona.

Elona's mind was thinking the same thing. "Imagine something else, my love," she said. "Think of that first day at the riverside."

Laszlo smiled and groaned as another stitch pulled his skin. He squeezed his eyes shut and imagined the music from the accordion and his voice filtering into the chaos. He started singing softly as his mind was transported back to that time when he had first met the love of his life. Laszlo opened his eyes as Elona gazed worriedly at him. "You know what, Elona?" he said.

"What, my dear?" she replied, her brow filling with worry.

"I need to marry you when this is all over," he said, a small smile creasing his mouth.

Elona smiled broadly. "Oh, Laszlo," she said softly. "I will gladly marry you." She kissed him softly on the lips as the doctor finished the stitches.

The young doctor suddenly turned to Béláné and kissed her on the cheek. "You are the best assistant a doctor could ever have!"

Béláné blushed and kissed him back quickly as they scurried off to another patient.

Elona laid a warm hand on Laszlo's forehead. "You're all stitched up, my sweet," she said. "I will get you some water while you rest."

⟩

Nagy was in shock. He had been reappointed Prime Minister of Hungary. He stood and grasped the cup of coffee with shaky hands. There was going to be a brief ceremony in an attempt to quell the violence.

The Russian tanks had lost terribly. The fiercest areas of fighting were at the Radio Station and the Corvin Cinema. He had not expected this kind of intense fighting, nor did he want it. Nagy rubbed his thinning hair and exhaled deeply. He had a meeting with all his advisors soon. Imre Nagy wondered what the Soviets were thinking. He sometimes wished he could jump inside their heads and read their minds so he would at least know their next steps.

It was a dangerous line to cross, aggravating the Soviet Union. He knew this all too well.

Nagy was proud of the Hungarian citizens for putting the mighty Soviets up against the wall, but he was also afraid of what might come of this in the end.

He was amazed at his people's strength and conviction, though. The Soviets had deployed the 128th Guards Rifle Division from USSR to Buda, and the 33rd Guards Mechanized Division from Romania was instructed to flush out insurgents in the south-eastern areas of the city. The 33rd Division encountered the greatest resistance in the 8th and 9th Districts, especially around the Corvin Passage and Kilian Barracks. In this area, the losses were extensive. The Soviets lost 14 tanks, 9 armoured vehicles, 13 artillery pieces, 4 multiple rocket-launchers and 6 anti-aircraft guns in just three days. The Soviets knew that they were not only fighting citizens, but many of the fiercest battles were with the Hungarian Army now. They didn't know how many of the Hungarian Army soldiers had changed sides, but it was a catastrophic blow to the Soviets. These were no longer untrained citizens with farm rifles. The revolution was exploding into a trained personnel insurgency, with citizens most likely being commanded into military formations.

And the fighting wasn't just in Budapest. The revolution was spreading to all parts of the country. The first deaths had occurred in Debrecen, a city in the eastern part of the country.

Even though he secretly admired the insurgents, Nagy felt powerless to stop the fighting. He had tried everything. The Soviet tanks were sent in just before he took power, and he could do nothing to stop it. On October 25th, he had announced that he would begin negotiations for the removal of Soviet forces. On October 26th, he had met with local writer unions and student groups as well as the Borsod Workers' Council.

Nagy steepled his fingers over his forehead in thought, resting his elbows on the desk. Yesterday, he had announced a major reformation of his government, even including several non-communist politicians as Ministers. Nagy had even negotiated with Soviet representatives pushing for a ceasefire and a political solution.

The Soviet army was in dire need of rest. They had been in combat in the city streets for days under intense fire. Nagy wanted them out of Hungary just as badly as his citizens did.

It was clear that the government had two options: continue to fight and bring in more reinforcements to crush the revolution or take the initiative and show a willingness to negotiate. Nagy was trying so hard with the latter, more peaceful option.

But it seemed his efforts were in vain.

The Soviets had mounted an operation this morning to take Corvin Passage at dawn.

Nagy watched the purple skies outside his window, teasing with the first rays of light. He stood, exhaled and straightened his tie, walking out of his office to the emergency ceasefire meeting.

Jozsef was tired. He had been fighting for days. He hadn't seen his wife, Marika, and his children for an eternity. Jozsef was dirty and filthy, only wiping his face in the mornings with water.

His unit had remained at the Radio Station since the fighting had started. Yesterday, the fighting had decreased significantly, with Nagy even broadcasting messages about his government's willingness to negotiate.

That's when Jozsef learned of a planned Soviet attack to overtake the Corvin Passage at dawn.

He looked in the mirror and exhaled. Jozsef bent over the small bathroom sink and splashed cold water onto his face. He groaned as the cool water hit his cheeks. Any tiny relief was welcome in his life right now.

He grabbed a rag and dried his face, then drank his coffee in one gulp. He knew his family was safe, and that put his mind to ease. His wife and children were far away from the areas of fighting in the country. Jozsef had sent an urgent message for them to be sent to his cousin's farm outside of Budapest. He had received confirmation that they were safe days ago.

Hopefully, he would see them again one day soon. Jozsef yearned to hug his children and smell his wife's flowery hair.

He straightened in the mirror. "One day soon," he told his reflection.

But first, he had to advance his police unit towards the Corvin Passage to provide reinforcement for the insurgents. Dawn was coming soon, he thought.

Elona smelled his musk before her eyes opened. His body was incredibly close to hers, and it felt wonderful. She felt guilty for rejoicing in the daily intimacy with Laszlo during a revolutionary war. Although, it was the only time she had ever spent every night and morning with the love of her life.

She now understood that he was the man whom she'd been waiting for all this time. It sounded silly, even for a rational woman like herself, but the truth lay in her heart. She loved this man with all her might. Elona would do anything for him.

She heard him groan as he climbed on top of her. Elona's body responded instantly. Her thighs parted as his body settled on top of her pelvis. She opened her eyes and gazed into his sexy stare. He was the most amorous in the morning, she realized. Elona didn't know how he found the energy after fighting all day, but he was always eager to make love to her upon waking.

His penis slipped effortlessly into her moist vagina.

Elona gasped as the length of his penis entered her fully. He kissed her mouth to keep her quiet. They had found a private room on the second floor, but Laszlo was still afraid of other men hearing them having intercourse. He didn't want other men getting any ideas.

Elona kissed him back passionately as he slid slowly out of her, then back in. He was a slow, gentle lover, and she loved every minute of it.

"You're so beautiful in the mornings," he murmured.

"My hair's a mess," she mumbled back.

"I love your messy hair," he said, his voice husky and thick.

He thrust gently back inside her, pushing all the way to the end of her womb, filling her completely with his penis. Elona opened her mouth and groaned loudly.

"Shhh," he whispered, then kissed her again.

Elona felt so warm inside that she could not stop her groans. It felt so exquisite with his sweaty skin against hers and the scent of their lovemaking drifting through the room.

He thrust several more times, kissing her deeply at the same time. She moaned into his lips as he continued his slow thrusts into her vagina.

Then his penis grew miraculously larger, and she knew that this was the moment of his imminent ejaculation.

Laszlo's entire body tensed as he released his orgasm inside her. He groaned quietly, whispering into her neck. "I love you," he murmured.

"My sweet," she said, wrapping her arms around his naked chest. "I love you so much."

He relaxed languidly on top of her for several minutes before shifting off and sliding beside her. He cuddled Elona's shoulders against him tightly. Laszlo held her fiercely like this for several minutes, almost as if he was afraid he wouldn't see her again.

She murmured into his chest as he kissed the top of her head.

The skies were still dark outside, but the dawn was slowly creeping in. They had been fighting for days, and it seemed they were winning. The Corvin Passage was impenetrable, it seemed. But Laszlo knew different. Sometimes the strongest holds were taken by sheer force.

He smoothed her messy hair and spoke quietly. "What do you think of us leaving?" he asked. "We could go to another country and live a quiet life there, no more fighting, just us. We can get married there."

Elona tilted her head up. "But we might finally get our country back from the communists," she said, confused. "Why leave now?"

Laszlo kissed her head again. "The Soviets do not like defeat," he said slowly. "I have a bad feeling about this."

"You do?"

"Yes," he replied. "I do."

Elona hadn't thought about how the Soviets would react. She had only thought about her own needs and her country. "Where would we go?" she asked.

"Austria, for now," he said. "Maybe another country after awhile. We could check which ones are accepting Hungarians."

Elona thought it was a good time to mention something that she had been hiding from him. "It might be a good idea," she said. "I don't know how much longer I can survive in this war. I don't feel well. Every day, I feel sick in the mornings after we make love."

He sat up on his elbow in alarm. "You feel sick?" he asked incredulously. "You never told me."

"I was trying to find a good time to tell you," Elona stated, smiling with a weak grin.

"Tell me what?" Laszlo asked, frowning with confusion.

She grinned shyly. Elona wasn't sure how he'd react to this kind of news, but she had to tell him. "I think I may be pregnant," she said bluntly. Now, it was finally said, she thought, waiting for his reaction.

Laszlo looked to the ceiling briefly, and at first, she thought he was upset, but then his gaze slowly fell back to hers.

"Thanks be to God," he whispered to the heavens. His face broke into a wide grin, and his smile was so large she thought his face might crack. He began to laugh and hugged her tightly, rocking her. "I love you so much, Elona," he said, his voice thick with emotion. "We are going to have a family. I cannot believe my good fortune. You are the best thing that has ever happened in my life." Then suddenly, he became emotional. He tried to control it but couldn't. Several tears streaked down his cheeks as he hugged her tightly.

Elona kissed his shoulder and held him as the unexpected emotions flowed out of him. "I would gladly have your baby, my love," she whispered.

They spent several moments like this, cradling each other and imagining their future together. It would soon be dawn, and she knew he would be fighting again today. His arm had healed remarkably quickly, and he was back commanding the insurgents on a daily basis. Elona felt so proud of him, but she was also scared that he would return as a casualty again. It broke her heart every morning when he left.

Laszlo pulled away from her briefly and looked into her eyes. "This seals our fate," he said. "We will leave for Austria soon."

"Are you sure?"

"I have never been so sure of anything in my life before," Laszlo replied.

Then an explosion rocked the street outside.

7

Jozsef held the smoking rocket launcher tightly as the tank erupted into flames in front of his team. It was barely dawn as the Soviet tanks crawled into the Corvin passage. His team fired another rocket launcher into the second T-34 tank. It missed and hit the side of a building farther down the street. His team rushed around the side of the Kilian Barracks, preparing to shoot again, when a heavy artillery team emerged from the Cinema. Several anti-tank guns and rocket launchers were hastily positioned on the street, and the T-34 and T-54 tanks came under heavy fire.

Jozsef went into the barracks and awakened the drowsy army personnel who hadn't already awakened yet. There was a mass chaos of officers rushing to arm themselves and some already preparing to go outside.

Jozsef shouted, "The Soviets commanded the tanks to crush the Corvin Passage this morning!" He showed his armband. "We've been stationed at the Radio Building. I heard the news today. We need every armed personnel out there now." Jozsef pointed across the street. "Corvin Cinema has opened up a barrage already." Before Jozsef could say another word, an explosion rocked the street. They all rushed outside and watched as another T-34 tank caught fire, filling the air with thick black smoke. "Two tanks out!" Jozsef shouted enthusiastically.

An eruption of gunfire hailed down on them, and Jozsef ran for cover with the other officers, but he was too late. A stray bullet caught his hand, and blood spurted from the wound.

Jozsef cursed with a string of profanities as he ripped a cloth from his arm and squeezed it over his left hand. He peered into the street. It was most likely a stray insurgent bullet.

"Corvin has a hospital set up!" one of his crew shouted. "We need to get you there!"

Laszlo commanded the anti-tank gunners. He was proud of the civilians he had under his command. They learned quickly, although they weren't all civilians. Many were Hungarian soldiers that he had worked with in the past.

Tibor was commanding the rocket launcher team. Laszlo watched as the third T-34 erupted into flames.

Laszlo pushed the anti-tank gun with his comrades farther along when he spotted the T-54 tanks. They slowed, and he spoke quickly to his team. "Station where they don't see the attack coming," he said loudly over the heavy firing. The Kilian barracks had started opening fire on any remaining Soviet soldiers, taking some prisoners. He noticed some insurgents were lynching the enemy on nearby trees. Laszlo frowned with disapproval and noticed Tibor's team from the corner of his eye. They were joining the Kilian Barracks rocket launcher team. They marched in a strong show of force. "Everyone down!" Laszlo shouted as Tibor's reinforced team opened up on two T-54 tanks.

The noise was deafening, and Laszlo could barely hear or see afterwards. Black smoke crowded the streets, and his ears rang with a high-pitched ting. He checked his team, and everyone was unhurt. Laszlo cautiously stood as the firing ceased. He saw Tibor wave him on. The streets were filled with flames, and a strange calm descended like a heavy cloud. Everyone slowly stood. Laszlo checked his watch. It had only been a half hour of fighting, and the insurgents had already taken out three T-34 and two T-54 tanks.

The streets were suddenly quiet.

Laszlo instructed his team to bear arms, and they slowly advanced past the burned-out T-54s with Tibor's team in front of them.

Once they had passed the wall of smoke, what they saw made them smile for the first time in five days.

Several Soviet tanks and armoured vehicles began retreating. Laszlo could overhear several Soviet commanders calling out to their own men. "Return to base!"

"Ceasefire discussions!" another commander shouted. "Hold your fire!"

The remaining armoured vehicles began backing up.

The insurgents whooped in delight.

Jozsef stumbled into the Corvin Cinema, his face pale and his hands shaking. Just making it across the street to the Cinema was a circus with death. The explosions and gunfire were constant. His team had finally heard a brief ceasefire and quickly raced across the street.

A young woman noticed his armband in the Cinema and motioned him to an operating table. "I will get someone," she muttered hastily, then left.

Jozsef stared up at the ceiling, trying to will the pain away. Then he heard a familiar voice.

"I know this man," Elona said, approaching the table. "Jozsef, my dear. How are you feeling?"

Jozsef smiled. "You don't know how happy I am to see you, Elona," he said. "I think I've lost a lot of blood. I'm feeling weak. You must notify Marika and my children."

"I will make sure Laszlo takes you to your family once this is over," Elona said softly, unwrapping his hand and inspecting the injury. "It is true, you have lost a lot of blood, but it looks like you'll be fine. I will get a doctor to stitch you up right away. Hold onto your finger with firm pressure like this." She showed him where to place the pressure and turned to find Béláné.

Elona rushed around the emergency room commotion and searched for her friend. After several moments, she exhaled and sighed heavily. Elona could not find her. She scratched her head in disbelief. Béláné should be here, she thought. Elona turned around, blatantly confused about her friend's sudden disappearance. She rushed along the emergency tables and found a pleasant older female doctor that was just finishing a surgery.

"Please come," Elona pleaded. "My husband's friend has lost a finger. He is losing a lot of blood as we speak."

The retired doctor looked up and wiped her hands. "Take me to him."

They both rushed through the melange and returned to Jozsef. The retired doctor inspected the wound expertly and delivered the grave news. "You have lost half your finger," she said. "And you've lost a significant amount of blood." She grimaced. "We will have to amputate the remainder of the finger and stitch you up immediately to stop the bleeding."

Jozsef felt a strange dizziness cloud his brain.

Elona looked down at him in concern. "Jozsef," she said. "You will be alright. Do you hear me?"

His eyes fluttered closed as the blackness overtook him.

ᐅ

Elona stayed by Jozsef's bedside until he awoke. She grasped his good hand. "You are here with us at Corvin Cinema, Jozsef," she said reassuringly. "Your left hand is bandaged up. The doctor saved your hand. You will be alright."

Jozsef blinked. "But my finger is gone?" He looked down at the white bandages covering his left hand.

"Yes, it is," Elona answered softly. "I'm sorry, there wasn't anything else we could do."

Jozsef stared up at the ceiling for several minutes amidst the hustle of the emergency area. Many nurses and doctors were working hard to repair the wounded. He felt the warmth of Elona's hand and wondered how much longer this fight was going to last. Would any of them even live to tell the story?

It was only his finger, he concluded. It could have been a lot worse. "I suppose it was only a finger," he finally said, weariness taking him over. "I have four more on that hand." He smiled weakly.

Elona chuckled gravely. "Well, you can certainly look at it that way," she said, her brow furrowing in concern as she glanced repeatedly towards the entrance of the Cinema.

Jozsef noticed her sudden apprehension. "What is it?" Jozsef asked, concern wrinkling his brow.

"It's Laszlo," she said. "He's still out there."

Elona scanned the front entrance with trepidation as Jozsef fell back asleep. Her heart hammered in her chest. If Jozsef was shot by a stray bullet, then Laszlo was surely in the line of fire also. Her mind went through every crazy scenario of doom, and she tried valiantly to stop the worrying and breathe.

Several shouts started outside, and a chill crept up her spine. A few soldiers began entering the Cinema, some wounded and some exultant. She left Jozsef and began to push her way to the entrance as a large number of insurgents returned from fighting. Some were holding their arms and bleeding, but most of them seemed triumphant. Elona tried to dispel the negative thoughts and continued searching for Laszlo.

Then she saw him enter with his team. They were triumphantly shouting after returning from heavy fighting.

Someone yelled, "We won! The Russians have retreated!"

Elona's hopes soared. She pushed her way through the crowd and finally reached him. She hugged him desperately, then kissed him roughly. "I'm so glad you're not harmed," she murmured between kisses.

He melted his mouth against hers and hugged her tightly as the remaining soldiers returned behind him.

Béláné entered the Cinema amongst the second group of insurgents and triumphantly shouted with several others. She wore an army jacket and had a large rifle slung across her shoulder. Elona looked up and stared in disbelief as her friend clearly had joined the fighting! This must have been why she couldn't find her anywhere in the hospital, Elona concluded.

Béláné ran to the young doctor, Gabor, and kissed him roughly. Elona chuckled in surprise as the young doctor kissed Béláné passionately back.

Elona and Laszlo joined the happy couple, smiling gaily. "I am so happy for you!" Elona laughed, still in shock at her friend's revolutionary transformation.

"We have won!" Béláné shrieked proudly, holding onto Gabor's hand. "I am happy for you, too, Elona. We have vindicated Gizella's death." Tears formed instantly in Béláné's eyes. "She didn't die for no reason," Béláné stated, her voice becoming hoarse. "We fought for her memory and won."

Elona hugged her friend warmly and smiled. "Yes, we have won!" she agreed.

Béláné returned the warm hug and began to sob from the release of adrenaline. Gabor stood silently aside as the women consoled each other.

Laszlo broke the hug by grasping Elona's hand. "Let's go join the celebrations!" he said.

Elona turned and saw that many of the citizens, nurses and insurgents had begun gathering in the center of the cinema. Many were laughing with relief while several bottles of vodka were being handed around. Many people were crying in joy, like Béláné and Elona, while the adrenaline of the past week slowly eased out of their bodies.

The large group ate together, munching on bread and sausages. Laszlo sat close to Elona with his hand on her knee. Then they heard the news.

The Nagy government had declared a ceasefire. There would be an afternoon radio speech. Elona hugged Laszlo as tears fell from her eyes.

He kissed her gently. "I know we have won, my dear," he said slowly. "But me, you and our child are still leaving for Austria tomorrow."

Chapter 23

It was a day like any other, but somehow the sun felt warmer, and the morning felt brighter. Elona hugged her friend as they packed. Béláné couldn't understand why they were leaving when the country was finally becoming normal again. Imre Nagy's broadcast had recognized the revolutionary organizations, guaranteed impunity for the insurgents and disbanded the AVH. The government even reinstituted national holidays and the Hungarian coat of arms. A sense of normalcy coated the streets, and people were beginning to resume their lives.

"Why are you leaving?" Béláné asked incredulously.

"I am pregnant," Elona said. "We are going to Austria to build a family."

"Oh, Elona!" Béláné shrieked. "Congratulations!" she smiled but held back. "Why Austria?"

"Laszlo doesn't trust the Soviets," she explained. "He said they never admit to losing a fight."

"But we have the Nagy government again!" Béláné exclaimed.

"Yes, we do," Elona said. "But all the same, we are still leaving." She packed a set of suitcases full of clothes as she pulled more out of her bedroom drawers. It was nice to be home again, she thought, wondering how long this normalcy would last for. Elona looked up with concern. "You should come with us, Béláné."

"No," she answered quickly. "I think I am falling in love with Gabor. It is fate that brought us together. I will stay to see this one through."

"I feel so happy for you both, and I understand completely," Elona replied. "Just keep it in mind if things change."

"I will," Béláné answered, picking up some of Elona's luggage pieces.

Elona grabbed the lighter suitcase and walked into the main kitchen with Béláné. Her father looked up as he sat at the table eating headcheese and crackers. "Elona," he said solemnly. "I wish you didn't have to go."

"Apu," she exclaimed, hugging him. "I will miss you so much." Elona gripped him strongly as her mother joined them at the table. "We lived so many years without you," Elona said. "At times, we thought you were dead."

"Well," Apu said, rubbing his scruffy grey beard. "The insurgents freed me, and the Nagy government has officially ended my prison sentence. I am alive and here to stay now."

Elona kissed him on the cheek. "At least us youngsters did something good in this country!" she said joyfully.

"You did good, that's for certain!" Apu replied, wiping his mouth. "I am relieved to be back home."

Elona stopped and picked up her luggage again. "I am happy you're home too," she said, emotion threatening to tear her resolve down. "I must meet Laszlo soon." She paused, catching her breath. "You know, I will visit when I can. I will always be here for you both. You can visit us and your new grandchild too."

Anyu kissed her on the cheek. "Don't worry, you'll only be in Austria," her mother stated calmly. "It isn't that far away."

"Yes," Elona agreed hesitantly. "We haven't decided quite where we will live yet, but we will definitely let you know." Elona shifted nervously from foot to foot. "Are you sure you don't want to come with us?" she asked for the millionth time.

Anyu pursed her lips stubbornly, and Apu chuckled in a deep voice. "I'm not going anywhere," Apu stated firmly. "Anyu and I will stay in Hungary forever. It is our lifeblood. No matter what political turns this country takes, this is our home and will forever be our homeland. No one can convince us to leave."

Elona could see the tension in her father's face and regretted asking again.

Anyu nodded and put her arm around his shoulders. "I am staying wherever your father is," she said firmly. "We will see our new grandchild one day soon. Do not worry about that."

A car horn beeped in the distance. Elona looked up sharply. "That's Laszlo!" she said. "I must go now. I love you both so much!" She hugged her parents warmly as Béláné grabbed as much of the luggage as possible.

"Go," Anyu said with tears in her eyes. "Go start your new life. You deserve it, my sweet Elona."

Laszlo peered his head through the front door. "Elona," he said calmly. "I still have many errands to tie up before we leave. I'm sorry to rush you. I have found a house for us to stay in while we prepare to leave. It may take a few more days than I thought. Do you want to stay with your parents longer?"

"I want to be with you, my sweet," she replied, beaming with joy. "I have everything packed." She pointed to her luggage as Laszlo grabbed them from Béláné swiftly. He nodded to her parents. "Anya, Apa," he said, acknowledging them with the more formal words.

Elona smiled, then quickly hugged her mother and father one last time and said her goodbyes to Béláné.

Laszlo's Mercedes pulled up in front of the barracks as Jozsef exited the building. He ran to the car, quickly sat in the passenger seat and slammed the door.

"All ready to see your family again?" Laszlo asked.

"Yes, thank you, my friend," Jozsef replied, looking down at his bandaged hand.

"They will be thrilled to see you," Laszlo said. He swerved the car onto the road and smiled at his friend. The Nagy government had not requested the vehicle returned yet. He assumed that he would receive some kind of impunity for his actions and possibly be demoted. Although, it didn't matter. Laszlo would never return to the military, but he would utilize the car until they requested it back.

"I don't understand why you are leaving," Jozsef said as they drove by homes which were bombed. There were suitcases of cash left outside of the wrecked homes for the victims, which appeared to be untouched. Laszlo was proud that his countrymen did not loot the cash donation boxes. The streets still looked grim, but people were beginning to scatter along the neighbourhoods, returning to work and home. Life was reverting back to normalcy amongst the scars of war within their communities.

"You should come with us," Laszlo said, a slight pleading in his voice.

"I have three children and a wife!" Jozsef responded indignantly.

"They can come too," he replied.

"There is no reason to flee," Jozsef said in protest.

Laszlo drove in silence as the mutilations of war passed by their windows. Elona had made sure that he drove Jozsef home to his wife and children as promised. Laszlo fished for a cigarette in his pocket absentmindedly and pushed down the urge. He was trying to quit smoking. "You know Soviets as well as I do," Laszlo said. "They never like to lose a fight."

"But they have lost now!" Jozsef exclaimed.

"For now, yes," Laszlo stated, pinching his eyebrows together. "We may stay a few more days and try to convince our friends to come with us."

"No," Jozsef stated stubbornly. "I'm staying. I cannot leave my family. Bringing them with me would be near to impossible. Hungary is stabilizing, Laszlo. Our country is finally recovering from ten years of communist Russia. Even Tibor is back working for the new Hungarian army. Everything will be fine."

"Yes, Tibor told me," Laszlo replied, fidgeting his hands nervously along the steering wheel. His desire to quit cigarettes was strong, but the nervous withdrawal tremors were disturbing. He drove in silence for several kilometres before nearing Jozsef's home. It appeared that the house was unscathed. Laszlo slowed the vehicle and pulled over to the side of the road. "It is your choice."

Jozsef nodded and opened the door eagerly.

Laszlo ducked his head down to meet Jozsef's eye. "Just know that the option remains open," he said. "We are going to Austria. If you have to leave, we'll be here for a few more days."

Jozsef grinned, happiness spreading through his loins as he caught sight of his wife at the front door, running towards him. "Okay, thanks for the ride!" Jozsef yelled back as he raced to meet Marika.

Laszlo watched the two embrace and wondered if Jozsef was right to stay.

Something in his gut urged Laszlo to leave. Right or wrong, he needed to listen to it.

Nagy was relieved that the violence was mostly behind them. After the ceasefire had been declared, he had broadcasted the new government reforms in his afternoon radio speech. It was well received by the people. He had changed his wording, and instead of a counter-revolution, he spoke of the uprising as a great national and democratic movement which had come about directly from the grave crimes of the preceding era.

Most of the reforms had fallen in line with the demands of the October 23 demonstration. Negotiations with the leaders of the insurgent groups began. Based on an agreement with the Soviets, Russian troops would begin to withdraw from Budapest. The Soviet government had made a statement of its intent to respect the sovereignty of its Warsaw Pact allies. The Revolution had triumphed, and Nagy was glad because it had paved the way for serious reforms.

This morning, Nagy was preparing to talk to his newly appointed Hungarian defence minister, Major General Pál Maléter, regarding the complete withdrawal of Soviet troops from Hungary. The meeting had been set for November 3 with Soviet officials and his defense minister in attendance.

But something bothered him. "Why have such massive reinforcements and troop movements been noted, particularly from the 7th and 31st Guards Airborne Divisions?" Nagy spoke angrily, with a slight tremor in his voice. "If they are withdrawing as they said, then why are massive reinforcements arriving?"

"I do not have the answer to that, Imre," Miklós answered. He wished he could be of further help. He was reinstated as Press Secretary of the newly reformed Nagy government and was proud of his country but did not get involved too much with the military movements. "Maybe Maléter can bring this up during the Soviet meeting?"

Imre Nagy shook his head sadly. "That would amount to suicide," Nagy replied softly. "Besides, I already asked them."

"What did they say?" Miklós asked.

"They said the movements were in preparation for leaving the country," Imre answered.

"Do you believe them?"

"No," Imre replied stonily.

Silence descended into the office. Nagy steepled his fingers and thought for a moment. He knew the Soviets better than anyone. He was afraid that they might be underhandedly planning an attack. Nagy released his hands, tapped his temple and then rubbed both his temples worriedly.

"What do we do now?" Miklós asked, his brow furrowing with concern.

Nagy looked across the desk and rubbed his temples further. "I will declare today that Hungary will be withdrawing from the Warsaw Pact," he said. "Hungary should be neutral like Austria."

Miklós stood. "Should I prepare a broadcast for this new development?" he asked.

"Yes," Imre Nagy stated confidently.

Miklós nervously lit a cigarette and exhaled the smoke into the room. "This may anger the Soviets," he said calmly, trying not to overstep his boundaries. "Are there any safeguards we can implement?"

Nagy nodded. He was glad Miklós had asked the question because he had already thought this through. "Yes, I have already asked the Western powers and the United Nations to defend Hungary's neutrality," Nagy replied. "I have pleaded with them to mediate our disputes with the Soviet Union as well."

"Do you think they will agree?" Miklós asked, a tendril of fear squirming through his veins. "The United States may not wish to be at the crosshairs with the Soviets. The world is in a precarious position with Russia right now."

Imre Nagy stood and walked with Miklós out of the office. He straightened his tie and prepared to meet with his defence minister. "True," he said confidently. "But Hungary has shown that we can win against the Soviets."

Miklós frowned worriedly at the arrogant statement. Hungary had won for now, but they were far from achieving real independence.

꒐

Laszlo kissed Elona gently and opened the passenger door for her. She gently slipped into the car seat, straightening her dress as Laszlo closed the car door. He returned around to the driver's side and sat behind the wheel. He had argued with Tibor vehemently about him coming to Austria with them. He stubbornly refused. Laszlo shook his head and started the vehicle.

The engine roared to life, and he smiled gently. "Off to Austria it is," he said finally.

Elona smiled. "I would follow you anywhere, my dear," she said sweetly.

He laid his hand on her knee and started driving towards the Austrian border. He would leave the vehicle alongside the road near the Hungarian border and telephone the barracks later so they could retrieve the vehicle. Laszlo had no intention of theft. He just wanted the convenience of driving his pregnant wife to the border instead of walking.

The drive was pleasant but cold. The weather was cooling significantly, and winter would soon be here, Laszlo thought. He glanced over to see how Elona was fairing.

Elona seemed to glow with pride and motherly love in the passenger seat. She absentmindedly placed her palms on her flat belly. She was not showing a bump yet. It was too early. Elona yearned to be a mother and wished to somehow accelerate the pregnancy process. She was fearful but hopeful. Elona didn't want to lose another child, and she wanted so much to marry Laszlo. Legalities were forcing them to wait until the divorce was finalized with Ferenc.

"What are you thinking about?" Laszlo asked, smiling. "You look so deep in thought."

Elona smiled sheepishly. "I just want to have a healthy baby," she replied honestly. "And I want to marry you as soon as possible." She laughed a bit, trying to make light of this small piece of information.

"We will marry," Laszlo said. "You can mark my words." Laszlo veered the car around a blind bend. A row of trees and bushes obscured the mountainous turn up ahead. He tapped the steering wheel decisively. "Once that divorce paper is signed, we will be in front of a marriage commissioner or priest, whichever is the quickest."

Elona grinned and laughed. "I love you, my dear," she said, smiling as they neared the blind corner.

Laszlo nodded and agreed. "You mean everything to me, sweetheart," he said as he steered the car sharply around the bend.

It was daylight, and they could see their future rolling in the countryside ahead of them. They had only three large suitcases to take with them to Austria. It was a good day.

As they cleared the bend, they both saw the armoured vehicles. They were travelling in the opposite direction in the distance, towards Budapest. Laszlo quickly parked the car in a sheltered spot of overgrown bushes.

"What is that?" Elona asked with a tremor in her voice, pointing in the distance.

Laszlo inhaled deeply, the anger rising in his throat. "Those are Soviet armoured vehicles," he answered.

"I thought they were pulling out of Hungary," she replied. "It looks like the opposite. A whole lot of them are going towards Budapest."

Laszlo fought with the desire to have a cigarette. His worst fears had come true. He wasn't sure what to do. Keep going to Austria or go back and get his brother and friends. His mind swirled in a dozen different directions with several different outcomes, and each wasn't good.

"What is going on, dear?" Elona asked, fear laced in her voice.

"The Soviets are sending reinforcements to squash the new government," he said solemnly. "This is what I felt deep in my gut. It is happening. The revolution will not win against this massive force."

"Is it really that bad?"

"Yes," he responded gravely, pointing. "Look."

They both quietly watched the enormous procession of tanks and APCs lumbering eerily toward Budapest.

After several minutes, Elona spoke, breaking the silence. "What will we do?" she asked.

Laszlo waited until the last tank had passed, then restarted the car. "I know a back road," he said, swerving the vehicle onto the highway. "We are going back to warn our friends and pick up my brother. I will take him by force if I have to."

CHAPTER 24

Major General Pál Maléter headed the Hungarian delegation negotiating with the Soviet officers on November 3. It was a promising negotiation, although there were several points that the Soviets disagreed with. Maléter was hopeful that within the day, if he had enough time, they would come to an agreement.

The way the Soviets had arrived at the Parliament building in Budapest had alarmed him, though. There were many more Soviets than just the seven members in the room. Nagy had assured him that it was an important discussion concerning the future of Hungary, and Russia had sent their best negotiators.

But Maléter wasn't fooled. He was, after all, the tank officer who had supported the uprising in Budapest. He was an army colonel for many years. Maléter had been promoted to Major General and Minister of Defense within the new Nagy government. He suspected that something wasn't right, but his position within the government meant he had to persevere until the negotiations were complete.

He swallowed his pride when discussing the negotiations with Nagy.

"I know they are being difficult," Nagy said. "But what did you expect?"

Maléter nodded, deciding not to argue. He stuck to the facts. "They have instructed us to meet later this afternoon at the temporary Soviet headquarters at Tököl Air Base to continue the negotiations."

Imre Nagy stood. "Then that is what our delegation must do."

Maléter nodded and swung around, leaving the office angrily.

Nagy watched Maléter's back as he walked down the hall. A shiver ran up Nagy's spine. Maybe he was wrong, and it was time to flee.

"You are coming with us!" Laszlo shouted.

Laszlo and Elona had travelled at high speeds over several back roads returning to Budapest. They were standing inside the Corvin Cinema, watching Tibor collect the last remaining weapons. Tibor halted when his brother shouted. There was something in the shrill of his brother's voice that reminded him of his childhood and the era of the Germans.

Tibor laid the weapons on the large table and put his hands down to his sides in surrender. "What would you have me do?" Tibor shouted back. "Flee and allow Gizella's death to be for naught?"

The front door suddenly opened, and they all froze, then instantly relaxed when they saw who it was.

"What are you guys doing here?" Béláné asked in obvious surprise. "I thought you were already in Austria."

Elona walked over to Béláné and hugged her warmly. After several moments, she pulled away and looked into Béláné's eyes. "We are here to save your lives," Elona said strongly. "We risked everything, turned around and came back to rescue our family and friends."

"What is going on?" Béláné asked suspiciously.

Tibor motioned with his hands all around the cinema as if it was all of Hungary. "They want us to abandon our fight for our country!"

"We risked our own lives coming back for you!" Laszlo thundered angrily. The windows ricocheted from the force of his booming voice, and everyone stood silent.

Elona pleaded with both of them. "It is true," she said. "We could have been killed coming back. There were hundreds of Soviet tanks and armoured vehicles on the highway. There were so many that we couldn't even count them. They are coming to Budapest. Make no mistake; if you stay, you will all die. The Soviet reinforcement army is on its way."

"If they haven't arrived already," Laszlo said, his voice lower. "If I know anything about the Soviet's army tactics, they will strike at dawn tomorrow."

Tibor stood transfixed to the spot. "We just buried Gizella finally," he said solemnly.

Laszlo laid a sympathetic hand on his brother's forearm. "Gizella will forever be a hero on the soil of Hungary."

Tibor's eyes moistened, filling with emotion.

Laszlo hugged Tibor briefly. "You must let her go, brother," Laszlo said softly. "She wouldn't want you to die too. Gizella would want you to live and be strong."

Tibor stood motionless as his brother embraced him. The last few weeks of emotion cascaded out of him, and he sobbed on his brother's shoulder.

The two women watched with heavy hearts as the brothers embraced.

"Come with us, Béláné," Elona said convincingly. "If we are wrong, then you can always come back."

Tibor turned at Elona's words and glanced at Béláné, then Laszlo.

"She's right," Laszlo agreed. "You can always come back if we are wrong and the Russians don't attack."

Tibor picked up a few rifles. "I will take these back to the Barracks, and then we will leave," he said decisively. "We will warn them too."

After a moment's indecision, Béláné spoke. "I will come," she said finally. "I can always return like you said."

A flood of relief poured from Laszlo's mind, and he smiled. "Thank God."

Tibor picked up all of the rifles and carried them across the street to the Barracks. The women and Laszlo piled into the sedan, awaiting Tibor's return.

Elona watched the clouds grow dark and turned to Laszlo. "What about Jozsef?" she asked.

"He was at the Barracks earlier," Béláné said.

"I will go get him, too," Laszlo said. He quickly jumped out of the car and ran across the street to the barracks.

Maléter arrived at the Air Base and joined the delegation on the tarmac. They all walked up to the doors of the temporary Soviet headquarters.

A massive group of soldiers loitered about the base. Maléter sensed something was wrong. The soldiers were tense but appeared as if instructed to look relaxed, it seemed.

Maléter's shoes clicked on the pavement as he walked along with his entire defence delegation. The sound of multiple shoes clicking on the large tarmac was somehow eerie and final. They straightened their shoulders and continued until they arrived closer and closer to the door. The Soviet soldiers began forming a circle around them, loosely at first, but then it grew thicker and thicker until they were surrounded by Russian soldiers.

They stopped at the makeshift building, and a door flew open. A Soviet general glared in their faces. "You are under arrest!" he shouted. "All of you!"

The Soviet soldiers circled around them tighter. It was futile to resist. The entire Ministry of Defense was being detained.

The Mercedes raced out of Budapest to the Austria border. The countryside was calm. Only a few families were seen travelling by foot to the border. Laszlo knew where the mass emigration points were located. So many Hungarians had been using bridges and canals to flee during the fighting. The recent ceasefire had calmed the country into believing the danger was over.

Laszlo had chosen a wooden bridge on a lonely country road to cross over to Austria. But now he questioned his decision.

Laszlo parked the vehicle in the bushes and staked out the area. Only a few Hungarian families loitered near the bridge. Laszlo wondered why they weren't crossing. "Let's go, men," he said. "I want the women to stay in the vehicle for now. We will find out if it's safe."

As they approached the bridge, Laszlo, Tibor and Jozsef staked out the area, ensuring it wasn't a Soviet trap. After several minutes, they returned to the women and nodded. The women joined them.

Once they all arrived at the bridge, their hearts sank. The sound of sniper fire cracked into the air.

Everyone ducked, then cautiously looked up. A member of the family on the bridge had been shot, and the others were running to the safety of the bushes.

Several other Hungarians stood near the edge of the tree line. One man held a baby in his arms. They looked at Laszlo in fear, shaking their heads.

"We are trapped," Béláné said. "There's no escape to Austria."

Laszlo looked at Tibor and Jozsef. He couldn't believe that the Soviets were shooting fleeing Hungarians on the wooden bridge. Laszlo frowned. They could not accept defeat now. They would all be executed. Laszlo's face translated into a silent conversation with the two other officers.

Jozsef grimaced. "You were right," he whispered solemnly as the truth dawned on him. "The Soviets are mounting a secret offensive. We must find a different route." He turned to go back to the car, and Laszlo grabbed his arm roughly.

"Where do you think you're going?"

"I'm going back for my wife and children," Jozsef said strongly. "Then we'll find another route."

"No, you're not!" Laszlo bellowed.

Jozsef narrowed his eyes and stood firmly. A heavy silence fell on the group of Hungarians as the two men stared down at each other.

Finally, after several minutes, Laszlo spoke. "You will be arrested and executed," he said. "You have committed treason."

Jozsef stood silent for several more seconds, then, making a decision, stepped quietly towards the bridge. "Then what do we do?" he said dejectedly. "Commit suicide going over this bridge?"

Laszlo grabbed his arm. "No," he said, looking towards the south. "I know of a canal farther away. It is more remote and not well known."

Tibor nodded. "I know which canal you're talking about," he said. "We used to play there as children."

Elona pointed at the tree line. "What will we do about the family here?" Elona asked. "That man has a baby."

"We will offer to take them," Laszlo answered. "We don't have much room in the vehicle, but we must try to save them."

Elona peered into the distance. No more shots were being fired, and the countryside was calm but cold. The family stared across at them in the bushes. "Where do you think the sniper is?" Elona asked.

"It sounds like the shots are coming from the far-left side of this riverbank," Laszlo said. "The sniper needs a clear shot at the bridge crossing." Laszlo motioned towards the treeline. "Jozsef, come with me. We will approach the family. The snipers can't see us here. Everyone else, return to the car."

Béláné, Tibor and Elona crept back to the car and waited as Jozsef and Laszlo returned several minutes later with three people and a baby. The displaced family sat on everyone's lap, squeezing into the Mercedes. The baby was eerily quiet, as if the infant knew something had gone terribly wrong.

Laszlo started the car and drove slowly away. He kept to the country roads of his childhood. They drove in silence, every person pondering what their future might be like now.

After several minutes, the man with the baby spoke. "Köszönöm," he said simply.

Laszlo nodded. "You're welcome," he replied solemnly.

The canal wasn't as far from the bridge as Elona had thought. After less than ten minutes of driving, they arrived at the waterway. Laszlo hid the keys under the driver's seat and closed the unlocked door as everyone piled out of the car.

The group gazed across the canal and exhaled in exhaustion. It was wider than he remembered, Laszlo thought. Tibor's face acknowledged the same disappointment. The water was higher than usual, and snow had begun to freeze along the shoreline.

Slowly, Laszlo walked towards the canal, laid his suitcase down and took off his jacket. The women watched as they gradually realized that he was preparing to enter the icy waters.

Laszlo turned and caught Elona's eye. "We cannot take anything," Laszlo said sadly. "We will need to leave our possessions here. We cannot cross with them. Only small items that you can strap to your body."

Elona walked towards him and stared across the canal at Austria. She laid her luggage down dejectedly and removed her coat. She grasped Laszlo's hand, and they entered the cold water together.

Tibor, Jozsef and Béláné watched solemnly as Elona and Laszlo crossed the icy waters. Elona struggled as the water suddenly rose to her shoulders. Laszlo lifted her higher through the deeper section. They continued crossing together, not looking back once.

The remaining friends glanced at one another, then placed their luggage on the shoreline and removed their jackets. They entered the canal together. The waters hit them with a gurgle and a splash as the cold November wind blew ferociously along the waterway. They shivered and continued across.

The remaining Hungarian families observed in astonishment as the ragged group of revolutionaries walked through the icy waters, crossing the canal to Austria.

The displaced Hungarians shuffled their feet looking back at the car, clearly indecisive. After several moments, the man with the baby held the infant to his chest and walked to the shoreline. He walked slowly into the icy waters with a shiver. The man continued, submerging his legs and wading bravely across the canal. The waters quickly rose above his waist as he struggled against the cold wind.

The rest of the Hungarian family hugged each other, then followed into the icy waters towards freedom.

CHAPTER 25

Imre Nagy heard about the arrest of his entire Defense Ministry. Miklós stood close by. They had fled together. Imre stood in the broadcast booth at the Radio Station with anger and fear bubbling in his heart.

He grabbed the microphone at 5:20 am, his hands shaking. He spoke into the piece. "My fellow Hungarians, at dawn today, Soviet forces have begun an attack on our capital, a massive intervention against their word!" Nagy shouted passionately, his voice rising. He faltered and swallowed. "They promised not to do this!"

Imre didn't have a script or anything prepared. He just spoke earnestly from his heart.

"Our troops are fighting! My fellow Hungarians, seek shelter!" he shouted into the microphone, swallowing hard.

Miklós watched nervously and looked around as if a team of Soviet soldiers were preparing to arrest them right now. "We must go," he whispered.

"I plea for the United Nations to intervene in this matter! America must seek to stop this crush of communism," Nagy shouted. "No country will be free from the Iron Curtain if the Soviets are left to destroy sovereign governments at their will!"

Miklós opened the door and waved Imre to join him. "We must flee!" he said softly. "The Yugoslav Embassy will shelter us! We must leave now!"

Imre Nagy stared down at the microphone as if it was the last thing he would ever say to his beloved Hungarian citizens. "Pray for us all!" he shouted, then raced out of the broadcast room with Miklós.

⑅

The Austrian soldiers had a refugee base already set up on the opposite side of the canal. Several soldiers were in the field with binoculars when they saw the group crossing the field. They were walking cautiously across the snowy windblown country-side with their hands up. Two armed Austrian soldiers marched out to meet the group. They weren't allowing anyone with weapons of any kind to enter the country.

The Austrian soldiers strode slowly, aiming their rifles at the group. When they neared the Hungarians, a shiver of respect raced through them. They lowered their rifles and waved the group towards them. They stared incredulously at the Hungarian's soaked clothes sticking to their thin frames. One soldier shouted, "Let's get these people some blankets and fresh clothes!"

"Thank you," Laszlo said, shivering.

The soldiers marched back with them to the refugee camp and handed the group over to be processed.

A few moments later, the soldiers noticed another group arrive, just as wet. They shook their heads and went back out to pick up the next group of refugees. Little did they know, that in five more hours, a massive surge of thousands more refugees would be running for their lives to Austria.

Clouds of black smoke littered the skies over Budapest as the Soviet army decimated the insurgents. Close to 30,000 Soviet soldiers entered Budapest, and the outcome was not even in question.

A few hot spots remained, primarily in the Corvin Passage, although the wounded piled high. The Soviet Army concentrated on the Barracks, knowing that it was the most formidable pocket of fighting and the Hungarian Army must be taken out.

Bodies were littered along the streets. More than 2500 Hungarians and 722 Soviets had been killed, with many more wounded.

By 8 am, the Radio Station was seized, and the remaining insurgents had fallen back to fortified positions. Civilians were the most heavily wounded. Since it was impossible for the Soviet army to differentiate between civilians and insurgents, they randomly fired into buildings. The streets shook with explosions as the tanks crept slowly along the streets of Budapest.

Hungarians ran to their homes wherever they could to escape the carnage, but unfortunately, many were killed in doing so.

Imre Nagy looked out the window with Miklós as the streets shook with violence outside. He put his hands together over his face and wept silently.

Miklós patted him on the shoulder. "We will stay here at the embassy," he said. "When we have a chance, we can escape to a country willing to offer us refuge."

Another tank explosion hit a nearby building and rattled the street. Imre looked up in alarm.

"We are safe here," Miklós said reassuringly. "They cannot attack the embassy."

Imre gazed up to the ceiling and placed his hands in prayer. "Hungary and its future are dying today. So many people and so much hope." Imre swallowed. "God save our brave Hungarians."

                                          ⌐

Elona sat at the rough table across from Laszlo, eating warm porridge. The refugee camp was already full, and thousands more were arriving every day. Austria was overburdened, and it showed. They had been here only a few days and were already told they would be bussed to Vienna soon for refugee processing.

Elona spooned another mouthful of warm porridge to her lips. Laszlo smiled at her unexpectedly and grasped her hand.

"We'll be alright, my sweet," he said softly, his voice several octaves lower than normal.

She could tell that he was just as weary as everybody else was. The refugee camp was overcrowded, and they had a small cot to sleep, food and shelter. Only the basic necessities.

Her belly was growing. She had terrible bloating and an urge to urinate often. Elona prayed the baby would be strong enough to make it through the pregnancy during such dire circumstances.

Laszlo sensed her thoughts. "The baby will be alright," he said. "We are strong people. If we made it out alive, so can she."

Elona chuckled. "You think it's a girl?" she asked, a smile on her face. Elona spooned another mouthful of porridge in and grinned.

"I think we should pick names," Laszlo replied, smiling. "We need something to help us feel joy again. What better than a newborn baby?"

Elona grinned widely. "I suppose so," she said. "What names do you like?"

"Mary is a nice name," Laszlo answered. "And for a boy, maybe Sandor."

"Mary and Sandor it is then," Elona replied heartily.

The noise of the cafeteria was considerable, so they had to speak loudly. Laszlo squeezed her hand. "Everything will be alright," he said.

Béláné, Tibor and Jozsef sat down with their trays. Tibor spooned the warm porridge into his mouth hungrily as the other two picked at their food.

"What is the silly grin for?" Béláné asked, stirring her porridge.

"Well, Tibor," Elona said. "We haven't told you yet, but you're going to be an uncle."

Tibor froze with the spoon lifted to his mouth. "What?" he said incredulously. He placed the spoon down. "I'm going to be an uncle?"

"Yes," Laszlo said proudly. "Elona's pregnant with my child."

Tibor slapped his brother's arm. "It's about time!" he jested.

The entire group laughed.

"Honestly," Tibor said. "I am looking forward to a normal life, and I think having a brand new nephew is a wonderful way to start it."

"Or niece," Laszlo interjected.

"Whatever it may be," Tibor said. "The baby will be loved by us all."

They all laughed and finished their breakfast.

⟫

Laszlo, Elona and the others arrived in Vienna aboard a large transport truck. The large refugee center was bustling with a huge influx of Hungarians. Almost 200,000 displaced citizens had fled in total, 20,000 to Yugoslavia, and the remaining 180,000 escaped to the Austrian border.

Austria had appealed to the United Nations for assistance placing the Hungarians in other countries. It was an enormous number of refugees in such a short period of time. The United States of America had offered refuge for 30,000 Hungarians, Australia had pledged assistance for 14,000, and the United Kingdom followed with promises to accept approximately 10,000 displaced Magyars. Perhaps the most surprising was Canada's overwhelming response. The faraway country was accepting 37,500 Hungarian refugees. The government of Austria was accepting the largest number of refugees to stay permanently, but they were in dire need of help. The country could not house and feed everyone.

Many people wanted to stay in Austria to be close to family, but when they found out about the high number of arrests that were happening when refugees re-entered Hungary, most people knew that their homeland was not home anymore.

"I am going back," Béláné said as they looked over the options for the different countries.

"I don't think that's wise," Elona responded.

"I am not military," she replied.

"But you participated in the fighting," Tibor interjected.

"How would they know?"

"I heard the Soviets are browsing through all the photos," Laszlo commented as he picked up an application to Canada.

Elona peered up at him suspiciously. "That's a faraway country," she whispered immediately.

"I know," he replied quietly.

Béláné had an Austrian application in her hand. "I cannot leave my fiancé in Hungary," she said.

"Did you have any photos taken of you?" Tibor asked.

"I believe there were some," she answered. "I was a nurse! I saved lives!"

"So was I," Elona retorted. "And I'm not going back."

Béláné rolled her eyes. "You are marrying a lieutenant!" she replied as if it was an obvious answer. She fiddled with the Austrian application.

"Wait," Elona said, sensing something. "Did you hear from the young doctor?"

Béláné blushed. "Yes," she confessed. "He had sent a letter. Gabor said that he loved me and didn't want to live without me." Béláné rolled the Austrian application in her fingers. "I can't just ignore him. He said the Soviets are not persecuting him for saving people's lives during the revolution."

Elona held Laszlo's hand firmly as they stood near the Canada booth. "Please, Béláné," she pleaded. "Don't go back. They may find out you participated in the fighting."

Jozsef overheard the conversation. "You are both lucky, Elona," he interjected. "You and Laszlo have each other. Béláné and I have left our loved ones in Hungary." His shoulders jutted out angrily. "Don't expect to understand what that feels like!" Jozsef's face turned a slight shade of red. "I'm sorry, but I agree with Béláné. I want to go back to see my wife and children too."

Béláné jutted her chin out in defiance at the extra support. "See?" she said. "Jozsef understands."

Elona curled into Laszlo's arms. "I apologize," she said resignedly. "You both will have to make those hard decisions, I suppose."

"I don't know for sure yet," Béláné replied. "We will see what happens."

Chapter 26

Nagy was nervous. They had awoken and made the decision to leave this morning. It had been more than two weeks being holed up at the Yugoslav Embassy. It had become a stalemate with the Soviets. Nagy could not trust them. He had to guarantee his safety before leaving the building. Negotiations were progressing ridiculously slow with the Soviets. They countered everything he requested until, finally, things changed yesterday.

"They honestly said that they would guarantee our safety?" Miklós asked incredulously.

"Yes, they finally agreed," Imre answered.

"Do you believe them?"

"I do," Imre replied. "We have no other choice. What are we to do?" He waved his hand around as if encompassing the entire building. "We cannot live here at the Embassy forever!"

Miklós frowned. "I understand," he replied softly. "But they have lied before. The Soviets cannot be trusted."

"We have negotiated our safety, Miklós," Imre replied, the irritation showing in his voice. "I have tried my best." Imre Nagy swung his coat over his shoulders and shrugged it on, threading his arms in. "They have asked for us to return to parliament. Kádár has signed a written safe conduct of free passage."

Miklós nodded. They both knew that János Kádár was appointed the new Communist Party leader and the new Prime Minister of Hungary. Miklós and Nagy trusted Kádár. "Okay," Miklós replied. He bent down, slipped on his shoes with a small shoehorn and stood confidently, smoothing down his suit. "Let's go then."

Imre Nagy nodded confidently and was escorted to the door with Miklós and other supporters in tow. His heart beat loudly in his temples as the door opened.

Nagy stepped out with Miklós and the others. They were freed! The door closed behind them, and they barely took ten steps before they saw the group approaching.

Nagy felt his hopes sink.

A large group of Soviet soldiers surrounded them as they prepared to walk to parliament.

A decorated colonel approached Nagy directly. "Imre Nagy, Miklós Vásárhelyi?" he spoke harshly. "You are to follow me." The Soviet soldiers formed a thick blockade around the group.

"Where are you taking us?" Nagy asked.

"You will find out when we get there," the colonel answered vaguely.

Elona cuddled with Laszlo on her small cot as they looked over the application to Canada. They had filled out the form with the assistance of a Canadian interpreter. Elona felt nauseous this morning and not because she was moving to a faraway country but simply because of the pregnancy. Elona wondered how she would feel being on a boat. She shuddered at the thought.

Laszlo had his arms wrapped around her and rested his palms on her small belly. Her abdomen had a slight bump but only noticeable when she was naked. Elona felt warmed by his touch, like he was somehow protecting the new life inside her body.

"We are leaving for Canada," Elona said introspectively.

"Yes, we are," Laszlo agreed. He began rubbing her small belly in circular motions through her sweater.

"It feels so surreal," she said. "Just three weeks ago, we were fighting for Hungary. Now we are leaving to a cold country in the north."

"The representative said that many southern parts of Canada are not as cold as people think," Laszlo countered. "And we are alive. That is the important thing."

"Yes, true," she replied. "Thanks to you." Elona curled into his embrace, then turned her head, sensing his breath changing. He looked into her eyes with so much love that it brought tears to her eyes. She kissed him tenderly. His gentle warm lips were soothing to her soul. She had found the man who she had been searching for all this time. It wasn't the greatest circumstances, but that was life, she thought.

After several moments, they broke the kiss and settled back into their embrace, watching the busy refugee camp they had been relocated to in Vienna. She peered through the mass of people and smiled when she saw her friends.

Jozsef and Béláné approached and sat down on the opposite cot.

"I have some news," Béláné said.

Elona sat up. "What is it?"

"I am going back," Béláné stated. She gestured with her hands, trying to stop any arguments. "I know what you're thinking. Gabor has assured me that I will be safe."

Elona didn't know what to say. She felt that anything she said would be disputed. Béláné was intent on returning to her lover. "I will pray for you," she replied softly.

"What about you?" Laszlo asked Jozsef.

"I will go back too," he said, exhaling heavily. "But I won't do anything until I know more about how they are processing policemen who changed sides."

"They won't be treating you with open arms," Laszlo stated.

"Possibly," Jozsef replied. "But I cannot just leave my family behind."

Laszlo quietly nodded. The pain Jozsef and Béláné were experiencing was valid.

"What are your plans?" Jozsef asked Laszlo.

"We have applied as refugees to Canada," Laszlo answered. "My brother did as well. We will be living a new life in Canada."

"That's a big step," Jozsef replied.

"Yes, it is," Elona said softly. "You should both come."

Jozsef smiled. "Maybe."

"Did you hear about Imre Nagy?" Laszlo said.

"No, did you hear anything?" Jozsef asked.

"Nagy was arrested and taken to Romania," Laszlo replied. "Immediately after stepping out of the Yugoslav Embassy."

"It was that quick?" Jozsef asked incredulously.

"Yes, it was that quick," Laszlo said solemnly, hoping the context would help Jozsef realize the graveness of the situation. "They are arresting political leaders and hundreds of insurgents." He placed a hand on Elona's knee. "Hungary is no longer home for us. It is not safe."

Jozsef inhaled sharply, then gazed down at his severed finger. "We will see what happens in the next few days," he stated, almost to himself.

"I'm still going back," Béláné said confidently. "I am leaving early tomorrow morning."

Elona frowned. "Well, it sounds like you've made up your mind," she said, standing. "One last hug before you go. We may not see each other again for a very long time."

Béláné stood, and the two women embraced strongly as if it was their last hug.

Béláné approached the border guards early in the morning. "Are you sure you want to do this?" an Austrian guard asked. "They have been arresting people as they returned."

Béláné frowned and looked across the field. "I have to," she said. "The man that I love is waiting for me." She inhaled and then blew out an exasperated sigh. "And the country I love more than anything is my home. I cannot forsake it."

"Okay, Miss," the guard said. "We cannot walk any further with you. Just keep walking towards that bridge in the distance. The Soviet guards will meet you."

Béláné had a moment of intense hesitation and then told herself to put one foot in front of the other. She started walking confidently to the border with her heart in her throat. She was terrified, but something spurred her on. It was love; she knew this. She shuffled another foot in front and kept walking. Béláné couldn't imagine living in Canada, far away from the man who had been through so much with her. It was like she had finally found the man who was meant for her. Gabor had inspired her and made her feel whole. They had even talked about having a family.

Béláné could not just desert him.

The walk to the border was farther than she thought, but each second was filled with fear and doubt. She wondered if this was the best choice in her life or the worst mistake. Béláné squared her shoulders, trying to dispel the thoughts.

She was following her heart, and that was something she could die for.

As the border came into view, Béláné saw the Soviet guard station. They noticed her immediately and began shouting.

She raised her arms over her head in surrender. "I have come back to be with my future husband!" she pleaded.

"Keep your hands in the air and walk slowly," a guard shouted back. "If you make one wrong move, you will be shot."

Béláné continued slowly with her hands up until she neared the guard's station. A soldier walked out to her and waved for her to continue approaching.

Finally, she made it safely to the border checkpoint.

The guard looked at her suspiciously. "What is your name?"

"Béláné Havrilla," she answered nervously.

"Your papers!" the guard shouted obscenely loud.

Béláné shuffled in her pocket and slowly pulled out her identification.

The guards looked through everything. Finally, after several nerve-wracking minutes, one of the guards shouted. "This woman is coming home," he said. "Allow her to proceed."

Relief flooded her entire body as the guards processed her return to the country and waved her on. She would be reunited with Gabor, and she couldn't be happier.

The airplane's engines started, and the sound was almost deafening. Elona covered her ears as Laszlo patted her leg. Tibor and Jozsef sat across the aisle. Tibor smiled, grateful for the chance to embark on a new life. After what had happened to Gizella, anything from here on would be a better future. Jozsef, on the other hand, was distraught. His entire body crumpled into the seat as if someone had shot him and left him for dead. His eyes were red and swollen, and his hands shook with a tremor. Jozsef's life was taking a turn that he never wished for but was forced to accept.

"It will be alright, Jozsef," Tibor said. "Canada will be good to us. After what we've all been through, anything will be better."

Jozsef couldn't even process the meaning of the words Tibor was speaking. Everything had left his blood, it seemed. He had left his wife and children behind. Nothing could ever compare to the heartbreak he was experiencing right now.

Laszlo leaned over and peered at his friend. Worry creased his eyebrows, and he fell back against the passenger seat. He knew that it had been a very difficult decision for Jozsef, and he almost felt the anguish emanating from his friend. There were only two choices, and one was barely even a choice.

Both Laszlo and Jozsef were told quite plainly by Austrian border officials that they were being sought by the new Hungarian government for treason. Canada had agreed to offer them both asylum. Tibor was a lower-ranking officer, so the Soviets had made a deal for his return without reparations, which he had promptly refused.

But Laszlo and Jozsef were quite another story. They were both high-ranking officers and would be arrested upon arrival. Laszlo was happy to leave and had his new life awaiting him in Canada, but Jozsef wasn't as hopeful.

The grief on his friend's face told the story of his torn heart and ego. Nothing could ever make Jozsef's life right again until he was allowed back.

Laszlo squeezed Elona's hand. He wished one day that Jozsef could reunite with his family. He had hopes for the new government in Hungary. They had been brutal in taking Hungary back, but the Soviets had reformed some things already. It wasn't the same country as before, and if that was the only consolation for the team of uncommon revolutionaries today, then it was a small beacon of hope.

The plane lifted off as it gained speed and flew into the clouds towards Liverpool. They were told they would board a ship in England, and it would take them to Canada.

Elona smiled weakly, a moment of nausea crossing her lips. She swallowed the urge to vomit as the plane levelled out in the sky. She had never flown before nor boarded a ship, so this was all new to her. The baby in her tummy had just started kicking, and she felt the movements randomly at the oddest times.

"Are you okay, my love?" Laszlo asked, squeezing her hand reassuringly.

She grinned and swallowed down the rising bile. Her face had an odd paleness to it. "I feel ill," she answered. "But we are together. I would go anywhere with you. Even across the world."

Laszlo smiled and nodded. "I love you, my darling," he said. "We are going to build a new future across the ocean. And it will be better than anything we had before." He lifted her hand and kissed her knuckles softly as the plane continued to England.

The plane had landed safely, and after a few rough days, they had begun boarding the Empress of Britain. The ship's destination was St. John's, Newfoundland. The boat had been chartered by the Canadian government for transporting the Hungarian refugees. They were being taken care of by the Canadian government, and nothing had ever felt so good.

Elona stood against the glass windows as the ship began to drift into the Atlantic Ocean. Laszlo held her waist and was genuinely worried about her. She had been quite sick, looking pale and weak. He hugged her and reassured her repeatedly, but it wasn't enough.

As the large ship ventured into the cold Atlantic waters, the December winds buffeted against the windows. The gentle sway of the ship was too much, and Elona ran to the bathroom, grasping her mouth. Elona rushed to make it to the bathroom in time, afraid that she would be retching the contents of her stomach everywhere.

Laszlo rushed after her and waited impatiently outside of the women's washroom. He heard the massive waves licking the boat and tapped his foot nervously. Elona had been in the washroom for longer than he liked, and his senses were on high alert. He fidgeted from foot to foot, wondering if he should just storm into the washroom and find her.

When another woman approached the washroom, Laszlo stepped forward. "Excuse me, Miss," he said politely. "My pregnant wife is in there, and I'm worried. She was nauseous, and I assume she has vomited. Could you please see if she is okay?"

"Of course!" the woman replied in Hungarian.

"Her name is Elona," Laszlo added worriedly.

"I will find her for you," she answered and disappeared into the washroom.

Laszlo clenched his fists nervously and looked at the large naval clock where most of the passengers were seated. The boat was overcrowded with hundreds, maybe even thousands, of Hungarian refugees. It would be a long trip, they were told. Laszlo's jaw twitched from the force of his teeth grinding against each other. He told himself to breathe. They would get to Canada alright, he reassured himself.

At that moment, the washroom door opened, and Elona appeared with the woman. "Here she is," the woman stated, unwinding her arm from Elona's waist and handing her over to Laszlo.

Laszlo smiled. "Köszönöm," he said, then immediately focused his attention on Elona.

He bent down and lifted Elona's chin, forcing her to look up at him. She looked somewhat better, but her face was still pale. "Are you alright, dear?" he asked, concern creasing his forehead.

"I'm fine," Elona replied weakly, wrapping her arms around Laszlo's waist. "I am just sick to my stomach."

"Most people would get sick on a transatlantic voyage," he said sympathetically. "I can't imagine how it feels to be several months pregnant as well." Laszlo smoothed her hair and kissed the top of her head.

"I vomited up all of our lunch," she said quietly.

"Oh my," Laszlo responded. "Well, we will find you some water and warm tea. The British seem to love their tea. I saw a table with many refreshments on it." He hugged her warmly and whispered in her ear. "It will be alright, my dear. I promise."

Elona snuggled her nose into his chest and inhaled his manly scent. Somehow his closeness soothed her worries. "I trust in our future," she said quietly.

Laszlo smiled and smoothed her hair lovingly again. He kissed her head one last time and pulled away a bit. "I do, too," he said. "Let's go find you some hot tea."

Tibor and Jozsef ate and drank, filling their bellies with as much food as they could. It felt like they had been starving for many weeks. The two men began to form a close friendship as they sailed across the Atlantic on the nearly month-long voyage. It had been a gruelling three weeks when they finally reached St. John's.

The rocky land appeared before them as the men laughed joyfully, seeing the new country awaiting them.

Jozsef was becoming more accustomed to the idea of leaving Hungary after he had met so many other Hungarians on the ship facing the same troubles. The people were all huddled together, some in family groups, some solitary. Many bonds were formed from collective tragedies and hardships. He found out that many others had also left their families behind. Some women wept the entire way only to have hope shine in their eyes as they approached the new land of Canada.

Tibor slapped Jozsef's back lightly in comradery. "We will be Canadians soon," he exclaimed.

Jozsef smiled as another man named Mike slapped his shoulder also. "Do not worry," Mike said. "We will see our families again!" Mike was a tall, strong Hungarian soldier who had also left his wife and three children behind.

Jozsef grinned as the three men joined in a chorus of well wishes. When Laszlo and Elona walked over to the group, several other women joined as well. Elona was still sick but had managed to keep some food down. She was finally becoming somewhat accustomed to the mid-Atlantic swells. Laszlo hugged her protectively as they joined their new friends, old friends and family.

Newfoundland's rocky shorelines beckoned them as the sun rose behind them. The boatload of weary Hungarian refugees had a chance at a new life, and they were going to make it count.

Chapter 27

The toddler ran at full speed across the hall, slipping on a small wooden toy and careening forcefully into the new accordion on the floor. Elona had just purchased the instrument for Laszlo's birthday this year. She let out a tiny gasp of horror and raced to her daughter.

The young girl was momentarily stunned. As the pain of the fall registered in her mind, she suddenly wailed at the top of her lungs.

Elona let out an exasperated sigh and bent down, tending to her daughter. She peered at the expensive accordion. It appeared to be fine. Elona grimaced and tried to pick up the small girl, but her body was too tired. Her swollen belly poked out in front of her. She was only three months into her third pregnancy but was growing weary already. Constantly chasing after her energetic daughter was exhausting.

"Mary!" Elona scolded. "You must be more careful!" She tried bending down to pick up the wailing toddler but, instead, slid down onto the floor with her back resting against the wall. "It's alright, my sweetie," she cooed. "Anyu will kiss it better." Elona gently kissed her daughter's small leg, inspecting the tiny scratch.

Mary's crying ceased almost instantly. She curled into her mother's bosom and wrapped her tiny arms around her momma. "Anyu," she mumbled in affection.

Elona cradled her daughter and began humming a soft, soothing tune. She remembered the day she had fallen in love with Laszlo as he sang alongside the Danube. The sweet memory filled her heart with warmth. Elona hummed the song, but it strangely turned melancholy to her ears. Elona began to weep silently for her old country and the devastation that continued to torment people there. She worried about her mother and father. They had written and said everything was fine, but Elona distrusted the government so much. She knew she could not trust the letters to accurately reflect what they were really going through. But they were alive, and that was a relief.

It was June 1958.

Secret Hungarian trials had commenced after the Soviets regained control of Hungary. Imre Nagy was transported from Romania back to Hungary along with Miklós. They were imprisoned, and for several weeks Miklós was paralyzed with fear. Several guards had taken him from the adjacent cell and moved him to another block. Miklós had screamed and was convinced that he would face a horrible fate. But as it turned out, Miklós had been spared.

Imre Nagy had heard, later on, that his friend had been sentenced to five years in prison. He was relieved to hear that Miklós Vásárhelyi would not suffer the same fate as himself. Major General Pál Maléter and the majority of his defence ministry were not as lucky.

The international community was disgusted by the Soviet invasion of Hungary and declared it atrocious and extreme. As far as the Soviets were concerned, they had no choice but to follow through with the new Kádár government policy. Imre knew that he should never have trusted Kádár. Not that he was an untrustworthy man but that the Soviets had given him no choice. It was either obey the Russians or face death himself. So Kádár complied and formed the new government according to the Soviet's wishes.

The secret Hungarian trials proceeded but were not allowed to be followed publicly. Imre Nagy, along with Pál Maléter and many others, were charged with attempting to overthrow the Hungarian People's Republic and were sentenced to death by hanging. It was not the ending that Nagy had hoped for, but he prayed that one day the world would see the injustice and condemn the Soviet government for their brutality. He looked up at the ceiling in his cell and wondered if one day Hungary might be free because of the work he did.

Nagy sure hoped so.

Laszlo was at the steel factory working as a blacksmith when he heard the news about the execution of Imre Nagy.

Several Hungarians were also working at the factory, and they all stopped for a moment of silence during lunch. A spontaneous vigil descended upon the Hungarian workers as they briefly met each other's eyes. They had survived, but many had not.

Laszlo held his hands briefly in prayer and thanked God for his life and his family. He prayed for Nagy, for Hungary and all the people they had left behind.

CHAPTER 28

Béláné Havrilla sat on the cold steel bench in the grey room. She had been arrested on July 25, 1957. A shiver ran through her spine when she heard about the news of Imre Nagy's execution. She wondered if such a fate awaited her as well.

She had lived a heavenly seven months with Gabor before she was arrested. The government combed through news photos and arrested everyone who was identified in the pictures as fighting in the revolution. Béláné had appeared in a prominent photo alongside another insurgent with their rifles ready and smiles upon their faces.

Béláné had been living in the women's prison for almost a year, awaiting her fate.

Her love for Gabor may have costed her life, she thought sadly. Béláné wondered how Canada was for Elona. She looked down at her short nails and splayed her hands flat upon her lap. She could have chosen Canada, but she didn't.

Maybe they would spare her life. Béláné heard that some people were only serving prison sentences. She crossed her fingers and hoped in her heart that she would be one of the lucky ones.

Laszlo arrived home and immediately took the two-month-old baby boy from the bassinet. The boy was crying up a storm, and Elona was in the shower. Mary was playing with her bottle on the floor in the hallway. "Apu!" she yelled as she ran into her father's legs.

Laszlo mussed her hair and cradled his infant son, Sandor. "Shh," he cooed, trying to quiet the boy's crying. "Sandor, Apu's home. Everything is going to be alright." The boy wailed louder until Laszlo sauntered into the kitchen, opened the fridge and removed the breast milk bottle. He warmed the bottle in a pot of hot water for several minutes, then put the nipple to his son's mouth. Sandor sucked greedily and happily drank the milk.

"Mary, give me a few minutes," Laszlo said as the girl bounced around the house doing cartwheels. "Anyu will be out of the shower soon."

Laszlo watched as his infant son sucked the bottle hungrily. He smiled and was instantly grateful for his family and his life in Canada. He thought back to the days of the army and felt some nostalgia, but mostly felt panic and disorder in his brain. Working in the army had affected him greatly, and he never sought treatment from doctors, worrying that it would label him as somehow unfit to be an ex-soldier. So he swallowed down his anxiety, accepted his frequent nightmares and tried to calm his shaky hands.

He never told Elona, but she knew. There were many nights that he would awaken suddenly shouting. Elona would always soothe him and tell him it was alright. They were safe now.

Laszlo was blessed to have such a good loving wife. He gazed down and watched his son's eyes slowly drooping closed. As Sandor fell asleep in his arms, Laszlo heard the shower stop.

He could hear his wife grabbing a towel and brushing her teeth. He looked up and finally saw her towel-wrapped body and wet hair.

Elona's eyes were red.

Laszlo felt a shiver run up his spine. "What's wrong?" Laszlo asked, his hands starting to shake. They had been hearing such terrible news from Hungary lately. So many people were being executed. So far, Anyu and Apu were still okay. Jozsef's family was also unharmed, but neither Jozsef nor himself was allowed back into the country. They would be arrested and sentenced for treason immediately. A chill ran up his throat as he saw how distraught Elona was. He stood with his sleeping son in his arms. "Tell me."

"Béláné was executed last week," she said, her voice cracking and tears rushing from her eyes. "My mother just called this morning."

"Oh my dear," Laszlo said slowly. "I'm so sorry."

Elona sniffled the tears back. She took the baby, burped him and then laid him down in the bassinet. She turned around, and Laszlo was right beside her. Elona clung to him and let the tears fall from her eyes as they stood by their baby boy. Mary quietly stumbled over to her parents and wrapped her small arms around her mother's right leg.

Laszlo smoothed Elona's hair and pulled her into his warm embrace. "We are one of the lucky ones, my dear," he said softly.

THE END

FINAL NOTE TO READER

During the Hungarian Revolution of 1956, approximately 200,000 Hungarians fled the country. 180,000 of them fled to Austria, and the remainder to Yugoslavia. Austria was bursting at the seams to handle the large influx of refugees and appealed for help from the international community. The United Kingdom accepted approximately 10,000 refugees, the USA accepted 30,000, Australia received 14,000, but Canada accepted the second highest at 37,500 refugees. A whopping 80,000 Hungarians mostly stayed in Austria.

The Hungarian Revolution happened during a particularly precarious time during the Cold War when Americans were not keen on further aggravating the Soviet Union. Hungarians were left to fight on their own and bravely fought in overwhelming numbers. The amount of Hungarian Army soldiers who joined the insurgents are still unclear, but it was large enough of a number to plan and execute a full-scale military offensive.

Many of these soldiers fled after the revolution, and many died. Higher-ranking officers were not allowed back into the country until 1990. My father was one of them. He left three children and his first wife behind, hoping to return and never saw them again. He died in May of 1990, never having the opportunity to return.

This is the story of so many Hungarians. It is a sad story but also one of hope and strength. The Hungarian Revolution did change the way the Soviet Union treated Hungary and many other countries. It brought the horrors of communism to the international front page. The famous bloody water polo match between Hungary and the Soviet Union during the Olympics of November 1956 started a fire in everyone's hearts. For the first time, the entire world experienced the fight against communism and the emotions it provoked in so many Hungarians. The Magyars believed in reform, and they fought with their lives to achieve it.

The death toll was approximately 3,000 Hungarians killed and 13,000 wounded. On the Soviet side, 722 were killed, and 1,540 were wounded.

Among the people executed were Imre Nagy, Pál Maléter, many of the parliamentary defence ministry and a woman named Béláné Havrilla.

She was born in 1932 and grew up partially in an orphanage. She worked as a cleaner, then later toiled in a lamp factory. Béláné took part in the protests, then quickly became an emergency nurse within the Corvin group. Sometime later, she took up arms herself and fought together with another woman named Maria Wittner. On November 7, 1956, she escaped to Austria with many other revolutionaries. She returned successfully to Budapest in December 1956 upon the urging of her boyfriend. There were many photos taken during the revolution. Béláné and Maria appeared in one such prominent picture, holding rifles and wearing armbands. Béláné Havrilla was arrested seven months later on July 25, 1957, and was executed on February 26, 1959, after spending 19 months incarcerated. Maria Wittner was also arrested but was more fortunate and received a life imprisonment. Maria was released in 1970 and was awarded the Grand Cross of the Hungarian Republic. So many others, including Béláné and my own father, never received any recognition for their bravery.

I have included many non-fiction historical characters in this novel. Among them are:

Imre Nagy, de facto Prime Minister of Hungary 1953-1955, 1956

Miklós Vásárhelyi, party press secretary of the Imre Nagy government and newspaper journalist

Major General Pál Maléter, Minister of Defense during the Nagy Government 1956

General Matyas Rákosi, de facto Prime Minister of Hungary from 1945 to 1953, 1955-1956

Tamás Kiss, a leader of MEFESZ

Béláné Havrilla, Hungarian protestor, insurgency nurse and revolutionist

All the names other than those stated above are fictitious, and any semblance to actual persons is purely coincidental. Even though this is a historical fiction story, it is the tale of so many Hungarians' fight for freedom from communist rule. Many were forced to recreate their lives in strange countries; some left loved ones behind, many lost family members and the unlucky ones completely lost their lives.

Imre Nagy served as the Chairman of the Council of Ministers (de facto Prime Minister) of the Hungarian People's Republic from July 4, 1953 to April 18, 1955 and October 24, 1956 to November 4, 1956. After Stalin's death in March 1953, the Soviet Union had come under pressure from uprisings and was heavily criticized about the brutal Stalin governance. Moscow needed someone to appease the populace. Rákosi was forced to resign after eight long years of oppressive governance, and Imre Nagy was the man Moscow needed for reform. During his first term in office, Nagy took corrective measures and revived hopes of recovering the economy. A new system of compulsory delivery of produce was introduced, and opting out of the stifling agriculture co-operatives was initiated, which ultimately resulted in significant reductions in food prices. Nagy also reduced state control of media and encouraged debate on economic and political reform. In August 1953, some political prisoners were freed. It seems that Nagy was just what Hungary needed.

Unfortunately, Rákosi, a stout supporter of Stalin policies, was still working in the background within the Nagy government. In January 1955, Imre Nagy was summoned to Moscow. He was heavily criticized for being too radical with his reforms and ordered to correct his errors. Rákosi, finding a way to exploit the situation, began accusing Nagy of rightist deviation. Nagy was dismissed as Prime Minister in April 1955 and later stripped of his Party membership.

Rákosi was successful in his intentions and regained his position as Prime Minister in 1955. He repealed many of Nagy's reforms and backtracked the country into the past repressive Stalin-type leadership. After having a taste of positive reform, this infuriated many Hungarians.

In February 1956, after Nikita S. Khrushchev's open attack on Stalin at the 20th Communist Party Congress in Moscow, the Soviet Union was once more looking to make reparations. Rákosi was forced from power and ordered to Moscow, where he remained until his death in 1971.

Instead of bringing back Imre Nagy, Moscow chose Ernő Gerő as Prime Minister on July 18, 1956. This cosmetic move angered the public even more, and the revolution began to gain momentum.

The Petőfi Circle was formed by members of the DISZ newspaper, which included many students from Budapest Technical University, Szeged University and local workers. The group rapidly grew in numbers and even had a faction separate from the original group. MEFESZ was a democratic student organization, whereas DISZ was mostly Nagy's supporters of reformed communism. The two factions were at great odds with each other. During the fateful October meeting at the Technical University in Budapest, two founders of Szeged MEFESZ demanded to speak and one of them was Tamás Kiss. The crowd wanted to hear them. Several DISZ leaders left the Aula in anger and dismay.

But it wasn't over yet. In fact, MEFESZ had fueled the fire. By midnight, when the meeting had ended, the demands of the students were formulated into 14 points. Two more points were added by the next morning. Surprisingly, not one point had anything to do with student life. Each one of the points directly addressed the political, social and economic concerns of the country. During this precarious time in Hungary's history, students were held in high esteem. For many, they were Hungary's only hope for a better future.

The events of October 23, 1956, and the following days of the revolution were researched heavily, and the events themselves described in this book can be construed mostly as fact. During the uprising, soldiers of the Hungarian Army had sympathized with the revolutionaries and began supplying them with arms. The Hungarian Army soldiers were Hungarians, not Soviets. They were as emotionally invested into Hungary as the people were, sometimes more so.

Many of those Hungarian soldiers were executed, killed in action or forced to flee for their lives during the second Soviet intervention on November 4, 1956. Thousands of these brave soldiers never received a medal of bravery; most received treason sentences instead.

Imre Nagy was also accused of treason during the Soviet secret trials. During his imprisonment, he was repeatedly tortured by party officials. I chose not to include this gruesome detail in my novel.

Nagy was tried, found guilty, sentenced and executed by hanging on June 16, 1958.

During the years that followed, the Soviet government had stifled any discussion of the revolution. Many Hungarian refugees never spoke of the revolution for fear of repercussions.

It was not until 1989 that Nagy's remains were reburied. Over 200,000 people attended Nagy's reinterment. One of the young speakers at the funeral was Viktor Orbán. This young man went on to become the longest-serving Prime Minister of Hungary (2023).

In the end, Imre Nagy's legacy changed Hungary and the international community's stance on extreme communism.

In December 1991, the dismembered Soviet Union, under the leadership of Mikhail Gorbachev, officially apologized for the 1956 Soviet actions in Hungary.

October 23 is now a national Memorial Day in Hungary, in sombre remembrance of the 1956 Revolution and War of Independence.

May God bless all the lives lost, all the families uprooted, and all the souls never able to return to their country. The children, grandchildren and great-grandchildren born from these brave revolutionists all have the blood of unrecognized heroes in their veins. This is something we should never forget.

And remember, the strong are always stronger when they stand as one.

I'd like to include a short thank you to all my editors, proofreaders, cover design artists and researchers who helped me create this truly amazing story. One of the people who helped me the most was my 17-year-old son. Surprisingly, he has an intense fascination and wealth of knowledge regarding Soviet armaments, ammunition and rifles. I am concerned but delighted that he was able to help so profoundly with all the technical aspects of the war scenes. God bless our children! They are the future.

And one more big thank you, to you, the reader, for supporting authors. We cannot exist without you.